FAVORITE SON
Will Freshwater

Tom,
I hope you
enjoy!
Will

Dreamspinner Press

Published by
Dreamspinner Press
5032 Capital Circle SW
Suite 2, PMB# 279
Tallahassee, FL 32305-7886
USA
http://www.dreamspinnerpress.com/

Favorite Son
© 2014 Will Freshwater.

Cover Art
© 2014 TL Bland.
tlbland4456@gmail.com
http://thruterryseyes.com
Cover content is for illustrative purposes only and any person depicted on the cover is a model.

ISBN: 978-1-62798-772-1
Digital ISBN: 978-1-62798-773-8

Printed in the United States of America
First Edition
June 2014

For Stephen.

The first person I want to thank is Paul, for glancing my way on the DC Metro back in 2001 and inspiring the short story that eventually grew into *Favorite Son*.

I also need to recognize the small army of friends who trudged through various drafts and provided invaluable feedback: Lissa Hornstrom, Joe Scott, Chris Corkum, Christian Riddell, Gary Gebhardt, Shannon McGovern, Bob Kabel, Ken Shields, David Reitman, Will Kearns, Marilyn Desmond, Nance Adler, Jennifer Palmer, Robert Jaquay, Tony Tedesco, Lee Ruiz, Court Stroud, and Lynn DellaPietra.

A very special thanks to my dear friend Bob Smith, who provided encouragement along the way and reminded me that writing is editing, editing, editing!

This novel would not have been possible without the love and support of Maggie Cadman. Words cannot express how grateful I am for her keen eye and open heart.

Through the good writing days and the bad, Stephen Cremen was always ready to give thoughtful feedback and warm hugs. His unfaltering confidence in my writing was the fuel that kept the creative engine running.

Finally, I'd like to acknowledge Elizabeth North, Ginnifer Eastwick, and the staff at Dreamspinner Press for all their hard work and insight.

Prologue

HE WAS born under the sign of Cancer in the early-morning hours of a day late in June. The event was premature, unexpected by almost two months. His parents had gone to dinner and a movie—*Yours, Mine and Ours*, a comedy with Lucille Ball—where his mother had, quite literally, laughed herself into labor. He sometimes savored the fact that it was happiness that had called him into the world. He also wondered how different his life would have been if he'd been born in September, a Virgo, as planned. But fate and a funny redhead had other plans.

The year was 1968, and his blue-collar family had none of the modern miracles of technology to monitor the development of their unborn child. Time passed and the bump grew. Always the optimist, his mother had merely assumed that her unborn child was healthy and growing ahead of the curve. While there were guesses about the gender of the baby, no one ever thought to question the quantity of life inside her womb. Any concerns about her weight and size went unvoiced. The doctor was in charge, and he knew best.

His parents' shock over the timing of the delivery doubled when a second child followed the first. Father and Mother had secretly hoped for a son to round out their trio of girls, and for a short time, it seemed that God had answered their prayers. Each boy was named after a grandfather, Peter and John, and presented to their waiting family.

Having a spare anything is generally a good idea, but sometimes things that are too good to be true turn out to be just that. He was only an identical twin for three short days, a time during which he was rarely awake and most certainly unaware of the sibling sleeping next to him. Peter died of unexpected complications. Since John was half the weight of his younger brother and barely able to breathe—even with the help of a respirator—his parents had prepared for the worst. The odds were against him from the very start, but he made it through the first night and the next. Days turned into weeks as the family held its collective breath.

After almost a month, John Peter Wells arrived home. The proximity of his brother's death to their birth had fused their identities. In time, his parents surrendered their grief and refocused their attention on their only son. John thrived under their care, but even twice as much love could not replace what had been lost. Each new experience, every new beginning, was a painful reminder of another beginning's end. Thoughts of his brother's unlived life spun inside him like the wheel of a gyroscope, time pulling him forward in only one direction. As long as John stayed in motion, he would never falter from whatever course he set.

Chapter 1

STANDING ON the Metro platform, John Wells casually wore the look of success. The arriving train brought with it a rush of warm air that instantly transformed his well-coiffed hair into a mess. Even so, it was a look most guys paid top dollar to get at salons in the city. The double doors of the car slid open, and John sauntered inside with one hand holding his briefcase and the other gliding his hair back into place. He checked his reflection in the window and readjusted the thick knot of his silk tie. The sharp cut of his suit accentuated the curve of his shoulders. Everything was just as it should be. His image, as usual, was perfect.

"Doors closing," a synthesized voice chimed as passengers hurried into the car. John grabbed a seat and stowed his overstuffed briefcase in the space at his feet. Wobbling back and forth, the train started down the track. John closed his eyes and tried to get comfortable. No one would notice if he put his life on hold for a minute and stopped worrying about the growing list of things it was his job to remember.

It was an ordinary Thursday morning in Washington—except the cherry blossoms were finally in bloom. John spent most of his time on Capitol Hill, serving as chief of staff to Senator Patrick Donovan. His job was never easy, but he had never expected it to be. He was accustomed to hard days and long nights brokering deals and lobbying votes. As the senator's go-to guy, he was routinely included in the most important closed-door meetings. John's voice, however quiet, always carried. After countless victory parties, he had started to believe it would last forever.

That was before the rumors—guarded whispers that Donovan might not run for reelection. Although nothing had been confirmed, it would be a tactical mistake to ignore the possibility that the senator might step down. Lesser men would have been prone to panic, but John was a survivor. If the unthinkable happened, he would be ready with a backup plan. It would be easy enough to secure another job—of that much he was certain. John would be patient and watch for a sign. The next few days should tell.

Patrick Donovan was a political animal who still loved the hunt. He would never give up the senate seat he'd held for five terms unless there was bigger game to be had. John's career was in good hands. No matter what happened, he'd be rewarded for his years of loyalty and service. Leaving now would be premature. Starting over was not an option.

John settled in and studied the faces of the people around him. The Metro was loaded with specimens from every nationality and background, a veritable Noah's Ark, except passengers seldom travelled in pairs. The electric hum of the engine grew louder as the train picked up speed. *Tenleytown. Van Ness. Cleveland Park.* The routine of the morning commute was always dependable. Each twist and turn of the track was exactly the same as the day before. The faces might change, but most shared the same look of apathy and fatigue—even before the workday had officially begun.

John turned away from the harsh, artificial light and looked out the window. Dawn was changing the color of the sky from black to deep purple. A heavy haze hung over the darkened houses. People were either asleep or already on their way to work. Twice this week he had woken up alone. There was no point in rereading the text message from David. It was too easy to infuse the words with insecurities about their relationship. John grabbed hold of the handrail in front of him as the train lurched to the right. The feeling of the cold metal afforded him a momentary sense of control. He looked out the window at the suburban dioramas and tried to pretend that his own life was still on track.

Confident and reliable, John Wells was always the one on whom others could depend—the guy who got things done. He was the kind of man who doled out smiles like a candidate passing out campaign buttons. Too often, he used one to punctuate a clever anecdote or placate a difficult audience. There was a time when a smile had been something more than just a smart accessory to complement his Gucci loafers and French-cuffed shirts. But over the years, he had given so many away that he was starting to wonder whether he had used up his allotted share.

The doors of the train opened and infused the stale air with a blast of cold from outside. It had been a hard winter, and John was ready for spring. The demands of work and the stress of urban living had taken a toll. Capitol Hill was a stove where pots always boiled, ready to spill over if not carefully tended. One or two were simple enough to manage, but John was a cook with one lid. Survival meant anticipating the next crisis and knowing when to cap it off.

John tried to swallow, but his mouth was dry. The red-brick houses beyond the station reminded him of his first place with David. It had only taken a few hours to load the combined contents of their apartments into the smallest U-Haul. But even sparsely furnished, that house had always felt like a home. John's student-loan payments devoured most of his meager salary, so money was always tight. Cable TV and air-conditioning were luxury items they quickly learned to live without. Each night he fell asleep to PBS droning quietly in the background or the sound of David reading aloud from a favorite book. No matter how hot it got that summer, they always slept wrapped in each other's arms.

At the end of an impossibly long day, John would stumble, bleary-eyed, into some political event to find David waiting in a borrowed jacket and tie. He always managed to keep one special smile in reserve, just for him. Days melted into weeks as happiness blurred the boundaries of their two separate lives.

Now, John attended work functions alone. He could barely remember the names of David's friends or recall how many classes he was taking this semester. It was true that he had taken his partner for granted, but there was still time to set things right. Once the situation with Donovan stabilized, he'd take David away on that promised vacation—to London or maybe somewhere warm.

With a steady hand, John pulled his BlackBerry from its holster and scrolled through a queue of unread e-mail. He studied the words on the screen and waited for work—his drug of choice—to take hold. Each message was another hit that drove everything from his mind but the next urgent problem only he could solve. The subject lines usually told him everything he needed to know. Original ideas usually generated a dozen counterfeit replies. There was, however, a communiqué from the senator, a man who rarely lowered himself to join the rest of the world in virtual reality. Patrick Donovan preferred to infuse his communications with his distinct southern charm, a quality that was hard to convey through digitally transmitted words on a two-inch screen. The e-mail was brief and to the point. Their daily status meeting was cancelled. A red blip pulsed on John's radar screen and then vanished. The senator's time was always at a premium.

Squinting at his reflection in the window, John tried hard to remember the young man who had come to DC with a half-empty suitcase and a head full of ideas. The city and the nation were high on politics, and John was a devoted disciple to the cause. After three long years in law school, he was determined to avoid a sentence of indentured servitude at a big-name firm. John wanted to make law, not simply study or defend it. He set his sights on Capitol Hill, where staff changed and advanced in steady cycles with each new administration. Jobs were plentiful, but he wanted more than just another credit on his résumé.

Most Americans knew of Patrick Donovan and the political office that was synonymous with the family name. John arrived for the interview an hour early just so he could wait outside and study the temperament of the senator's staff. There was a certain amount of skill required to blend in, but mostly it was about observation and luck. The men in the office spoke the loudest, but it soon became clear that the women ran the show. A thoughtful discussion with the senator's secretary went further than a long-winded policy debate with one of his aides.

Despite a lack of political experience, he was hired on as legislative counsel and immediately set about making himself indispensable. John was new to the game, but he worked harder than anyone else and quickly honed his skills. His ability to ingratiate himself with others created a "halo effect" that extended to Donovan himself. Before long, the senator began to win key votes on important bills. Patrick Donovan's career flourished, and John's work was acknowledged, albeit discreetly, by his inclusion in the inner circle of the senator's closest advisors. At the young age of thirty-six, John Wells was already a resounding success.

The train stopped at Metro Center and the doors slid open. As he had done a thousand times before, John grabbed his briefcase and joined his fellow commuters as they poured out into the station in one flowing mass. The morning rush hour was in full swing, and people crowded the platform, all en route to different destinations but mindlessly herding in one direction. One foot shuffled in front of the other across the smooth stone surface. At every moment, he was acutely aware of his distance from the next person and the tiny bit of space his body inhabited. John was almost to the escalators when he noticed the rugged profile of a man leaning against the wall.

The man looked up as though someone had called his name. John turned away, but it was too late. The stranger had noticed him. John's skin flushed hot beneath his gabardine suit as the sound of screeching brakes echoed off the smooth, cavernous walls. Nearby, a public service announcement played over a loudspeaker. John inspected the shine on his wingtips, but he could feel the stranger watching. Without thinking, he stepped onto the moving escalator. *Head up. Shoulders back. Eyes forward.* The hard plastic handrail felt cold and slippery. He wiped his sweaty palm on the leg of his pants and hurried up the steps to the next level. Everyone seemed to be moving in slow motion.

John weaved through the lingering commuters and cut down an adjoining corridor to the connecting train. Counting slowly to himself, he stopped at the end of the platform and pretended to read a brightly lit advertisement on the wall. A minute passed and nothing happened. The recycled air inside the station was stale. With a mixture of relief and disappointment, he lowered himself onto a granite bench and sighed.

John's nerves were shot, and he needed a fix. Automatically, he unsheathed his BlackBerry and pressed the power button. He scanned the tiny letters, but there was no familiar rush to carry him away. Work was no longer enough.

The sound of heavy footfalls echoed in the distance. Even without looking, John knew the stranger had followed. He locked his eyes on a fixed spot and pulled his briefcase closer. Running lights flashed out a warning along the edge of the platform, and the faint hum of the Metro swelled into a roar. All around, the other commuters began gathering their things and moving forward in anticipation. John grasped the leather handle of his briefcase and quickly stood. Blood rushed to his head, but he managed to stay on his feet. In a matter of seconds, the train would arrive, and the crowd would surge onto it. The doors would close, and the Metro would carry him away. The encounter with the stranger would be nothing more than a momentary distraction in an otherwise ordinary morning.

John started to go, he almost did, but something held him back. A rush of wind from the arriving train mussed his hair and blew his tie over his shoulder. This time, he made no effort to readjust his appearance.

The stranger was dressed in civilian clothes—a pair of khaki pants and a pale blue button-down shirt. His brown hair was cropped short, and he wore a neat goatee that seemed a natural part of his face rather than a fashion statement. John noticed an expensive pair of headphones hidden discreetly under the collar of his shirt and followed the cord down into a leather messenger bag slung across his chest. Everything about him was ordinary. Fiddling with the button on his suit jacket, John pushed his feelings back in place. He was used to a certain level of disappointment when it came to his personal life. He was just about to write off the whole encounter as a symptom of his general fatigue when the stranger smiled and recaptured John's attention.

"Doors closing," a synthesized voice chimed, and the train glided away.

The two men were completely alone.

"How are you doing?"

John shifted his weight from one foot to the other and considered the question. It would be easy enough to slip into the casual banter that filled up the hours of his day, but words seemed too imperfect to communicate what he was feeling. Now, more than ever, he wanted to step out of his well-ordered routine and become someone else. Without thinking, John dropped his briefcase onto the ground and took a step forward.

"Hi. I'm Peter."

His brother's name slipped out of his mouth of its own volition, but somehow it felt truer than anything else he could have said. John was sick of second-guessing Donovan, and his arms were tired from trying to hold on to David. It couldn't hurt to give reality a little break and indulge a harmless fantasy. Peter was now a character in the story.

"My name's Paul. It's nice to meet you."

Peter extended his hand and tried to keep it from shaking. He could tell a lot about a man by his handshake. Too soft was a sign of weakness. Too firm was an open declaration. Paul knew how to exert just the right amount of pressure from his fingers and palm to squeeze, but not crush. Standing tall with his head held high, he exuded a natural confidence that was stronger than any pheromone. Peter saw a different version of himself reflected in Paul's unbroken gaze. He liked the way it felt to be looked at that way.

The silence between them became acute. Looking down, Peter realized he was still holding on. An old man in a dark coat and matching fedora shuffled by and smiled. It was an awkward moment but not unwelcome.

"Sorry about that."

Dizzy and disconnected, Peter felt as if he'd been drinking on an empty stomach. He pulled his hand back and shoved it deep into his pocket. The watch on his wrist reminded him that it was getting late, and he would soon be missed. He needed to excuse himself and walk away. It was fine to pretend to be someone else for a few minutes, but the real world was waiting for him aboveground.

"I couldn't help noticing that you were looking at me back there."

It was a statement—not an accusation—but it was enough to make Peter blush. A strange, bitter taste in his mouth made him worry that his breath smelled. He looked to his right and then back again as Paul stepped forward and adjusted the strap of his bag. *No wedding ring.* John made a mental note.

"Listen, I've really got to be going," Paul said as he reached into his messenger bag. "I'm late for work... and I tend to be late a lot." In one fluid motion, he extracted a business card and pressed it into the breast pocket of John's finely tailored suit.

"Call me."

Paul didn't bother to wait for a reply. He backed away slowly and offered another dazzling smile to seal the deal.

Peter picked up John's briefcase as the lights at the edge of the platform began to blink. His timing, as usual, was perfect. The next train glided into the station, and Paul became a stranger once again. The doors of the car opened and Peter stepped inside. It was another train, a different line, but everything was the same. Gripping the handrail tightly, he crossed back over to the other side.

The rest of his morning would be more predictable. *Gallery Place. Judiciary Square. Union Station.* The train would move forward and deliver him to his destination. He would go to work and do his job.

Tonight, he would take the same line back and try to ignore the fact that the house he shared with David was no longer a home. That relationship, or some version of it, would survive. These brief moments meant nothing in a life that was at its best—and worst—consistent.

"Doors closing," a voice announced. "Doors closing…."

The train moved slowly down the track, and Paul turned around for one last look. Safe inside the car, John smiled.

Chapter 2

THE SUN was barely up, but at the Hart Senate Office Building, the business of deal making had already begun. Still charged from the encounter in the Metro, John strode down the hallway. He was careful to avoid making eye contact with the junior staff. To acknowledge their presence, with even a glance, would invite solicitation from those who needed his help. Social exchanges were merely business transactions, and trading information was about alliances, not friendship. The friction of the daily grind had given John layers of calluses. Thick skin kept him from feeling regret or disappointment, even if it kept him from feeling much of anything at all.

A young woman pushed open the polished doors of the senator's office and walked toward him with a file in one hand and a large coffee in the other. She wore a simple black skirt that effectively disguised the better part of her figure. She'd pulled her hair back in a tight bun, and her skin was free of makeup. She was attractive. Some might even call her pretty, if she would only stop trying so hard to prove them wrong.

"Good morning, sunshine," John whispered in her ear as he grabbed the cup from her hand and downed a gulp. With a halfhearted smile, she abandoned her coffee and continued down the hall. After so many early mornings together, she knew how much he needed it.

"You have a meeting in seven minutes on the new appropriations bill," she called out over her shoulder. "That's *seven* minutes. The file is in your office. Also, the pile of messages on your desk is growing faster than the national debt. Please return some calls."

"Yes, *Mother*," John replied and took another swallow. He looked back and waited for an acerbic reply, but she ignored the taunt and kept right on walking.

Melody Donovan had been John's research assistant for ten years. It was her job to find the facts to support what he already knew. She had been with him since the very beginning—back when every new piece of legislation was a chance to change things for the better. Side by side, they had fought the good fight and celebrated each victory. But recently, the real wins were too few and far between. Backroom deals and political compromises had worn down the sharpness of their convictions. Now, their swords were too blunt for battle. Politics required a sacrifice of ideals. That was a price John was willing to pay.

The lights in his office were already on and another cup of coffee was waiting on his desk. John forced back a yawn as he grabbed the file. He tried to skim the report, but the words on the page were a blur of letters and punctuation. It was becoming painfully clear that he needed more than caffeine to get through the morning.

How many late nights had he spent on the phone with Melody? It used to be a thing between them—to talk at the end of the day while John waited for David to get home from school. Now, the calls lasted until one of their phones ran out of juice. Conditions at home were rapidly deteriorating, but no matter what happened, he would always have Melody. She was his only true friend, but she was enough.

The clock on the bookcase chimed out the hour. Without thinking, John grabbed the fresh cup of coffee and tossed the empty into the trash. Melody's admonition rang in his ears as he hustled back through the main office and ducked out the door. He was almost to the elevator when he spotted the senator at the far end of the hall. At well over six feet, Patrick Donovan was an imposing man whose physical presence was enough to part the sea of lobbyists in his path. He walked with his head tilted downward to hear the murmurings of Stan Wilson, a political strategist who had recently been brought on as an advisor. When the moment was right, the senator made eye contact. John knew the look.

Wilson was known for unmaking deals and breaking promises. He was a man who was feared—but not trusted. While most people denounced his tactics, his success proved that it was the principles of Machiavelli, not the Founding Fathers, which drove national politics. The ends still justified the means. So far, John was unimpressed with the quality of his work, but traces of his influence were beginning to manifest.

"Good morning, Stan," John said with the smile reserved for close friends and bitter enemies. "It looks like you're already engaged in a serious discussion. What could be so pressing this early in the day?"

"Nothing you need to worry about," Wilson said dismissively as he offered his own toothless grin. "You just make sure to keep the trains running on time."

John reminded himself that this guy was slippery—easy to underestimate, difficult to read, and impossible to charm. Subtle derision of his work would backfire. Wilson's past successes lent a certain weight to even his clumsiest ideas. John needed to find his Achilles' heel, and Melody Donovan was his secret weapon. She knew her facts almost as well as she knew her father. Stan Wilson was a player, but he was only one man. John and Melody were a team.

"There's something important that I need to discuss with you."

John listened carefully to every word, but the senator's southern drawl made it difficult to discern anything from his tone.

"Meet me for lunch at the Metropolitan Club at noon."

Donovan punctuated the request with a short nod and then disappeared into his office with Wilson in tow. John made a mental note to debrief Melody, then slipped into the stairwell next to the elevator and closed the metal door securely behind him. The cinder block walls and primitive fluorescent lighting reminded him of a bomb shelter. Several flights down, a trio of distorted voices sounded like a badly tuned radio. Smooth leather soles scraped up the concrete stairs. A door slammed shut as John exhaled and leaned against the wall. This stairwell was his secret spot—the only place left in the Hart Building where he could stop and think without interruption. Lunch with the senator was a reserved privilege; even Melody rarely got much time alone with him. John suddenly began to wonder what his own father would have thought of his only son's success.

JACK WELLS lived with his extended family in a house on a hill that overlooked the steel mills of the Monongahela Valley. Handsome and athletic, he was the personification of other men's dreams. Every Friday night, he ran a football up and down the high school playing field to the sound of cheering fans. Each Saturday morning, he sat in the kitchen and watched his mother wash the soot from their windows with vinegar and hot water. Jack's father and uncles were all steelworkers. The sweat and dirt on their faces told him everything he needed to know about the world inside the gates. Molten steel was the color of the sun and almost as hot.

Jack dreamed of making touchdowns—not iron—and a college scholarship was his ticket out. Four years passed quickly for the star athlete. He measured his academic career by yards and quarters, not semesters or grades. By the end of his senior year, Jack had three undefeated seasons under his belt and the attention of every pro-sports recruiter in the state. His success as a professional athlete was practically guaranteed.

It's said that pride goes before a fall, but all that Jack felt on that cold November afternoon was frozen ground. *Crack.* The sound came from inside his body as tendons tore and his left knee split. One wrong turn and his days of running plays were over. After graduation, Jack returned home and traded his helmet and cleats for a hard hat and steel-toed boots. He married his high school sweetheart and tried to forget the sound of the crowd chanting his name. In time, he learned to live with memories instead of dreams—until that fateful night in June.

Although premature, John quickly grew into his father's image—a sculpture of muscle and bone. He was taller and larger than the other kids—the boy who always stood out in the class picture. He excelled academically and spent most of his time studying in the library. His classmates branded him a "loner," then worked hard to avoid him and make sure the label fit. The coaches expected him to carry on his father's legacy, but John had other plans. Jack Wells had spent years mastering a sport he could no longer play. All of his hard work had been for nothing. John would forge a future that no one could take away.

MELODY STEPPED into the stairwell with a full day's worth of exhaustion on her face. It was always the same. John could never hide from her for very long. She offered him a weak smile—the only one she had—then closed her eyes in silent reproach.

"I missed the committee meeting."

"Yes, I *may* have heard that from a couple of people," she said with a tinge of sarcasm. "One of whom may or may not have been the senior senator from Alabama."

"And when Senator Parsons isn't happy...."

"No one in Alabama is happy." They finished the sentence together. Melody moved in closer and leaned her full weight into John's shoulder. Public displays of affection were strictly forbidden, but alone in the stairwell, he could allow a brief lapse of decorum. In truth, John was grateful for human contact. It reminded him of better days.

"I'll circle back and smooth things over with Parsons. You worry too much."

John waited for Melody to remind him that worrying about him was pretty much her full-time job, but she refused to return the volley. Lately, the casual banter that got them through the daily grind had gone missing. John thought he knew all of Melody's moods, but this was one he had never seen. Eventually, they would have to stop with the silent treatment and talk it out. Unfortunately, time was the one thing he could not spare today.

"Sorry Mel, but I've really got to go."

John tried to focus his attention on his friend instead of his watch, but Melody knew his schedule better than he did. He kissed her on the side of her head, then slipped back through the door and sprinted down the hall. There were people to meet and deals to make. It was time to put the distractions of the morning behind him and get back to work.

JOHN TALLIED up the number of moving violations as the yellow cab raced up Constitution Avenue. It was almost noon, and the sidewalks were overflowing. In DC, lunch was an event, not a meal. Most people thought discussing business over silverware and an untouched plate of food made the subject matter more palatable. John had never bought into the concept. Normally, he used travel time to return calls or reply to e-mail, but all he could think about today was his impending lunch with the senator. Pushing his body back into the worn leather seat, John let out a sigh of relief. Donovan had finally granted him a private audience to discuss his plans for the future. After weeks of speculation, he was about to get some answers.

Despite its distance from Capitol Hill, the Metropolitan Club was a central hub for the power elite. The brown façade of the building stood in stark contrast to the gleaming white exterior of its distant cousin on Pennsylvania Avenue. The architecture was Italian, but there were no graceful arches or ornate tracery to soften the facade. The club was not a home and did not offer welcome—even to its members. Its declared mission was the vigorous pursuit of social ideals, but the rules of conduct reflected the clarity of intent of those who passed through its doors. The dress code required jackets and ties at all times, and the use of cell phones was strictly prohibited. Members and guests were even forbidden to exchange business papers in the public spaces, since such vulgar displays would confirm what everyone in DC already knew—an invitation to the club was a golden ticket.

John entered the building through the main entrance and ascended the grand staircase into the lobby. A thick red carpet cushioned the sound of footsteps, and yards of ivory silk hung from every window to diffuse the sunlight. The common area was expansive, but the dense silence was almost like being under water. John mentally mapped out the various caucuses in session. People spoke in hushed tones with facial expressions that were louder than their words. Somewhere, a clock marked time that was passing more slowly than it did in the real world. John was used to owning space. It was rare for him to feel intimidated and rarer still to be humbled. But at the Metropolitan Club, he was a guest. He would enter no farther until escorted by the member who had invited him.

Patrick Donovan's world propagated. It did not recruit. John had tried to break in before and failed. In high school, he was sure that an Ivy League degree would change the mettle of his character. A Yale alumnus had invited him to lunch at the HYP Club to discuss his college application. John arrived early and strategically positioned himself on a hard wooden bench by the door. Watching the sharply dressed members come and go was a pleasant diversion, but as the minutes ticked by, his enthusiasm changed to dread. An attendant finally noticed him waiting and rang up the member.

After almost two hours, an apologetic host escorted John into the dining room. Mother had suggested he skip the menu and order the chicken; she forgot to warn him to avoid anything prepared with Cajun spices. The first bite of the blackened dish took John completely by surprise. His voice, between coughs, was barely audible and water only made it worse. By the end of the meal, his freshly pressed shirt was soaked with sweat. One wrong choice had turned the interview into an unrehearsed comedy. Yale managed to survive without him, but the experience had left an indelible mark.

An invisible clock chimed out the hour. Punctual as always, Donovan emerged from one of the private meeting rooms off the lobby. At his side was Senator Sam Matthews, the Hill's newest rising star. Matthews had managed to defeat his Republican opponent in Texas, a state that had not elected a Democrat to statewide office since 1994. An unexpected burst of laughter from Donovan disturbed the preternatural quiet of the room. The gallery of elites glanced up just long enough to register the meeting. Matthews was not at the club by coincidence. In fact, it was doubtful that he was a member. The confluence of power was intriguing, even to the most casual observer, but John was the only one who seemed to appreciate its true significance. Matthews was still an unknown commodity. He needed to align himself with someone whose maturity and tenure would make up for his own inexperience. It was only natural for him to gravitate toward a venerated statesman like Patrick Donovan.

The two men were all handshakes and smiles as they approached. John buttoned his jacket and discreetly wiped his palm dry. He stepped forward and opened his mouth to speak, but Matthews brushed right past him. John quickly withdrew his hand as his face flushed red. Matthews had dismissed him as a zero—someone beneath his notice. Despite his record of accomplishments, John's collar, not his blood, would always be blue.

"You're here. Good."

The senator's waiting smile was a salve for the sting of rejection. John drew in a deep breath and let it out slowly. It was enough to be respected by a man like Donovan. In the end, his opinion was the only one that mattered.

"Sam Matthews is a smart guy, but he's too confident for his own good. Some time on the Appropriations Committee should fix that pretty quick."

With a light step, John followed Donovan up the stairs and down the softly lit hall. An older black man dressed in a white dinner jacket was waiting at the entrance to the dining room.

"Good afternoon, James!" the senator called out as the waiter escorted them to a table. The man received the greeting with reserved politeness, but refrained from speaking or making eye contact. He had served the senator—or men like him—for the better part of forty years. He was as much a part of the club as the paneled walls and Persian rugs. Even so, he had never allowed himself to believe that he was indispensable.

With the warmest of smiles, James unfolded the napkins and presented two freshly printed menus. Donovan nodded in acknowledgement, but the waiter was already hurrying back to the kitchen for Donovan's sweet tea with extra ice. John adjusted his chair and unbuttoned his jacket.

"So, sir...."

The clink of silverware on china punctuated the silence that followed. John reached for his water and took a long drink. Lowering the glass, he tossed out one of his most effective smiles. It was the senator's favorite and usually had the intended effect of stroking his temperamental ego.

"Do you have any idea why I asked you to join me here today?"

Donovan let the weight of the question linger before he continued. Experience had taught John not to answer and to indulge the senator's mercurial moods.

"I invited you here to talk about my plans for the future."

Ping. A bright red dot pulsed onto John's radar.

"Tomorrow night in Boston, at the fund-raiser for the Donovan Civic Center, I am going to announce my candidacy for president of the United States."

It is rare when real life takes on the feeling of a movie—when the dialogue and scenery blend together to create an effect usually reserved for Hollywood. John sat perfectly still and stared at the senator across the pristine table. Historic news demanded reverence.

"A national campaign is never easy. It will be a bloody battle. The press will try to twist my voting record to make me look like a Yellow

Dog Democrat who's out of touch with the values that have made this country great."

The knot in John's stomach tightened. He had heard this speech before from candidates who tried to hide their true politics in the soft wool of patriotism. It worked for some but only for those whose relative anonymity allowed them to selectively redact their pasts. After thirty years in the political spotlight, Donovan would need more than campaign rhetoric to keep his opponents from marginalizing him.

"To succeed, we must be strong enough to make tough choices to protect ourselves from these attacks. We need to act decisively and do whatever is necessary to achieve the loftiest of political goals."

The speech was practiced, though not very well. Donovan's words belonged to someone else. Stan Wilson had programmed the invisible teleprompter that was feeding the senator his lines. He was using his considerable influence to reshape the future candidate into the man he needed him to be.

"John," Donovan said in a voice that finally sounded like his own, "I am going to ask you to make a tremendous sacrifice."

Suddenly, the track of the movie that was playing switched back to real life. The leading man was once again his trusted friend and mentor. John took a deep breath and waited. He already knew he'd do anything to get Donovan into the White House. Nothing else mattered.

"I need you to resign as chief of staff."

John blinked hard and tried to clear the spots from his eyes.

"After you transition your responsibilities, I'll do everything I can to help you find another job. I'll speak with Senator Parsons about a position on his staff."

Donovan's words rang hollow now that the deed had been done. From here on out, anything he said would just be dialogue.

"You know that you're like family to us. That's something that will never change."

Donovan paused to take a drink from his sweating glass of iced tea. "Like family" was not the same as family. That was the lesson John was being made to understand. He had deluded himself into believing he actually mattered. In reality, he was nothing more than currency—human tender—that could be saved or spent. Seconds passed and his vision cleared. John still felt dizzy, but the blow had fallen short of its intended mark.

John carefully refolded his napkin and laid it back on the table. He knew that Donovan would be ready for a counteroffensive. Lobbying for his job would make John look desperate, and attacking Wilson would be an all-out declaration of war. Each scenario he considered would put into motion a series of responses that would escalate the conflict. John knew the man in front of him and the hidden levers that needed to be pulled to throw the machine into reverse. The only way to win the battle was to refuse to fight.

"Patrick."

John forced back a smile as he registered the almost imperceptible look of shock on the senator's face at the bold use of his first name.

"I simply don't know what to say."

Nothing was further from the truth. John's tone was flat and unreadable—a slow burn was necessary to achieve the desired effect. He lowered his head and pretended to study the white tablecloth beneath his outstretched hands. Donovan had been reading from a well-rehearsed script, but it was time to go off book. The senator needed to be lulled into a false sense of security until John could find a way to unseat Wilson.

"I'll do whatever you need me to do."

Donovan's shoulders dropped in relief. There would be no harsh words of recrimination—no ugly scene to tarnish the senator's sterling image. The end would be dignified. As usual, John would make it easy.

"Very good," Donovan said as he reached across the table to pat John's hand. "I knew I could count on you. There'll be other opportunities for you down the road. I'll see to that."

John fought the urge to recoil from the paternalistic gesture. The senator's reassuring words were for his own benefit. Patrick Donovan only surrounded himself with the brightest and the best. John's dismissal would send a resounding message that he was no longer an asset. Once word got out, his career would be finished.

The waiter returned to the table at just the right moment. Although more subdued, Donovan used the interruption as an excuse to move on from the unpleasantness of the situation. Turning from John, he casually smiled at the aged man who was patiently waiting for his order.

"What's good today, James?"

The senator always asked the same question, even though he already knew the waiter's stock reply.

"Everything is good today, sir."

"I'll have my usual then." There would be were no surprises at lunch today—at least none that were on the menu.

John smiled and pushed his feelings back.

"I'll have the chicken."

James poured the senator another sweet tea and then disappeared back into the kitchen. Donovan's hand trembled slightly as he poured an extra helping of ice into the glass. He misjudged the amount, and the amber liquid overflowed onto the tablecloth. John pretended not to notice.

"There's another sensitive matter I need to discuss with you," the senator said in a low voice as he dabbed at the mess with his napkin. "I have an important role for you to play at the event in Boston."

John's heart began to flutter at the prospect of redemption.

"Melody has been acting a bit odd lately, and her mother is concerned." The senator tossed the soiled napkin onto the table and looked John squarely in the eye. "After the announcement tomorrow night, the press will descend. You know my daughter's history and her penchant to overreact under pressure. We can't risk her doing anything that might draw negative attention to the campaign. I need you to stay close and watch over her. You're the only person I can count on to handle this with complete discretion."

John felt a weird throbbing sensation in his right temple, as if his head was being squeezed. He was being forced out of his job, but only after he performed a final act of servitude for the Donovan family. Anger was an invisible color that was seeping out of his pores onto the white linen tablecloth. With a steady hand, John took his napkin from the table and placed it back on his lap.

"Of course, sir. I'll take care of Melody. Whatever you need—I'm still your man."

The senator smiled to acknowledge what he already knew to be true.

The rest of the lunch was uneventful. Conversation was required in such an intimate setting, but John understood his new role as "emeritus counsel" and limited his questions to topics that did not challenge the senator. After the meal, Donovan decided to forgo his usual coffee. It was a decision that surprised the waiter, but not John. Timing was everything, and the senator knew when to make an exit.

The two men walked back through the lobby and stopped just short of the doorway. Donovan seemed apprehensive about facing John in the light of day and riding back to the office together. Anticipating the awkwardness of the moment, John was ready to defuse it.

"I'm sorry, sir. I forgot to mention that I have an appointment in Georgetown this afternoon. Can you make it back to the Hill on your own?"

Donovan's eyes narrowed and his smile disappeared. Too late, John realized he'd crossed a line. The senator carefully considered the situation and weighed the discomfort of a cab ride together against the idea of a member of his staff so obviously managing him.

"I think I can manage just fine without you," Donovan said to himself as he fumbled with the heavy wool of his overcoat. John made no move to help him.

The sting of the words felt good. Somewhere, deep inside, both men suspected Donovan had made a decision he would come to regret. Still, right or wrong, it was done. Without a word of farewell, the senator pushed open the doors of the Metropolitan Club and left John Wells alone in a world where he did not belong.

Chapter 3

MORE ORANGE than yellow, the sunlight was getting stronger with each passing day. Spring had finally sprung in the manicured patches of green around the city. Soon, it would be summer. Walking quickly down the sidewalk, John loosened his tie and unfastened the top button of his shirt. Traffic on the street was gridlocked behind the flashing hazard lights of a delivery truck, and angry horns blared like an orchestra tuning instruments. Somewhere close, the thumping bass of a car's radio added percussion.

Connecticut Avenue looked the same, even if everything else in his world had changed. John knew the city—the direct routes that got him where he needed to go. There was always another appointment to make or meeting to attend. Reaching his destination was more important than appreciating the journey. Now, freedom was a lens that brought things into focus. It was harder to measure the passing of time when there was nowhere he needed to be.

Skirting the outer ring of Dupont Circle, John slipped into a Starbucks. The lunch crowd was long gone, and the day had drifted into a sleepy pocket of afternoon. Even without a queue of customers, the barista at the counter hurriedly took his order. *Tall. Skinny. Americano.* There was no need for pleasantries or conversation. Conveniently, the customer had been stripped away from the business of service. With practiced efficiency, a second young woman assembled his drink and delivered it across the stainless-steel counter. In less than a minute, the transaction was complete.

At least the ceramic mug that held his coffee was not disposable. Right now, he needed something solid to hold onto. John exited through the side door and pulled a heavy cast-iron chair into the sun. The scraping sound of metal on concrete announced his presence to the empty sidewalk. Wounded and weary, he settled back and stretched out his legs. Warmth from the steaming mug radiated though his hands and body. The pungent smell of coffee triggered an unexpected flicker of memories.

There was a time, not long ago, when John had embraced the city like a lover. From the grungy restaurants in Adams Morgan to the stately halls of the Capitol—it had all been more than just a backdrop for his career. Back then, his life was like clay, not marble. Anything was possible. John began to chuckle at the irony of his current predicament.

"Laughing alone. That's not a good sign, Peter."

Standing in front of the café door, Paul crossed his arms and intentionally tilted his head in a way that accentuated his profile. He dropped his messenger bag on the ground and sat in the nearest chair without waiting for an invitation.

As a bead of sweat trickled down the skin beneath John's shirt, he feigned indifference. Whatever happened between them in the Metro was purely accidental—the confluence of a series of unplanned events. This, however, was something completely different. The randomness of meeting Paul again so soon threatened to elevate their encounter to the status of serendipity. From this point on, any further exchanges would be acts of volition—something premeditated that came with consequences. Considering the chaos swirling in his life, there was only one sensible thing to do.

The grinding engine of a passing bus gave John a few extra seconds to think. He was about to make a quick exit when Paul reached across the table and grabbed his hand. The boldness of the gesture took them both by surprise. As their fingers intertwined, John unexpectedly felt his resolve falter.

"You know, I really have to get back to work. I'm running late, and I...."

"...tend to be late a lot." Peter finished his sentence.

Paul's eyes were full of unbroken promises, and Peter's smile was warmer than the afternoon sun. Their mutual attraction was compelling, but was the possibility of a fleeting romance worth risking the security of a long-term relationship?

"So, how about we pick this up again some other time? Say, tomorrow night?"

What Paul lacked in subtlety, he made up for in swagger. Peter's imperfect world might be spinning in the wrong direction, but he knew what he wanted—even if John didn't.

"I'd like that very much." It was Peter who answered the question.

"Wait! No, I can't," John quickly interjected.

The light in Paul's eyes went dark. He squeezed Peter's hand tightly in his own, then released it and began to gather up his things.

"I want to see you again, but I have to be in Boston tomorrow night. I work for Senator Donovan, and he's making an important announcement."

"Important announcement, huh," Paul said with a cynical laugh. "Is it more important than spending time with me?"

"I know that's hard for you to believe, but it'll probably end up being the biggest news story of the week."

Inside, John was struggling to regain control. History was about to be made, and he was determined to be part of it. Despite the odds, he'd find a way to adapt and become whatever kind of man the senator needed him to be.

"Hey, Peter, are you in there?" Paul asked as he waved his hand in front of John's blank face.

"Yes, sorry. Just too much work and not enough play."

"Well, we're definitely going to have to do something about that. You've got my card. Call me when you get back."

The glimmer in Paul's eyes was still there, but its effect had been diminished by his obvious disappointment. He was a man who was used to getting what he wanted when he wanted it. Delayed gratification was just a fancy term for putting off a chance to have fun.

Peter knew his other life—the one John had spent years building—was teetering in the balance. An affair, no matter how discreet, would tip the scales. It was time to end this dangerous flirtation before it went any further. He started to speak, but Paul was already on his feet, weaving toward the street through a maze of tables and chairs.

John stayed seated and watched him trot off to his waiting job. He was hoping for a sign—a wave or a smile to dispel his doubts—but Paul was late. This time, there would be no looking back.

BACK ON the Hill, the Senate was in session, and the afternoon was packed with a rush of eleventh-hour negotiations. Business as usual was the order of the day. John returned to the office and tried his best to carry on. Despite a heavy workload, his brief absence seemed to have gone unnoticed—even by Melody. Technically, he was still in charge, but the news of his "unplanned departure" would break soon enough. For a few weeks, perhaps as much as a month, he would continue to manage the day-to-day issues until a successor was named. Then there would be a small send-off party and some token reward for his years of service.

The memory of Donovan's words mocked John's overinflated sense of self-worth. Maybe the senator—and everyone else—really could manage without him.

The sky was an inky black when John finally switched off the lights. Not surprisingly, he was the last to leave the office. After all, his days belonged to the senator and a job that refused to share him with the rest of the world. Only at night, after the political engines had throttled down, could John head home and reclaim some essential part of himself.

David had made that possible.

Loving him had always been easy—an involuntary reflex that was as natural as breathing. That was before John's job changed everything. Work used to be a verb that explained what John did—not an adjective that described who he was. In the evening and on the weekends, David talked for hours about school and his classes, but John rarely offered any information in return. War stories were for Melody. Eventually, David gave up and retreated to the safety of his books. Silence was better than disappointment. John had erected barriers to protect his partner from the stress and insanity of political life. Now, after so many years, he realized they were on opposite sides of the wall.

The security guard outside the building nodded good-night. The temperature was dropping, but John didn't bother putting on his overcoat. As he bounded down the marble steps and hurried along the path to Union Station, the cell phone buried deep inside his briefcase began to ring. The vote on the senator's clean energy bill was next week. That meant the call was probably from someone who was either getting on board or jumping ship. A year earlier, John would have spent the short walk to the Metro talking with David. He'd forgotten which one of them had stopped calling first, but the memory of those conversations made the ringing sound more urgent.

John searched for the phone by touch beneath the layers of papers and files. Just as his fingers reached the sleek metallic surface, the ringing stopped. Chiding himself, he removed the phone from the bag. The call was not from David. That time in their relationship had come and gone. From now on, information would be given on a "need-to-know basis." The nightly calls had ended for the same reason their relationship was falling apart. There was nothing left to say.

The screen on the phone told John he had one missed call. He entered the required code to retrieve his message and listened to the familiar voice on the line.

"John Wells—I've been thinking about you."

It was Eric Sloan, one-half of a power couple John and David had known for years. Although time had done little to deepen their friendship, keeping up appearances was a political and social necessity.

"I know how busy you are right now, but I simply must see you. Meet me for a drink tonight. You know where."

Eric rarely made demands, but when he did, he got his way. And tonight would be no exception. John knew it would be a tactical mistake to refuse his invitation. Rather than delay the inevitable, he pushed the return-call key and fell into an all-too-familiar role.

"Hey there, handsome," he said to Eric's voice mail. "I've been thinking about you, too. I'm on my way to Halo. I'll meet you there."

John flipped the phone closed and stuffed it into his bag. With a practiced gesture, he raised his arm toward the fleet of taxis circling Union Station. Spending an hour with Eric was better than going home. At least at Halo he could numb his pain with expensive alcohol. In a room full of people, he could pretend he wasn't alone.

Within seconds, one of the cabs flashed its lights and pulled over. John barely had time to shut the door before the driver zoomed back into the flow of oncoming traffic.

"Logan Circle."

The cab crisscrossed the District via a network of one-way streets. At every red light, the driver came to a screeching halt. Then, as soon as the light turned green, he floored it and took off at full speed toward the next intersection. The jarring sensation from starting and stopping was disconcerting—even for a seasoned traveler. Before long, the cab turned off Thirteenth Street and onto the roundabout.

Like the polar icecaps, the gay ghetto of DC was shifting. Dupont Circle was becoming passé. The cab had almost driven back to the turn where it had entered the Circle when it veered onto P Street. Despite the hour, cars jammed the street and alfresco diners packed the sidewalk.

With a loud screeching of brakes, the taxi ground to a halt in front of a large industrial warehouse that had recently found a second life. John paid the driver and slid out of the passenger side as a younger man brushed past him and quickly took his place.

There was no placard to mark the entrance, only the spectral projection of a shimmering white ring above the door. Halo was a nightclub that didn't need to advertise. You either knew about it or you didn't belong. The stoic doorman may not have known John's name, but he certainly recognized his type. Without missing a beat, he stepped forward and used both hands to slide open the heavy metal door.

John stepped inside the darkened foyer and allowed his eyes to adjust. All the bars in DC were smoke free, but the air was thick with the swell of voices and music. Huddled around the bar, boys disguised as men gave him the once-over. John knew he was a rare specimen—a wealthy man who was hot. That kind of status was flattering and annoying at the same time. Carefully making eye contact with all the right people, he sauntered toward the back where his friend would be waiting.

Eric Sloan was over forty, but he was still more attractive than most guys half his age. Completely silver, his hair was his only tell. Even from across the room, John could see an entourage flitting around the white leather sofa where Eric held court. Half-empty glasses covered the table in front of them. From the look of things, the party had been going on for quite some time. That would make their conversation more interesting, albeit less predictable.

John waited patiently for the right moment, then stepped forward and extended his hand. Eric laughed at the formality of the gesture and planted a dry kiss on his cheek. John detested such public displays, but his face didn't show it. The tinkling ice in Eric's empty glass signaled the others that he wanted privacy. In a matter of seconds, they were alone.

John ordered a drink and sat down. His muscles ached from the strain of another long day. Glad that it was almost over, he loosened his tie and let his body sink into the soft leather.

"So tell me," Eric asked as he raised his glass. "What have you been up to since we last spoke?"

Although his friend's tone was disarming, the question was loaded. News travelled fast around the DC Beltway, but it was unlikely that anyone in Eric's social or political networks knew of the senator's plans. Experience had taught John not to react in these kinds of situations. If Eric was going to fish for information, he'd have to offer some bait.

A waiter with a silver tray appeared at their table. Under normal circumstances, it would have been the perfect opportunity to change the subject. But as the server bent down to deliver the drinks, John's attention wavered. Dressed entirely in black, the boy had the face of an angel. He lingered for a moment to acknowledge the older man's obvious attention. There were other patrons waiting, but he knew how to earn the tips that paid his rent.

"Looks like you might need more than just a stiff drink tonight."

John threw back the rest of his cocktail to hide his reaction to Eric's keen observation. Even though the alcohol filled his body with artificial heat, it was important to stay cool. Being "monagamish" was currently in vogue. Most couples had given up on fidelity, deluding themselves with the notion that they'd evolved beyond the point of "rules and absolutes." Like skyscrapers, the structures of these modern relationships were designed to shift and sway without damaging the foundation. John was still old-fashioned when it came to love, but trying to defend his values at Halo was like ordering a salad at a steak house. It was better to smile and let people assume the worst.

"I'm sorry. That comment was insensitive in light of your current domestic situation."

John had no idea what Eric was talking about, but his tone suggested he should. Apologies in their social circle were rarely offered and almost never sincere. As the music changed, Eric pushed his knee against John's leg. The gesture was adolescent, but tolerable. Alcohol was already causing John's inhibitions to slip. Reluctantly, he let his head fall back and stared up at the exposed pipes and network of vents in the dark recesses of the ceiling.

"David is an idiot," Eric whispered under his breath. "He'll never find anyone better than you."

"What do you mean?" John asked, raising an empty glass to his lips. Without waiting to be summoned, the waiter promptly reappeared with another round of drinks. John took his without even glancing at the young man who had been so captivating a moment before. Suddenly, the faces around him were no longer beautiful.

"You're too smart to play dumb. It's time to face facts about David's extracurricular activities."

It was obvious that Eric was feeling none of the effects of the alcohol he'd been consuming. His tone was serious now that the true purpose of their meeting had been revealed.

"God knows I've had more than a few of my own indiscretions. A couple hours with one of the local boys can be fun, especially when there's someone to come home to at the end of the night. But adultery is a mortal sin that the members of our little circle—the people who matter— are loathe to forgive."

To Eric Sloan, this was just another piece of business that needed to be resolved to ensure the preservation of the status quo. John's feelings meant nothing in the grand scheme of things. He would have to end his relationship with David. To object, to do anything else, would make him part of the problem instead of the solution.

"Don't worry. I'll take care of the situation right away."

Clusters of curious men watched eagerly from the sidelines. Although no one could overhear what was actually being said, the pantomime between the two men was enough to fuel a fair amount of wild speculation. Around the lounge, heads turned and whispers circulated. The onlookers would judge Eric by the company he kept, but the Sloan armor could withstand a few minor dings.

John stared across the table at his doppelganger. There was a time when he would have appreciated Eric's professional detachment. A thick emotional veneer protected him from caring too much. However, John was finding out what it felt like when that hard shell shattered. He needed to act quickly, before all the strength drained from the cracks.

Acting on survival instinct, he slipped his hand through Eric's thick mane of silver hair and pulled him closer until their lips touched. The kiss had no real passion behind it, but it lasted long enough to convey his intended message.

"I know this isn't easy," Eric said as John stood to leave. "But remember, you have my full support."

THE SCRAPING sound of a key in the lock startled John. He had been asleep on the couch too long to wake up quickly, but not long enough to have gotten any real rest. David went through his usual routine of closing up the house for the night and setting the alarm. He lit a small lamp on the writing desk and casually sorted through the day's mail. Despite the late hour, his movements were almost graceful—as if the best part of his day had just begun. Sitting up, John quietly made his presence known.

John knew David had grown accustomed to spending these hours alone. With an audible sigh, he tossed the pile of letters onto the table and headed for the stairs. John hurried across the room to block his escape.

"Let's not do this again tonight. I have class in the morning."

"I'd be inclined to agree with you," John said, ready to deliver the speech he'd practiced on the cab ride home, "except for the fact that *technically*, it's already morning. Three a.m. might be a new record—even for you. Honestly, I have to wonder why you even bother coming home at all."

"I wonder that myself," David responded defiantly. "Why do I keep coming back to this place when we fight almost every night?"

John stepped forward and closed the distance between them. He was breathing hard, and his heart was racing.

"Because I'm your partner, and this is your home... *our* home. How does that inconvenient fact keep slipping your mind?"

"I haven't forgotten anything, but we both know that things have changed. It's time to stop pretending."

John's efforts to provoke David were useless. Standing on the edge of the cliff, both men were ready to jump.

"So, what?" John's voice unexpectedly cracked. "I'm just supposed to pretend I don't know what you've been doing behind my back?"

"I'm tired of all your accusations and judgments. I'm sick of talking *at* you while your nose is buried in your goddamn BlackBerry. I won't apologize or feel guilty for finally giving up on us and trying to find some happiness for myself."

John knew it was the closest he'd ever get to an admission from David. He bit down hard on his lower lip and let the pain fortify him. It was time to end things once and for all. John opened his mouth to speak, but before he could form the words, David grabbed him forcibly by the shoulders and kissed him hard on the lips. The certainty John had felt a moment before melted.

Like drowning swimmers, both men grabbed and clawed at one another as they stumbled back to the sofa. Trembling hands traced familiar paths. Lips touched and shared breath—too sweet—passed between them.

David undid the buttons of John's shirt and parted it down the middle. With complete abandon, he sank his teeth into tender skin as his partner arched his back and cried out in pain. Before John knew what was happening, his belt was unfastened and his clothes were on the floor. It had been a long time since they'd been together like this, but things were still moving too fast.

Stopping just long enough to slip out of his pants, David pulled John into position and began to push up against him. John tried to switch places, but each thrust drove him deeper into the cushions of the couch. Muscles tightened and twitched as the tension mounted. Sooner than expected, David gasped and buried his face in a pillow.

John realized his mistake too late.

Neither man spoke as they disentangled their bodies. Naked and unspent, John watched David gather up the clothes from the floor. When he was sure he had everything, he switched off the light and headed upstairs to bed.

Although tired and lonely, John knew he could not follow. David was right about one thing. After tonight, there could be no more pretending. Accepting the inevitable, John settled back onto the couch and pulled a blanket over him. In less than a minute, he was asleep.

Chapter 4

JOHN ROLLED onto his side and tried to dislodge his body from the crater it had made in the couch. After lying in the same position all night, his muscles were stiff, and his backside felt heavy and numb. The urge to surrender to sleep was like gravity, threatening to pull him under. With some effort, he swung his legs around and planted his feet firmly on the floor. As John stood up, the lap blanket covering his naked torso fell away.

"Shit."

His pants and shirt were gone. In his haste to make a quick exit, David must have grabbed both sets of clothes off the floor. Still, it hardly mattered. Wrapping the blanket around his waist, John shuffled toward the kitchen to make coffee. Fresh anger was already brewing. After last night, it was clear David had been planning his exit for some time. All those nights away from home had bolstered his confidence and dispelled any doubts about whether he could make it on his own. Each new friend provided a foothold in a world that did not include John.

Hot water hissed through a paper filter as a steady stream of dark liquid trickled into the glass pot. Staring intently at the machine, John tried to ignore the pounding in his right temple. It seemed like a cruel axiom that the more urgently he needed coffee, the longer it took to brew. Even before the pot was half-full, he pulled David's favorite mug from the cabinet and filled it to the rim.

The breakfast room off the kitchen got the morning light, though John could not recall ever having taken the time to enjoy it. He'd spent the better part of the last decade investing a small fortune furnishing rooms that were rarely used. The Italian biscotti jar on the counter had never held a single cookie, and the espresso maker next to it only surrendered a ration of coffee when it was coddled and wooed.

Yellow sunlight reflected off the dark surface of a heavy walnut table. David had discovered the piece a few years back in the basement of an antiques shop in Georgetown. Although John had initially bristled at the cost, it didn't take much coaxing to convince him to make the purchase. Buying such a table with its price tag and pedigree was another resounding affirmation that he had arrived.

John sat down and tried to appreciate the view. Just outside the French doors, brilliant pink blossoms bloomed on newly planted trees. Despite his marital infidelities, David had remained devoted to their garden. Taking a long sip of coffee, John winced at the bitterness. The hard wooden chair pushed relentlessly into his bare bottom. He tried shifting his weight, but the furniture in the breakfast room had been designed for style, not comfort.

"Is it Thursday or Friday?"

Another hit of caffeine helped John reorder his disjointed thoughts. *Friday. Donovan. Boston.* The significance of the impending event jolted him into motion. He left his unfinished mug sitting conspicuously on the table and hurried upstairs. The door to the bedroom was ajar, but the room was dark. John searched the shadows for some sign of life, but beneath the mounds of pillows and blankets, the king-sized bed was empty.

John shifted open the plantation shutters and tried to remember the next step of his morning routine. On the floor outside the bathroom, he nearly tripped over a mound of damp towels. Hastily, David had scrubbed away any evidence of last night.

John snatched up the pile with both hands and hurled it into the wicker hamper. The force and weight of the bundle sent the entire contents of the laundry basket flying. Stooping to gather up the clothing, he realized that most of the outfits were brand new. Just recently, David had begun acquiring a variety of tight T-shirts and designer jeans for the nonacademic events on his social calendar. John picked up a pair of stylish underwear and admired the fabric. Although the wardrobe had been purchased with his money, none of it was for his benefit.

John charged over to the bed and tore off the linens. He pulled so hard at the fitted sheet that the mattress shifted off its frame.

"How could I have been so stupid?"

The empty room did not answer.

Anger was pointless, and his tired eyes were too dry for tears. John needed to conserve his energy and come up with a game plan. With some effort, he pushed the mattress back into place and sat down to think. Past experience was a good indicator of what would happen next. Negotiating a division of property would be quick and painless. Everything, including the house, was his. David had always been better at spending money than making it. But even without his job, John could live comfortably on his savings for a while. Money was the least of his concerns.

A blaring ring called him back to the present. Like a faithful soldier, John snapped to attention and marched across the hall to the den. A familiar calm descended as he picked up the handset of his private landline.

"Hello?" John said into the device as he walked back into the bedroom and grabbed his bathrobe from a hook on the closet door.

"Thank god you answered. It's me."

Melody was the only person who knew him well enough to be so familiar. John's first instinct was to tell her about David. As his "work spouse," she already knew most of the gory details anyway. But commiserating would have to wait. Today, he needed an ally more than a friend.

"I'm sorry if I woke David, but I got worried when you didn't answer your cell. Dinner with my father last night was a complete disaster." Melody sounded almost as bad as John felt.

"Listen, I know how you feel about doing anything spontaneous, but I was wondering… whether you might consider…."

"Cut to the chase, Mel. What do you have in mind?"

"Let's run away." The suggestion was something John would have expected to hear from a teenage girl, not a seasoned political aide. "We could grab an earlier flight to Boston and spend the whole day together."

Her anxious tone suggested that Melody Donovan was less than comfortable with her father's political plans. Over the years, she had managed to survive each of the senator's grueling reelection campaigns, but a presidential race would be a different beast. The national media would be relentless, and the political attacks on Donovan would eventually turn negative. The small measure of private life Melody had managed to sequester would quickly disappear.

In this time of crisis, she had turned to her best friend. It was only natural to assume that he would be beside her through it all. John knew Melody would fight for him even if that meant standing up to her father. While the senator would never keep someone on staff to appease his daughter, her opinion mattered. Melody Donovan was the one person Stan Wilson could not marginalize. She alone could openly oppose him without fear of reprisal.

"Have I stunned you into silence, or are you trying to come up with an excuse to bail on me?"

"Sorry, I've got a lot on my mind this morning." A younger version of David smiled at him from a sterling silver frame on the credenza. John was trying to keep up with the conversation, but a jumble of feelings and memories were proving to be a distraction.

"Okay, let's go to Boston—right now—this morning." His response was completely out of character, but John couldn't resist the temptation to jump on a plane and check out for a little while.

"So at least we'll have today." Something about Melody's tone immediately caught his attention.

"Hey Mel, is everything okay? Are you all right?"

"I'll make the travel arrangements and meet you at National in an hour. For once in your life, Wells, don't be late."

John started to reassure her that he would be there on time, but the line was dead. He spoke Melody's name to call her back, but she was already gone.

THE WHEELS of the plane grabbed hard on the runway. Air roared through the engines as the brakes fought back against the speed that had kept the aircraft aloft. John yawned and did a modified stretch within the confines of his seat. The flight had been short, but he'd enjoyed almost a full hour of uninterrupted sleep. Even without looking, he knew Melody was awake. Despite her obvious fatigue, she could rarely manage to get any rest. Still, some quiet time with a book had done her good. She looked more relaxed, and the tension in her face was gone. Making the trip together had been the right decision.

After a few carefully executed maneuvers, the plane came to a stop. The flight was only half-full, but the double chime that signaled their arrival sent the passengers into a mad frenzy of activity. Cell phones powered up and bags were yanked from overhead bins. Before long, bodies packed the narrow aisle, inching forward toward the exit. Melody ignored the impulse to move and kept right on reading.

> He saw that all the conditions of life had conspired to keep them apart; since his very detachment from the external influences which swayed her had increased his spiritual fastidiousness, and made it more difficult for him to live and love uncritically. But at least he *had* loved her—had been willing to stake his future and his faith in her—and if the moment had been fated to pass from them before they could seize it, he saw now that for both, it had been saved whole out of the ruin of their lives.

"*The House of Mirth?*" John asked as he shifted impatiently in his seat. "Isn't Edith Wharton a little heavy for your day off?"

"I'm just rereading an old favorite."

The plane was emptying fast, and the cleaning crew was already collecting newspapers and refolding blankets. One of the male flight attendants stopped briefly to steal a glance at the handsome couple. A quick look from John told him he had misjudged the relationship.

"A penny for your thoughts?"

Melody didn't answer.

"Hey, I thought we agreed that I would be the moody one on this trip."

John's tone was playful, but something was definitely off. Melody had barely spoken to him all morning. He'd made a few feeble attempts at conversation, but her persistent silence gave him the perfect excuse to grab some shut-eye.

"Can we table any serious discussions for later? I really need a break."

It was clear to John that Melody was battling more than simple fatigue. He knew from experience that the number of hours she slept each night varied with her moods. Invitations to join him for dinners in Georgetown and weekend boat trips to Annapolis were politely declined. The senator had confirmed that calls from his wife usually went unanswered.

Fourteen-hour workdays left Melody exhausted, but John was hopeful things would change when the Senate adjourned for the summer. The heat and humidity would slow the pace, and the extra hours of daylight meant shorter nights alone. Melody had even mentioned something about taking some vacation time to see the new Impressionist exhibit at the Guggenheim.

The aisle was finally clear, and the plane was empty. It was time to go. John watched his best friend gather her things and tuck her book into the outer pocket of her bag. Compared to the onerous limitations Melody would be forced to endure as a member of the first family, his own domestic problems with David seemed less important. Thinking with his heart, John grabbed her hand and kissed it hard. The spontaneous display of public affection made her smile.

Inside the terminal, the human current pulled debarking passengers onward. Down in baggage claim, impatient travelers huddled around empty carrousels. It was a different city, another airport, but one thing was the same: everyone had baggage.

As a rule, John travelled light. *Four shirts. Three sweaters. Two pairs of corduroy pants.* He still remembered the contents of the footlocker he'd dragged off to college. The strange-looking clothes inside had been selected by his mother from the L.L.Bean catalog and delivered by mail order. Money was tight, but his parents maxed out their only credit card to make sure their son looked the part. Nervous about a few of the more dubious fashion choices, John had hidden the fawn-colored "duck boots" in a bag under his bed until he saw his peers in similar footwear trudging through the snow.

Now, after fifteen years, he was back in Boston.

Once he made certain Melody was beside him, John tightened his grip on the handle of his carry-on bag and headed straight for the nearest door. Outside, a lane of mismatched cabs was waiting. The nearest driver sprang to life at the sign of a fare and tossed their luggage into the open trunk. With practiced efficiency, he jumped behind the wheel and flipped on the digital meter. John fastened his seat belt and called out their destination through a small, square opening in the Plexiglas divider. The cabbie paused just long enough to make eye contact in the rearview mirror and then punched the gas.

The cab's engine squealed in protest as it propelled them away from the curb and across two lanes of heavy traffic. Ignoring the blaring horns of the cars behind them, the driver smiled and turned up the volume on the radio. It was, after all, Boston.

The taxi maneuvered through airport traffic and detoured underground onto the expressway. The Central Artery/Tunnel Project, more notoriously known as the "Big Dig," had provided an efficient and discrete system of roads hidden beneath the city. It was the most ambitious urban-infrastructure project in history, but the $14.8 billion spent to complete it had ultimately provoked Congressman Barney Frank to ask, "Wouldn't it be cheaper to raise the city than to depress the Artery?" Even though construction was still underway, the project had already changed the face of Boston forever.

John stared out the grimy window and counted the lights inside the tunnel. He remembered how he'd spent the better part of his freshman year learning how to get around the city. Manic drivers and patched-up potholes taught him to keep his eyes on the road ahead and ignore anything too far to the right or the left. Fortunately, those same lessons had prepared him for a career on Capitol Hill. Now, all the familiar routes John had once travelled were buried beneath public parks and improved commercial spaces.

In a remarkably short time, the cab resurfaced on the other side of the city and made a sharp turn into a crowded driveway. It would take another century for the Boston Harbor Hotel to acquire the patina of the Metropolitan Club, but what the building lacked in pedigree, it more than made up for in grandeur. The driver stopped and parked beneath the five-story archway that served as a gateway to the waterfront. Perched at the top of the hotel, the glass rotunda would be the perfect setting for Senator Donovan to make history.

John paid the driver in cash and handed their bags to the bellhop. The rate for their two-night stay would probably seem more like a mortgage payment than a hotel bill. His close association with the senator created the illusion that he was accustomed to staying in such places. But mere proximity to wealth did little to diminish the vivid memories of family vacations spent in shared rooms at a Holiday Inn. Even though John had never found a way to escape from that past, he'd become pretty good at hiding from it. With an exaggerated flourish, he offered Melody his arm and guided her through the door.

One look explained how the Grand Lobby of the Harbor Hotel had come by its name. Exotic orchids floated in long, slender vases, and soft light from the chandeliers made the marble floors look like melted chocolate. Unimpressed by the opulent trappings, Melody headed straight for the front desk while John lagged behind to admire a fleet of wooden ships on display. The senator was an avid sailor and would have enjoyed the workmanship of the models. After tonight, however, there would be no time for such distractions. As a presidential candidate, Donovan would be insulated from most aspects of the real world. Soon, Stan Wilson would have the senator moored under a layer of protective glass.

Melody reappeared with the room keys and a handful of gaudy tourist brochures. John turned toward the elevators, but she spun him around in the opposite direction and walked him out the door.

"Wait! Where are we going? I want to see my room."

"Later!" Melody said as she pulled him across the driveway and out into the street. The horn from a passing car startled them both into a sprint.

"What are you doing? Trying to get us killed?" John asked once they'd reached the safety of the sidewalk. "I want to go back to the hotel."

"No way, Wells. If I leave you alone, even for five minutes, you'll be on the phone and ass-deep in e-mail."

Melody was right, and John knew it. He was happy to see that the light had returned to her eyes. It would be a welcome change to spend an afternoon with someone who had no secret plans or hidden agendas. All she wanted was a few hours off the grid.

"Well, if we're going to do this, then we have to do it right." John took the brochures from Melody's hand and tossed them into the nearest trashcan. "If you want to see Boston, the *real* Boston, then follow me."

A familiar ringing stopped him cold in his tracks. John reached for his BlackBerry and stared intently at the screen. Although it was still early, his unplanned absence was undoubtedly creating some disruption back at the office. Worrying the hard plastic with his thumb, he weighed his options. As chief of staff, he was always on-call, but a command from the senator—or a message from David—would ruin the whole day. Concern about the deep creases that had reappeared on Melody's face overrode his sense of duty and obligation. John double-checked to make sure the phone had powered down and then tucked it inside his jacket. When he turned back toward Melody, she was staring at him in disbelief.

"I guess the senator will just have to manage without me."

Chapter 5

JOHN LEANED his torso against the metal railing and stretched the upper portion of his body out over the harbor. Overhead, a flock of seagulls floated on drafts of air. Like a delicately balanced mobile, the birds dangled from invisible wires until a gust of wind sent them scattering. Gazing up at the blue sky, John smiled. He was eighteen again and ready to play. With a keen sense of direction and a healthy dose of adolescent enthusiasm, he dragged Melody down the final stretch of the Harborwalk toward the New England Aquarium.

Just ahead, to the left of the entrance, a rocky crag and forty-two thousand gallons of seawater re-created a slice of Massachusetts' coastline. At the first sign of an audience, the exhibit's inhabitants broke into song. Visitors always expected the harbor seals to bark like sea lions. But the pups communicated in short, high-pitched yelps while the older animals vocalized with deep, low roars. As if to make the point, one of the mature males waddled forward and let out a low moan that sounded like a prolonged burp.

"Is it me or does that big one sound an awful lot like Senator Parsons?"

"Don't be ridiculous," Melody deadpanned. "Parsons has a southern accent."

The attendant inside the ticket booth was not the man John remembered. He had the right South Boston accent, but his face was too young and his eyes were too bright. Back in college, John could get into the aquarium with a quick nod and flash of his student ID. Now, he had to buy a ticket like everyone else.

Except for a few puddles of light, the main hall was mostly dark. Elementary school kids darted back and forth, calling out each new discovery to one another. Inside the penguin exhibit, a waddle of rockhoppers sported spiky crowns of yellow feathers that plumed like punk-rock haircuts. Miniature hands reached into the Touch Tank to stroke the sleek backs of cownose rays.

Yelps and giggles echoed off the smooth concrete walls. The children's laughter was infectious, and John was glad to see that Melody was not immune. Squeezing her hand tightly, he guided her through the obstacle course of small bodies and up the walkway that spiraled around the Giant Ocean Tank. Her unexpected smile made his happiness complete.

Light from the ceiling filtered down through one hundred and fifty thousand gallons of fresh seawater. The eerie blue glow that radiated from the observation windows somehow made the space around the tank seem even darker. Still, it was bright enough to illuminate the schools of tropical fish swimming around the coral reef. John leaned against a stone pillar and stared into the tank. *Goliath grouper. Sea nettles. Lionfish.* It had been more than fifteen years, but he still knew each genus and species by heart.

"So, you're really a closeted fish nerd?" Melody asked, stepping forward and pressing her hand against the glass. "How did I not know this about you?"

"Well, it's not usually the kind of thing you put on a résumé." John quietly chuckled. "I'm full of surprises."

"Ditto."

A wave of eager children rushed up to the observation window. In a matter of seconds, their little heads were bobbing around like buoys. Even in the half-light, John could see that Melody's smile had retreated into the darkness. There were a dozen places left that he wanted to explore, but it was already time to go. The rest of the afternoon was for Melody. Their next stop would surely brighten her mood.

After an hour inside the aquarium, the sunlight outside seemed doubly bright. Tourists loitered on the benches around Christopher Columbus Park, and lunchtime shoppers mobbed Quincy Market. John suggested stopping for something to eat, but Melody refused. As usual, she seemed cruelly indifferent to her body's needs. Arguing about it would be a waste of time. The Donovans were, for the most part, stubborn to a fault.

Instead, John marched her down the street and across the red-bricked plaza that surrounded Government Center. Unlike the rest of the city's new construction, it was a scar on the face of Boston that never seemed to heal. At the far end of the block, they hurried down a flight of stairs and into the subway. Fluorescent lighting accentuated the thin layer of dirt that seemed to cover every surface. A piercing shriek cut through the air as a Green Line train rounded the sharp curve that led into the station. John winced and quickly covered Melody's ears. The Boston T was less sophisticated than the DC Metro, but it certainly had more heart.

Although he'd never been much of a Red Sox fan, John knew the area around Fenway Park. The Back Bay Fens was a favorite cruising spot for gay men, but it was also the city's cultural epicenter. Art lovers usually opted for the MFA, but as a former Bostonian, John had a more intimate destination in mind.

Even though the four-story Venetian palazzo was home to one of the finest private art collections in the world, the exterior of the Isabella Stewart Gardner Museum always reminded John of his elementary school. The museum was laid out according to Mrs. Gardner's specific tastes, and anyone named "Isabella" was entitled to lifetime free admission. Upon her death in 1924, she bequeathed her home to the city on the condition that none of the exhibits could ever be changed. Even after several pieces of art were stolen in 1990, the curators, true to their charge, left the empty frames hanging on the walls.

All of the rooms were tastefully decorated with paintings, sculptures, tapestries, and furniture. Rembrandt, Raphael, Michelangelo, and Botticelli. All the great European artists were in residence. Once inside, Melody became John's personal docent. With remarkable focus, she guided him through the galleries and explained the importance of each piece.

"I think my grandmother had a big plate like this on her kitchen wall."

"Actually, it's called a 'tondo,' which is a circular work of art with terra-cotta figures mounted on a wooden frame. It was made by Benedetto da Maiano circa 1495."

"But of course," John said in a faux British accent. He knew that Melody had a master's degree in art history, but her breadth of knowledge was truly impressive. She seemed to know a little something about every major work in the museum.

"Okay, you have to stop!" John said after they had viewed another three exhibits. "This is too much culture. I'm from Pittsburgh. I need a break."

The museum boasted a lush internal courtyard that was visible from almost every room. Three stories high, the atrium structure had a glass roof and a floor of Roman tile. Melody leaned out from one of the balconies like a modern Juliet. Ancient marble statues watched from the flowering gardens below. Right on cue, her Romeo stepped forward and took his place at her side.

"So what do you think of the museum? It's a little understated, but…."

"This place is incredible, and you know it," Melody said, playfully jabbing her elbow into John's side. He pretended to flinch.

Once, not so long ago, Melody Donovan had been an assistant curator at the Smithsonian. What was supposed to be a brief stint working on one of the senator's toughest reelection campaigns had somehow morphed into a full-time job. Each term of office brought another set of challenges and eventually the leave of absence became permanent. Over the years, her passion for art had cooled into a pastime. Supporting her father meant settling for pictures in books or a few stolen hours at the National Gallery.

The sun had dipped behind the Hancock when John and Melody emerged from the T stop at Copley Square. Arm in arm, they strolled up Newbury Street, looking in windows and enjoying the last few hours of their afternoon. It had been a long day, and John was tired and hungry. Melody spotted a French bistro on the corner and suggested they stop for a bite before heading back to the hotel. The fare was probably pretty good since the outdoor seating area was overrun with patrons. Rather than fight for a table, John grabbed some modest provisions for an impromptu picnic.

Despite the unseasonably warm weather, the Charles River Esplanade was nearly empty. Melody sat quietly as John unwrapped the sandwiches and passed her a cold bottle filled with neon-colored liquid.

"What's this?" she asked, trying to translate the French on the label.

"Haven't a clue," he replied through a mouthful of sandwich. "But it looked like it would be fun to drink."

Melody laughed and raised her bottle in a mock toast as the food in front of her sat untouched. John devoured his entire sandwich and half of hers while watching a steady stream of students cross the Salt and Pepper Bridge. Commuting back to Harvard or MIT, their carefree lives were a painful reminder of the mess that was waiting for him back home.

"It's over with David. We ended things last night." John chewed his food and swallowed hard. "He's been cheating on me for months."

Fragments of John's conversation with Eric conveniently filled in any gaps in the unfolding story. He waited for her to respond, but there was only silence. Finally, after almost a full minute, she let out a heavy sigh and took another swig from the bottle.

"Did you hear anything I just said?"

"Yes. I heard you quite clearly." Melody said, standing up and walking to the edge of the river. "Do you know how many sleepless nights I've spent listening to you complain about your love life? Each bitter fight you've had with David just strengthened your resolve to hold on. You're one of the smartest men I know, but you've been blindly devoted to someone who could never love you back."

"I should have known you'd disappoint me," John called out in his best imitation of the senator's voice. Melody let out a low, almost inaudible laugh and wiped away a tear. His pointed remark hit its intended target.

"Wow. Low blow. Honestly, Wells, how did you expect me to react?"

"Maybe you could try to care a little more about my feelings."

"Care *more*?" Melody said, throwing up her arms in frustration. "You can't imagine how hard I've been trying to care *less* about you!"

A safe distance away, John watched helplessly as something inside her broke loose.

"I'm tired of being your colleague and confidante. No matter how hard I try, I can never make myself into someone you could actually care about—a candidate who could ever be good enough to win your great, elusive love."

The words stung, but John reminded himself that this was Melody. As his most trusted ally, she was the person who knew him best.

"I never aspired to be your assistant or sidekick."

"Oh, come on! I've *never* treated you like a subordinate."

It was time for John to end this silliness. If Melody needed reassurance about her place in his world, he would give it to her. "You know you're my best friend."

"For such a smart guy, you can be pretty stupid. I never wanted to be your *friend,* John. I'm in love with you."

John tried to contain his feelings, but her words sounded like breaking glass. *Donovan. David. Melody.* He was fed up with all the deception and lies. Before he knew what was happening, his disappointment had caught fire. His arms went slack, but his hands were trembling. After being denied twice—at the Metropolitan Club and at home—John was finally getting a chance to fight back.

"So, being my friend was just an act? I thought you really cared about me. I trusted you!"

"John, wait, please let me explain…." Melody's voice faltered.

"No! I've heard enough."

John swept the remnants of their picnic into the trash and took off running. The afternoon was over. Getting his job back was all that mattered now. When he was far enough away, he dared a quick look over his shoulder. Melody was standing right where he'd left her, staring out across the water. For a moment, John considered turning back, but it was too late. He had already made his choice.

Chapter 6

IT WAS a Friday night in Boston, and cabs had their pick of fares. Everyone had somewhere they needed to be. Stepping between the double-parked cars on Beacon Street, John waved both arms. The nearest T stop was only a couple blocks away, but his legs were burning, and his shirt was damp with sweat. Finally, after a half-dozen failed attempts, he spat out a litany of curses and started back on foot.

By the time John reached the hotel, people were milling about on the red-carpeted sidewalk, and the driveway was full of black sedans. The official start time for the event was almost an hour away, but it looked as though most of the A-list guests had already arrived. Flashes twinkled as photographers memorialized the occasion for the local papers.

John needed to do a quick change and find the senator before people started asking questions he couldn't answer. At the side entrance, a guard from Donovan's private security detail stood watch. *Brian. Ted. Robert.* John couldn't remember the man's name, but being "like family" was still enough to get him through the locked door. With a subtle nod, he brushed past and detoured down a narrow corridor to avoid the crowded lobby. The few guests who glanced his way looked right through him. Without his suit and tie, John was practically invisible. He was almost to the elevators when Donovan and Stan Wilson emerged from one of the banquet halls.

The senator's unexpected arrival created an undertow that pulled his adoring fans closer. Instinct told John to swim the other way, but he knew better than to fight the current. The crowd surged forward, and he moved right along with it. At the last possible moment, just as Patrick Donovan extended his hand, the couple in front of John faltered. Luckily, the senator was too busy basking in the glow of all the radiant faces to notice his chief of staff standing a few feet away. Perhaps he was so accustomed to having John around that he'd become desensitized to his actual presence. In any event, the procession continued on to the rotunda where the rest of the guests were waiting.

John knew time was running out, but he desperately needed some fresh air. Once the coast was clear, he bolted to the nearest exit and threw his body onto the metal bar that held the doors shut.

The temperature outside had dropped considerably, and the harbor smelled like fish in a freezer. Lights from the skyline shimmered off the water as boats bobbed rhythmically against Rowes Wharf. Five stories above, Donovan was getting ready to make history. By now, Melody would be back and dressed. Soon, she'd step onto the stage and take her rightful place at her father's side. Everyone else seemed to be moving forward while John was standing still. Clapping his hands together, he laughed at the irony of the situation.

"Laughing alone *again*, Peter? You're either a really happy guy or mildly deranged."

Paul looked more like a movie star at a Hollywood premiere than a guest at a political event. For a moment John worried that his mind had finally snapped under the pressure. After all, the odds of running into each other in Boston were probably a million to one.

"What are you doing here?"

Paul narrowed his eyes and cocked his head. He seemed to be waiting for Peter to answer John's question. Finally, after a long, awkward silence, he offered up a clue.

"I'm here to do my job."

To John Wells, Paul was a complete stranger. The chemistry between the two men was undeniable, but a third unplanned meeting was more than just mere coincidence. It was time to stop flirting and start asking questions.

"And remind me again what it is you do?"

"I'm glad to see you took the time to look at my business card," Paul said, accepting the challenge to make a more lasting impression.

Peter reached into his pocket, but John was wearing a different jacket.

"If you *had* read it, you'd know that I'm a reporter for the *Washington Journal*. I got a hot tip that Patrick Donovan is making a big announcement tonight. In fact, it'll probably end up being the most important news of the week."

Internally, John flinched as Paul quoted him verbatim. Being careless with information was a mortal sin in politics. If Donovan found out that his chief of staff had let the news slip, there'd be hell to pay.

Good looks and boyish charm didn't change the fact that Paul had just become a serious liability. John willed his pulse to slow down as he assessed the situation. Any novice reporter could have cashed in on John's mistake. With a few phone calls and a little fact-checking, the *Journal* could have run a story based purely on speculation. But except for the local media, there was almost no coverage of the event. Paul had shown remarkable restraint and kept the tip a secret. Rather than report on a rumor, he'd followed the story to Boston to get the real scoop.

The newly introduced element of risk heightened the intensity of the encounter. There was only one problem. Paul was interested in a guy named Peter. Yesterday, it had hardly mattered. Their meeting in the subway was an unexpected anomaly—like a flash of heat lightning on a clear summer night. But now, a storm was about to break, and John was stuck with his deception.

The blue lights of a police motorcade reflected off the vaulted walls of the archway. That could mean only one thing. Donovan's close friend, the governor, had arrived from the statehouse on Beacon Hill. It was showtime. John had to act quickly to lock down the situation and get back inside. Instinctively, he shifted into deal-making mode. Paul may have had the element of surprise, but John still had the upper hand.

"Hey, handsome, how'd you like to score a private interview with the senator?"

Did he still have enough clout to arrange the meeting? John wasn't sure. But even if he didn't, he knew that Melody could make it happen. With a little prodding from his daughter, Donovan would acquiesce and spare a couple of minutes for questions.

"That would be amazing!"

John could tell by Paul's smile that he was intrigued.

"But that kind of favor doesn't come cheap. I'll get you some face time with Donovan if we can hook up later."

Paul leaned forward and stroked his goatee. "Wow, Peter. I'm not sure what kind of guy you think I am, but I don't trade favors like *that* with just anyone."

John's first attempt at a romantic gesture had come off as a cheap proposition. Paul turned and walked back into the hotel.

"Shit, I blew it," John said as he took off in hot pursuit.

Even though he knew the senator was waiting, it now seemed more important to remedy the situation at hand. John had just reached the tempered-glass door to the hotel when Paul turned around and smiled. He was clearly enjoying the minidrama he'd just created. By pretending to be offended, he'd turned John's advantage against him. It was a gutsy move, but John appreciated the maneuver. Paul hesitated for a moment and then pointed to his watch.

Raising both hands, John spread his fingers wide. *Ten o'clock.* Paul nodded once to consummate the deal. The lights along the harbor flickered on as the last bit of sun dipped below the horizon. Gripping the metal handle of the door, John watched as the new object of his affection disappeared down the hall. Back home, David was probably on his way to 30 Degrees or JR's for happy hour. More likely, he'd taken advantage of John's absence and invited someone over. The thought of another man in their bed was nauseating, but John had no right to pass judgment. After all, his unwavering devotion to the senator had been its own kind of infidelity.

It was a waste of time to fixate on things he could not change. The past was like the wake behind a boat—it would always be there, but it would never push John forward. Ready for a new beginning, he opened the door and stepped inside. At the elevator, he pushed the call button and turned his attention to the bellhop hurrying toward him. The man was in his early twenties with jet-black hair and darker-than-average features. *Black Irish.* John felt a familiar stirring as the elevator doors opened and he stepped inside. The bellhop stopped a respectful distance away and stared at a fixed point on the wall. Gripping the brass luggage cart with both hands, his knuckles were almost white.

"There's room for two."

John smiled and cast out his line.

"That's all right, sir. I can wait for the next one."

The young man had worked at the hotel long enough to know better than to take the bait.

"Suit yourself."

The next thirty minutes passed in a blur. The red light on the room phone was blinking, but there was no time to retrieve messages. Stepping into his polished wingtips, John inspected his reflection in the mirror. The man looking back was a formidable figure in his blue suit and red tie. Nothing about his appearance betrayed his new emeritus status. At least on the outside, he still looked like the man people expected to see.

One by one, John counted down each floor as the elevator delivered him to the lobby. Stan Wilson might be a shrewd political strategist, but he had misjudged Patrick Donovan's resolve. A man of many moods, the grand scale of the evening would make the old man sentimental. John was certain that one chance was all he needed to prove to the senator that he was still indispensable.

The elevator stopped on the fourth floor, and an elderly couple dressed for the evening entered the car. The man pushed the lit lobby button again for good measure while the woman fidgeted with her triple strand of pearls. The senator's wife owned a similar necklace, locked safely away in the vault, which she wore any time she was called upon to make a public appearance.

John remembered one such night five years earlier when he'd been invited to the estate in Virginia to celebrate the senator's reelection. Donovan had inherited a rare case of GlenDronach from his father that he kept in reserve for special occasions. The single-malt Scotch had been distilled in Scotland before John had even been born. Smoky and sweet with gunpowder—it smelled like victory. With any luck, he'd taste it again in November.

Once reinstated, John could begin rebuilding his life. Two brief interludes with Paul had left him wanting more than what he had settled for with David. John could sell the house in the suburbs for a hefty profit and move back into the District. Hell, he might even throw himself into restoring one of the neglected brownstones on Constitution Avenue. Marathon days at work would be counterbalanced with a personal life that was actually worth living. Evenings and weekends would be spent hanging out at hip cafes and shopping for fresh produce at Eastern Market. John would make time for cooking classes and travel to far-off lands.

Whatever he could imagine, he could do. Tonight, everything would change.

By the time he reached the rotunda, the room was packed to capacity with the senator's most ardent supporters. Guests sipped champagne from crystal flutes and admired the million-dollar view. Fragments of conversations floated through the air like lyrics to the orchestra's music. The senator had spared no expense. Even in a crowded room, it was easy to spot him holding court with the governor and a group of major donors. Donovan was impeccably dressed. His Savile Row suit was a noticeable upgrade from his usual wardrobe. In fact, everything about the elder statesman looked new and improved. His gray hair was now salt and pepper, and his trademark eyeglasses were gone. Stan had recast his candidate as the perfect blend of strength and experience. Only those closest to the old man—people like John—could appreciate the transformation.

Waiting for the senator to finish his conversation, John lingered in the wings. He had learned long ago how to read Donovan's gestures and interpret the subtle changes in his body language. Social exchanges were usually well choreographed. Once a meeting was over, it was over. As if to make John's point, the senator offered up a hearty laugh and a round of handshakes as parting gifts.

One of the guests called after him, but Donovan had already stepped out onto the empty terrace. Rather than wait for the perfect moment, John decided to make his move. With strategic precision, he set an intercept course. He was only a few feet from the open door when a hand on his shoulder altered his path. The air reeked with the unmistakable smell of expensive wool and cheap soap. John didn't need to look over his shoulder to know who was standing behind him.

Stan Wilson would never have dared to strong-arm Donovan's chief of staff before tonight. But oh, how quickly things had changed. He was just like all those bullies back in high school. Ironically, the same boys who had made John's life a living hell later begged for his help with term papers and final exams. Of course, he had obliged, but only after giving each of them a healthy dose of their own medicine. John learned the hard way that being needed was better than being loved.

Wilson steered John up a flight of stairs and over to a secluded seating area on the mezzanine. One of the senator's private guards appeared out of nowhere and took his post. His presence would ensure their privacy. Adjusting his sizeable girth, Stan sat down in one of the chairs and gestured for John to join him.

"What a night. What a night." A lack of eye contact with anyone made it clear that Wilson was repeating the mantra for his own benefit.

"Throwing Donovan's hat into the ring is the easy part," John said, calculating his next four moves. "The senator needs to surround himself with the brightest and the best if he expects to have any chance of winning. One wrong move—a single miscalculation—and he'll be out of this race before it even starts."

Smiling, John waited for his words to crawl under Wilson's skin. By the end of this conversation, he'd be buying John a drink.

Like a wax figure at Madame Tussauds, Stan's round, shiny face hardly looked real. *Snap. Snap. Snap.* He lifted his pudgy arm as high as he could and clicked his fingers three times. Promptly responding to the signal, a passing waiter hurried over with a silver tray of champagne. Wilson grabbed a glass and quickly waved the young man away. John sat empty-handed.

"Sorry, John. Did you want something?" The question was perfunctory.

"No thanks. I never drink when I'm on the clock."

White noise from the ballroom changed frequencies. Donovan's guests were growing restless. There were only a few minutes left for John to make his case and find the senator. With more bravado than brains, he pulled off his boxer's robe and stepped into the ring.

"Stan, I'm glad we're finally getting a chance to talk. I have some interesting thoughts about how Melody and I can contribute to Patrick's presidential campaign."

John leaned forward to speak, but his opponent raised both hands and signaled him to stop.

"Senator Donovan has already informed you of his decision to terminate your employment. It would serve no purpose for us to discuss it any further."

A sucker punch to the gut took John's breath away. Experience and insight into the old man's quirks might earn him a few points in the first round, but Wilson was going for the knockout.

"I wouldn't be so quick to write me off. You should know that I've always been kind of a dark horse. No matter how bad the odds, I always come out a winner."

"That's a particularly clever choice of words Mr. Wells—given the announcement the senator is about to make. But I already know *everything* I need to know about you. Any value you may have once had has been overshadowed by your homosexual proclivities."

The room tilted sharply to the right and the floor seemed to shift. Wilson had used the word "homosexual," but he was probably thinking of something more colloquial like "faggot" or "queer." John had heard this kind of hate speech on the radio and TV, but unfiltered homophobia was almost extinct on the Hill. If the real reason for John's termination ever got out, the same voters that elected him would shun the senator. Wilson's vitriol was cyanide, and Donovan was about to commit political suicide.

Although it was never discussed, the senator knew all about John's relationship with David. Why had his private life suddenly become a career-ending issue?

Stan was the key to decrypting Donovan's new political agenda. The two men were polar opposites, yet the senator had chosen an inflexible ideologue to manage his campaign. What kind of endgame were they planning behind closed doors? The simplest answer to a question was usually the correct one, but so far John hadn't been able to come up with an explanation that made sense. Now, as he scanned the room below and put names to faces, everything became clear.

Donovan had hired one of the savviest political strategists in the country. That fact, coupled with his recent alliance with Sam Matthews, a political conservative from Texas, could only mean one thing. It was still early, but the presumptive nominees were doing badly in the polls. If Donovan entered the race as a moderate, he could draw votes from both sides and steal the election.

But to succeed, the campaign had to stake out a position that was just to the right of the middle. Avoiding hot-button issues—like abortion and same-sex marriage—would be key. As an Irish Catholic, the senator's position on a woman's right to choose had always been murky. It was his voting record on gay rights that would be more difficult to redact, especially if the headlines were coupled with pictures of the senator and his openly gay chief of staff. Practically overnight, John Wells had gone from being an asset to a liability.

Flanked by his wife and the governor, Patrick Donovan crossed the stage and stepped up to the microphone. Except for Melody's absence, it was a perfect photo op.

"You really should have a drink," Wilson said as he rose from his chair and tried, unsuccessfully, to button his jacket. "It looks like you're going to need it."

Thunderous applause from the crowd drowned out John's feeble reply. The meeting, like his career, was over.

Hidden behind Donovan's eloquent words were the beginnings of his new political demagoguery. Transfixed, the audience listened as he spoke about his love of country and his dreams for a brighter future. In a few minutes, the senator's supporters would put down their flutes of expensive champagne and eagerly drink the Kool-Aid he was mixing. John rose from his seat and walked down the hall. The speech had just started, but he'd already heard enough.

Distance reduced Donovan's amplified voice to a buzz, but there was no way to escape the thunder of applause that followed the official announcement. *President of the United States.* Those words—like "forever" and "I love you"—meant nothing to him now. Turning back for one last look, John was stunned to see Melody standing a few feet away.

"Did he tell you about me last night, or did you figure it out on your own?"

The look on her face answered his question. After all, it was her job to find the facts to support what he already knew. Melody stepped forward and reached for his hand.

"Not here," John said, backing away. "Not now."

Nodding, she offered him a weak smile. In the dim light, Melody bore a striking resemblance to her father. That distinctive nose and prominent chin were pure Donovan. Only her eyes, dark and unreadable, were her own.

JOHN PRESSED the call button three times to hurry the elevator. There was nothing but work waiting for him back at his room, but he had nowhere else to go. Getting drunk at the bar would only make him feel worse, and he didn't feel like walking the streets of Boston alone. What he really needed was to borrow a page from David's book, but his date with Paul was still hours away. Perfectly timed, a now-familiar figure darted across the lobby and ducked inside the business center. John felt a second wind kick in.

Paul glanced up from his laptop as the man he knew as Peter entered the room. The main event in the rotunda was just getting started, but he was already hard at work drafting a story for his waiting editor. The article was brief and to the point. For now, the senator's announcement was the news.

"Finished."

A looming deadline always pushed Paul to his limit. Flushed with adrenaline, he looked like a runner who'd placed first in a race. The tip about Donovan had really paid off, and he was ready to celebrate. There was no reason to wait until ten to start showing his gratitude to his source. Taking John by the hand, he pulled him closer. The first kiss, when it finally came, erased any doubts about what would happen next.

Motionless, the two men stood in the elevator and waited for the other to select a floor. The age-old question—my place or yours—was too embarrassing to actually ask out loud. John's hand hovered in front of the numbered panel. Back at his room, there were messages waiting, and a late-night call from Melody would undoubtedly spoil the mood. The heart-to-heart talk they were destined to have would have to wait. Paul was worried about a different kind of distraction, but he was determined to finish what they'd started. Clearing his throat, he reached forward and selected his floor.

Flashing red lights from the street below illuminated the darkened room. As Paul quietly double bolted the door, John wandered over to the window to see what was going on. Down in the driveway, two paramedics were loading a stretcher into an ambulance. Their movements were slow and mechanical. There was no need to rush.

Ten stories up, the air leaked out of John's lungs as he shrugged off his jacket. It was too late to turn back now. One by one, his buttons came undone, and his shirt fell to the floor. Paul's goatee was like steel wool against his skin. Even so, John found he didn't mind the discomfort. Pleasure and pain—like life and death—were two sides of the same coin.

Chapter 7

JOHN PULLED back the covers and crept across the room to the window. Outside, a narrow shaft of sunlight winked at him from between two dark skyscrapers. It was still early, but dawn was breaking.

Waking up next to a stranger was incredibly awkward, but at least he hadn't gotten drunk last night. John's judgment was already impaired, and he'd conveniently left all his inhibitions in DC. Even sober, he was suffering the effects of a different kind of hangover. Forgotten muscles ached and chafed skin burned. Cold water would probably help John's face but not his head. What he really needed was another couple of hours of sleep—or at least a strong cup of coffee.

Back in bed, Paul's legs scissored in slow motion beneath the blankets. Arching his shoulders into a deep stretch, he emitted a low, satisfied growl that made John's abraded face turn an even darker shade of red. Sex with Paul was a full-contact sport and "fooling around" was anything but. Even though his head told him to sit out the next inning, John stumbled back to bed.

Mere proximity was enough to rekindle their spark. Rough hands inched tentatively toward familiar spots. In the dark, John had relied on his other senses—touch, taste, and smell—to find the way. Now, by the light of day, his eyes studied every curve and muscle. The dense, pink roundness of Paul's shoulder looked like a piece of ripe fruit.

"Ouch! Hey there, tiger—no biting," Paul barked playfully as he sucked in a breath. Ignoring the reprimand, John dove in for another long, scratchy kiss.

The blaring ring of the hotel phone startled them both. John expected Paul to simply ignore it, but after the third ring, he rolled out of bed and snatched the receiver. The senator's announcement was big news, and his editor was probably calling to check in. Propping up his head with a pillow, John stared at the ceiling and listened intently to the one-sided conversation. Physical exhaustion aside, he felt great. Although he'd only known Paul for a short time, their night together had renewed his sense of optimism. Without his job, the next few months would be hard. But with Melody at his side and a new boyfriend to come home to, he knew it would all work out.

Like a caged animal, Paul paced back and forth. He was obviously trying to keep the conversation short, but whoever was on the other end of the line was relentless. Each exchange seemed to make him more agitated. Finally, after a prolonged silence, Paul stopped and stared out the window.

"I'm flying home on the nine o'clock shuttle. I love you, too."

Paul placed the receiver back in its cradle and pulled on a crumpled pair of boxer shorts. Even under a heavy layer of blankets, John felt a chill. The conversation he'd just overheard made it painfully clear that Paul was involved with someone else. Last night had been nothing more than a one-night stand.

"Sorry about that, John."

And with those four simple words, the last vestige of his fantasy world faded.

Paul had known Peter's true identity from the very beginning. It was even possible that he'd staged their "accidental meeting" at the Metro. A seasoned political reporter, he would have seen Donovan's chief of staff on C-SPAN at least a dozen times. Paul might have initially questioned John's motives, but playing along with the charade made it easier to rationalize his own deception. One good lie had begotten another.

First David, now Paul. John was through playing the jilted lover. Quickly, he gathered his clothes and got dressed. At least he'd have an interesting story to tell Melody over breakfast. Paul pulled on a T-shirt and followed him to the door. At the last second, he reached for John and pulled him into a bear hug.

"I know it may be too much to ask, but I was hoping you could still arrange that interview with Donovan."

Breaking loose, John unfastened the locks and opened the door. As he stepped into the hallway, he turned around and looked Paul squarely in the eye.

"Of course I'll take care of it. A deal's a deal. And after last night, you've certainly earned it."

Deprived of more than just sleep, John wandered back to his room and slid the white plastic keycard into the lock. As he stepped inside, he heard the unmistakable crunch of paper beneath his foot. Bending down, he retrieved a plain white envelope—a copy of the hotel bill or some other business matter—and stuffed it into the pocket of his jacket. Whatever it was would have to wait.

BUZZ. BUZZZ. Buzzzzzzzzzzz.

Minutes or hours later, his BlackBerry flashed to life and rumbled across the surface of the bedside table. Mostly asleep, John forced his eyes open and crawled across the mattress toward the fluorescent glow. Deft fingers touched the bleating device, but the phone slipped from his grasp and bounced onto the carpet. Cursing loudly, he jumped out of bed and grabbed it a split second before the call went to voice mail.

"John Wells."

"It's Patrick… Patrick Donovan."

"Good morning, sir."

Suppressing a yawn, John quietly switched on the polite etiquette that had always defined their relationship. The more things changed, the more they stayed the same. He was ready to receive the senator's usual morning litany of questions and requests, but there was only silence. After a few empty seconds, John pulled the phone away to see if the call had dropped. When he brought the receiver back up to his ear, the unmistakable sound of the old man's sobs shook him awake.

"It's Melody. She's dead."

The words struck with immeasurable force. Reflexively, John raised his hand to protect himself from the blow.

Later that same day, the senator would announce the news of his daughter's death with heroic stoicism. Right now, however, he was crying freely over the loss of his only child. John knew he should offer some measure of comfort to the man he had once respected and loved. But with Melody gone, there was nothing left to say. Sinking to the floor, he disconnected the call and dialed the only number he could remember.

"Hello?"

"Something terrible has happened... and I really need...." Like poison, John tried to spit the words from his mouth, but David's sigh cut him short.

"I'm sorry, but I can't talk to you right now. This isn't a good time."

John's grief hardened into anger. It was an emotion that was more destructive, but infinitely easier to bear. Now, his pain had a target.

"What do you mean it isn't a *good* time? Is someone there with you?"

"That's none of your business," David said in a clinical voice. "You need to accept that our relationship is over and move on. I'm sorry you're having a crisis, but I can't be the one to help you through it. Find someone else to talk to. Call Melody."

Before he could explain what had happened, the line went dead. The tragic irony of David's final words echoed in his head as a new reality took hold. John's life was over.

Chapter 8

ALTHOUGH THE media had turned the Grand Lobby into a pressroom, John managed to slip out the back door of the hotel unnoticed. Waiting at Rowes Wharf, a small armada of water taxis was ready to whisk guests off to various ports around the harbor. Dizzy from an overdose of grief and exhaustion, he jumped onto the first launch and hunkered down in a corner for the short trip to Logan. Within minutes, the soothing motion of the boat had rocked him to sleep.

By the time he woke up and realized his mistake, it was already too late. In his haste to make a clean getaway, John had boarded the wrong shuttle and ended up on the other side of Boston. Clutching his overnight bag, he climbed onto the pier at the Seaport World Trade Center and considered his options. Time wasn't really a factor since the DC shuttle flew almost every hour, but going home today meant facing David and shepherding the Donovans through their horrible ordeal. Even though his colleagues sometimes joked that John was a glutton for punishment, descending into that kind of emotional hell wasn't something he was prepared to do.

The first order of business was to flush out the sludge clogging his thoughts. Since getting any quality rest was out of the question, he scoured the block for a cheap chemical substitute for sleep.

Exiting Dunkin' Donuts with a large coffee, John noticed a banner that spelled out PROVINCETOWN, and an idea took hold. Secreted away at the tip of Cape Cod, the quiet village would be the perfect place to crash for a few days and regroup. Hopped up on caffeine and adrenaline, John pulled out his wallet and hurried to the reservation window.

Inside the cramped office, a clerk was busy counting out tickets for the weekend voyages. She was an older woman with snowy-white hair that billowed around her chubby, red face like cotton candy. Shuffling over to the open window, she leaned forward and greeted John with a heavy South Boston accent.

"Good morning, dearie," she sang out in a loud voice, giving his hand a friendly pat. "And how are you on this glorious day?"

"Honestly? I've been better."

Standing tall, John coughed to clear the sound of grief from his throat and slid a wad of cash across the counter. The woman took it and smiled so wide that her eyes narrowed to thin slits. Over the years, she'd provided passage to more vagabonds than she cared to count.

"Here you are—one round-trip ticket to Provincetown. I just need your name, sweetheart."

STANDING ALONE on the upper deck of the ferry, he watched as the Boston skyline receded into the horizon. Heavy waves crashed against the metal hull, and billowy clouds, like ginned cotton, blanketed the sky. An unshaven face scowled back from the reflection in the window. Deep creases in his dress shirt and suit pants confirmed they'd been worn the night before. Still, none of the other passengers would notice or care what he looked like. To them and everybody else, Peter Wells was just another guy.

The Atlantic stretched out in every direction. Travelling by water made it easy to pretend that Provincetown was an island—a place cut off from the rest of the world. With no point to fix on, it was hard to tell how far they'd travelled or their proximity to shore. At sea, distance was measured by speed and time, not miles.

Peter hugged himself for warmth and relived his final moments with Melody. Last night at the window, he'd watched unknowingly as paramedics loaded her body into the ambulance. She'd seemed fine when he'd left her outside the rotunda. What could have happened? Shock and grief made the details of her death seem irrelevant. The fact that Melody was gone was all that mattered.

Finally, after almost two hours of sailing, a short, stocky lighthouse appeared at the end of a long, narrow peninsula. Bobbing in the water off the port side, Peter spotted the flashing green bell buoy that marked the entrance to Provincetown harbor.

The motors of the ferry ground to a hum as the craft adjusted its speed and course. At this time of year, the few private boats moored in the channel were safely tucked away inside their canvas cocoons. Only fishing draggers, crewed by sailors of Portuguese descent, were heading out with the tide.

It felt more like winter than spring, but at least the sky was clear and bright. Peter turned his face toward the weak sunlight and watched as the town rose up to meet him. The modest mass of land was packed tight with an odd mixture of buildings that were old or too obviously new. Hand in hand, two women walked along a thin ribbon of beach borrowed from the sea. An old dog trailed slowly behind them as his faithful companion, a boy of five or six, filled a pail with pebbles. The family stopped and came together to watch the ferry deliver a new batch of weekend tourists.

Making one last sharp turn, the boat maneuvered to the end of MacMillan Pier. With practiced efficiency, the deckhands tossed heavy ropes to their counterparts on shore who pulled the lines taut. Once he'd secured the vessel, the captain cut the motors, and the water went still.

Peter's ears quickly adjusted to the absence of white noise from the ferry's engines. Walking down the narrow metal gangplank behind the other passengers, he listened as fisherman called out to one another in husky voices, and seagulls demanded their share of the daily catch. The sound track was distinctly Provincetown.

Peter was almost to the end of the pier before realizing that he hadn't the foggiest notion of where to go. Looking anxiously to the right and left, he let his bag fall to the ground and nudged it with his shoe. With only a single change of clothes, he wasn't prepared for a protracted stay. Hell, even his toiletries were travel sized. To make matters worse, much of the town was still shut down for winter, and a sunny weekend would only increase the demand for rooms. As things stood, he'd be lucky to find a vacancy for the night.

Peter could appreciate the rich irony of the situation. After all, hadn't John Wells built a successful career out of expecting the unexpected? In all his years on the Hill, he'd rarely acted on impulse, and when he did, the results were usually regrettable. However, the only way for Peter to deal with the shifting volatility of his current situation was to trust his gut— even if that meant making some bonehead mistakes along the way.

It was an imperfect analogy, but like Brigadoon, Provincetown was a magical place that vanished into the mist each winter. John had spent many blissful summer days watching towering drag queens roller-skate up Commercial Street past crowds of gawking tourists. In April, however, the town was nearly empty. Peter scoured the streets looking for a place to stay, but each failed attempt further confirmed his worst fears. All the inns and guesthouses were either closed or booked for the weekend. After searching for a couple hours, he started to wonder whether it was time to give up and catch the afternoon ferry back to Boston.

A low, angry growl in the pit of his stomach produced a foul-tasting burp. It had been almost a full day since he'd eaten anything, but at least hunger was a condition that could be remedied. A few people were congregating outside a restaurant on the next block. Tightening the grip on his bag, Peter crossed the street and hurried up the sidewalk. For the first time in days, it felt as if he was about to catch a lucky break.

Forcing a smile, Peter bounded up three wooden steps and held open the door for an older woman who was just leaving. Inside the quaint cafe, the aroma of brewing coffee and baking bread sent another noisy tremor rippling through his belly. The half-dozen tables and mismatched chairs were vacant, but at least the place was open. Somewhere in the background, a woman on the radio sang a song about love.

"Be with you in a minute."

The voice came from a young man working behind the counter. Despite the weather, he was dressed in a faded T-shirt and khaki shorts. His name, Chris, was conspicuously embroidered across the front of his apron. He looked to be about eighteen, but loaded the slicer like a pro and watched as the razor-sharp blades divided the crusty loaf into twelve equal parts. Sliding the bread into a waiting plastic bag, he twisted it closed with a quick turn of the wrist. Finished, he clapped the flour from his hands and flipped back a layer of blond bangs that threatened to obstruct his vision.

"Sorry for the wait. What can I get you?"

"I'm not quite sure. What's good today?"

Chris gestured to a list of specials printed neatly on a chalkboard. Each dish was named after a local patron, like "Sam's Mac & Cheese" and "Oscar's Tuna Melt." John always made it a point to eat healthy, but Peter wanted something he could sink his teeth into. After reading the menu twice, he finally decided on "Sal's Reuben"—a corned beef sandwich on rye, slathered with Russian dressing and topped with a scoop of sauerkraut. Comfort food always reminded him of snowy afternoons in Pittsburgh with his grandfather at Isaly's Deli. Satisfied with his order, Peter grabbed a mug and served himself some caffeine.

Chris hummed along quietly with the music as he assembled the sandwich. When he was finished, he served it and refilled the coffee cup without bothering to ask. Peter figured his haggard look told the kid to keep it coming. Spreading a couple of paper napkins across his lap, Peter picked up the sandwich with both hands and went to work. The warm bread and salty meat melted in his mouth. After so much hurrying, it felt good to sit down and enjoy a meal. His plate was almost clean when he heard the bell above the café door jingle.

"Christopher!" A male voice of operatic caliber shattered the peaceful Zen of the room. "Thank goodness you're open! I simply *must* have a chai tea latte. Would you be a dear and whip one up for me? And I may need a cookie, too. No wait, I'm still on my diet. Make it a scone."

The source of the disturbance was standing at the counter with his hands on his hips. He was a pleasant-looking fellow in his early sixties, clean-shaven, with a round face and neatly combed hair. Wearing glasses that were stylish but practical, he'd dressed for spring in a blue cable-knit sweater and pink corduroy pants. Chris chuckled quietly as he pulled a gingerbread scone from the glass case and handed it across the counter. This customer was obviously one of his regulars and the feigned drama a well-practiced routine.

"Well, hello. Hell-loo! Are you new to town? Well, of course you are! You've got a face I certainly wouldn't forget."

Peter lifted his mug to acknowledge the greeting but not the compliment. Verbal foreplay between strangers was rare in DC, but it had been all too common back in Pennsylvania. Anticipating the social intercourse that was sure to follow, he downed most of his coffee and prepared for the worst.

"Goodness, but where are my manners," the man asked, giggling. "You simply *must* excuse me. My name is Byron."

Without waiting for a response, he sashayed across the room and offered his hand in greeting.

"Hi, there. I'm… um… Peter."

"Oh, my, my, my," Byron said with a serious look on his face. "You *do* have a firm handshake. That's a sure sign you're of hardy stock. You need to be sturdy to make it through our winters. The boys of summer are all sugar and fluff, but you seem like the rugged type."

"Thanks. I think," Peter said, as his thumb grazed the baby-soft skin of Byron's hand.

Wearing a sympathetic grin, Chris served Byron's steaming latte and offered Peter a chocolate chip cookie, on the house.

"Would you mind terribly if I joined you," Byron asked in a high, tentative voice. "It's so rare that I have anyone to chat with over my morning treat. That's actually what they call a chai tea latte here. 'Byron's Morning Treat.' It's more like my 'mourning' treat, and I drink it in the afternoon, but I seem to be famous for ordering it!"

Peter wiped his mouth and gestured toward one of the empty chairs. Byron could barely contain his glee as he took a seat and scooted in. Once situated at the table, he wrapped both hands around his latte and blew softly over the frothy surface. Purring with delight, he took two quick sips and popped a piece of dark gingerbread into his mouth. Peter watched him and wondered what would happen next. He was in a strange place talking with a stranger. John had recently done the same thing, and it hadn't turned out well. Still, what harm could come from some chitchat over coffee? Truth be told, Peter needed a break from his new full-time job of being alone.

"So, Peter…," Byron said as he broke off another piece of scone and used it to stir his drink. "What's your story? What brings you all the way out here to the end of the world?"

John slouched in his seat and asked himself the same question. What the hell *was* he doing in Provincetown? The answer was a definite nonstarter.

"Peter? Where did you go? Did I lose you *already?*" Leaning forward, Byron put both elbows on the table and rested his chin in his open palms. Framed by his hands, his face looked almost childlike.

"Sorry," Peter said, shifting in his chair. "I had a late night and an early morning. I took the high-speed ferry from Boston."

"Boston? Oh, I just adore that city! I loved it so much that it almost *killed* me. I finally had to move to Provincetown to get some rest. I made the move in '79, when this place was still a charming little town. Now, it's become a drinking village with a fishing problem!"

Peter forced yet another smile. He knew Byron was trying his best to be funny.

"I opened my bookstore—Reader's Cove—and I've been here ever since."

"Well, today is my very first day here," Peter heard himself say. "So, I guess this is where my story begins."

"Oh dear," Byron said as his eyes filled with emotion. "That was beautiful—very profound. Are you a writer, Peter? Are you a poet? I can tell you have the heart of an artist!"

"Sorry to disappoint you, but I'm not much of anything anymore. I'm just a guy who needs to buy some clothes and find a place to stay overnight."

Byron bit down on his lower lip and furrowed his brow. Pushing back from the table, he made a superficial assessment of Peter's appearance.

"Yes, you definitely need a Cape Cod makeover. Oh my, now doesn't that sound like a cocktail they'd serve at the Boatslip?"

Byron giggled heartily at his own joke. Peter laughed too, but more at himself than the attempt at humor. Byron might be a bit quirky, but he seemed to have a good heart. Melody would have liked him very much.

"Sorry. I'm afraid I'm not very good company."

Despite Byron's best intentions, their conversation was not going well. Catching Chris's eye, Peter gestured for the check.

"You know," Byron said without a trace of humor or irony, "sometimes it's easier to open up to a stranger than to a friend. I know we don't know each other, but I'd like to help, if you'll let me."

Peter surprised himself by accepting the small measure of comfort. It had been the hardest day of his life, and it was only half over. Maybe, just maybe, he could trust this stranger. After all, Boston was only a ferry ride away.

"Thanks. I actually do need some help finding a place to stay. I could also use a new friend, if you think you're up for the challenge?"

"You bet I am!" Byron said, raising his latte to signal his enthusiasm. "I love a good challenge, and I can always use another friend—especially one who looks like you. My goodness!"

Peter noticed that most of Byron's coveted scone remained untouched and insisted on paying the check for both their orders.

"Wow! It's my first real date in fifteen years!" Byron announced, winking playfully. "Christopher! Spread the word!"

The bell above the door jingled as the young man placed the money in the register and pocketed the twenty-dollar tip.

THE NEWLY built houses in the West End were far too large for their tiny lots. Neighborhoods, like badly pruned trees, were growing wild. As expected, Byron did most of the talking while he walked Peter through a thicket of streets. Provincetown was his home, and he took great pride in pointing out the subtle nuances that tourists usually missed.

After almost a mile, he stopped in front of a white picket fence and opened the gate. A proper house stood proudly in the center of a well-tended yard. The place was large enough to be a bed and breakfast, but the personal touches peppered around the property gave Peter the distinct impression that it was someone's home.

"Hey, I thought you were going to help me find a place to stay?"

"That's what I'm doing, silly," Byron chided. "Trust me! You have to learn to *trust* people."

Peter followed his companion up a stone path that snaked through the grass. Even from a distance, he could see the front door of the house was open—almost as if they'd been expected. A boyish skip in Byron's step gave the clear impression that this stop was part of some grand master plan. Normally, Peter would have been inclined to indulge his new friend, but it was getting late. He was just about to give up on Provincetown and hurry back to catch the last ferry, when Byron stepped onto the porch, singing out another greeting.

A sprite of a woman pushed open the screen door and stepped outside. Awash in the afternoon sunlight, her skin was luminous. Despite her advanced age, she was well dressed and wore her hair in an upswept style that complemented her narrow face. Barely over five feet tall, she walked to the edge of the porch and stared down her nose at Peter. After an unusually long and uncomfortable pause, she offered a subtle wink to let him know he'd passed inspection.

"Well, what a grand surprise!" the old woman said to Byron with a heavy Scottish burr. "And how are you today, my bonny lad?"

"I'm just fine, my sweet angel," he said, taking her hand and kissing it three times in quick succession. The intimacy of the gesture made Peter feel even more out of place.

"And who is this fine young fellow you've brought with you? Is this your new beau? Do I need to be tellin' Jasper that you're steppin' out with another man?"

"My lord, no!" Byron said, crinkling his face and bursting into what most of the locals knew as his signature laugh. "Honestly, woman—the way your mind works! Anyone can see that *this* one is far too old to be my cabana boy!"

"Hello, I'm Peter."

Eager for his new friend to take the spotlight, Byron faded into the background as the old woman stepped closer.

"And Peter," she said, speaking directly to him at last, "do you think you might trust me with your last name, too?"

Blushing, John looked away. Somehow, the old woman could tell he was a man with secrets.

"It's Wells," he said, quickly correcting his faux pas. "My name is Peter Wells."

"Oh my, but that's a lovely name. Thank you, dear. And I am Florence Woodside. It's very nice to make your acquaintance."

"Good afternoon, Mrs. Woodside. It's a pleasure to meet you as well."

Weightless and fluttering, grasping her hand was like holding a bird. Peter squeezed once and set it free.

"Now that we've made the necessary introductions," Byron said, clearing his throat, "it's time to get down to business. Is the cottage out back still vacant?"

"What are you doing?" Peter asked through clenched teeth. Ignoring the question, Byron smiled and kept his eyes locked on Florence.

"Why yes, dear," she said, nervously adjusting the sleeves of her white cardigan sweater. "As you know, it's been empty for some time."

"Perfect! Peter needs a place to stay, and you have a vacant cottage that needs a tenant. Voilà!"

In less than five minutes, Byron had gone from mildly eccentric to certifiably nuts. Peter needed a room for the night—not a long-term arrangement. Glancing at his watch, he realized that he'd never make it back to the pier in time. He was stuck in Provincetown for the night and fresh out of options. The idea of renting a cottage from Florence was unconventional, but considering all the problems waiting for him in DC, it might actually be crazier to rush right back home. He could easily extend his stay by a week or two. Considering what he'd just been through, a vacation would probably do him some real good.

Before Peter knew it, Florence was leading him by the arm toward the backyard. It was a familiar gesture—something Melody would have done to urge him along. Just around the corner, the cottage was waiting.

Nestled between two full-grown maples, the structure was a simple clapboard box with a gabled roof. Two four-paned windows flanked the fire-engine-red door. It was still too early for flowers, but the beds along the walkway were green with sprawling ivy. Oddly, the empty house still looked lived in. Tired wooden steps creaked as they climbed onto the porch. Slipping free from his arm, Florence turned the brass knob and pushed open the door.

Inside, the cottage was as simple and homey as the word implied. Each room was properly apportioned and decorated in a stylish blend of contemporary furniture and vintage pieces. The fifty-cent tour ended where it had begun, in the living room. Plopping onto the down-filled sofa next to Florence, Peter closed his eyes and pressed his head into one of the cushions. The idea of hiding out in this place for a couple weeks was tempting, but it was time for him to stop pretending he could just run away and become someone else.

"Mrs. Woodside. I'm afraid I have to…."

John had just started to explain why he couldn't stay, when the old woman cut him short.

"This cottage was my son's home—my boy, Bill. He passed away about a year ago."

Peter was struck by the enormity of the old woman's revelation. Like the senator, she'd had the misfortune of outliving her only child.

"I've just lost someone who was very special to me," he heard himself admitting out loud. "It's been really hard, and I'm not quite sure where to go or what to do."

"Well, Peter," Florence said, smiling as she took his hand, "I think it would be lovely if you'd stay here, even if only for a short spell. Perhaps we can be a tonic for each other."

Chapter 9

CHOOSING TO stay in Provincetown was the hard part. Once that decision was made, everything else fell right into place. There were no leases to sign or references required. Florence simply handed the key to Peter, and the deal was done. Byron showed remarkable restraint when he heard the news. Miming "hooray," he pressed his palms together and offered a muffled round of applause with his fingertips. Peter somehow managed to produce a passable smile to acknowledge all the enthusiasm, but his reserves were depleted, and there was still one thing left to do before he could call it a day.

"I've got to run back into town to buy some clothes."

"Oh dear, I'm afraid all the stores will be closed," Byron said without even bothering to look at his watch. "You'd have to drive all the way to Wellfleet or Eastham to find anything open at this hour."

A road trip was out of the question, especially since Peter didn't have a car. But eventually, he'd have to eat again, and finding food meant walking through town without a warm jacket. He was just about to ask Florence whether any of the local restaurants delivered when he noticed her giving him the once-over.

"You look to be about the same size as my Bill. All his things are still in the bedroom. Go right ahead and help yourself to whatever you need."

The thought of borrowing clothes from a dead man was disconcerting. However, considering the alternative, he'd take the offer under advisement. Byron wanted to stay and help him settle in, but there were no boxes to unpack or furniture to move. Picking up his carry-on bag, Peter tried, unsuccessfully, to stifle a yawn.

"Too much fresh air," he mumbled, covering his gaping mouth with the back of his hand.

As if sensing that her new tenant needed rest, not company, Florence walked Byron to the door and casually invited him back to the house for a nice cup of tea.

All the unsolicited kindness was touching, but Peter was ready for some time alone. As soon as his new friends were safely away, he ducked back into the cottage and shut the door.

Nothing—not even the familiar hum of a refrigerator—dared disturb the preternatural silence. It felt surreal, but strangely exhilarating, to have the whole place to himself. To calm his restless mind, Peter wandered around the living room, inventorying the contents of closets and drawers. Like a reverse scavenger hunt, he spent the better part of an hour discovering things.

Tucked away in the only bedroom, his borrowed bed was waiting. *Thud. Clunk. Clunk.* Peter dropped his bag onto the hardwood floor and kicked off his shoes. Collapsing from exhaustion, he pulled a heavy patchwork quilt over himself and drifted off.

When Peter opened his eyes again, the room was dark. Panic took hold as he thrashed beneath the weight of the bedding and searched for something familiar in the shadows. After a few tense moments, a flood of memories came rushing back. First Boston, now Provincetown. Twice in one day, he'd woken up in another man's bed. Propping himself up on a pillow, Peter threw back the covers and squinted at the glowing dial on his watch. *Seven o'clock.* It was still early, but he'd have to get moving if he wanted dinner.

Unused plumbing coughed and sputtered as a flow of rusty water turned the white porcelain sink brown. Peter pulled a bottle of shaving cream and a disposable razor from the full complement of toiletries in the medicine cabinet. Scratching at the edges of his five o'clock shadow, he studied his reflection in the mirror and tested the coarseness of his beard.

"Screw it," he said defiantly. Something about the dark mask suited his mood.

Peter's skin blushed a bright shade of pink under the pounding, hot water of the shower. Methodically, he coated and recoated his body with soap, trying to scrub away the residue of the last two days. When the water began to turn cold, Peter turned off the faucets and stepped out of the tub. Through a wall of steam, he reached for a bathrobe hanging on the back of the door. The skin on the back of his neck bristled as his wet hand brushed against the soft flannel. Bill Woodside's unfinished life was a painful reminder that Melody was gone.

Wrapping a towel loosely around his waist, Peter padded barefoot across the floor. The crumpled shirt he picked up off the floor undoubtedly smelled as bad as it looked. Tossing it to the corner, he grabbed his bag and dumped the contents onto the bed. Unless he had inadvertently packed a ski parka, options were seriously limited. It was time to push through his initial aversion and take Florence up on her offer.

A small brass key turned inside the lock of the wardrobe, and the mirrored double doors creaked open. The freestanding closet had five cedar-lined shelves and ample space for hanging things. Even considering his predicament, Peter found it difficult to imagine wearing a dead guy's shirts and pants. Still, John had borrowed a sweater or two from his college roommates. This was essentially the same thing—except he didn't have to worry about returning it.

Unexpectedly more comfortable with this self-negotiated arrangement, he picked out a dark-blue turtleneck. Soft cashmere scratched against stubble as he pulled it over his head and slipped on his own jeans. Closing the closet doors, Peter took a step back and stared into the mirror. The sweater was a perfect fit.

THE FRONT gate clicked shut behind him. Except for a few flickering stars and a rogue streetlight, the neighborhood was dead. Even the faint vital signs that had been evident during the day were no longer detectible. Choosing the most direct route, Peter zippered up his borrowed jacket and hustled into town.

Closed shops and empty sidewalks gave Commercial Street a lonely, haunted feeling. Looking up one side of the block and back down the other, he could just make out the spectral glow of the word "ESPRESSO" in red neon up ahead. By the look of it, at least one place was open for business.

Even though the food at Spiritus Pizza was unremarkable, the place was a tourist favorite. The benches out front were the best spot in Provincetown to waste time people watching. Late at night, after the bars had closed, hordes of gay men would hurry there for one last chance to either hook up or console themselves with pizza. Despite the passing decades, the no-frills décor of the place was pretty much the same. There were no other customers inside, but one of the ovens was open, and a glob of dough was waiting on the counter. Peter had just begun perusing the menu when the kitchen door flew open and a man emerged wiping his hands with a wad of paper towels.

"Hey, sorry to keep you waiting. You're the first customer I've had all night."

Peter intentionally avoided making eye contact with the handsome guy standing in front of him. Still raw from his encounter with Paul, he was in no mood for games. The man was tall—well over six feet—and wore a plain gray T-shirt that accentuated his impressive physique. With short blond hair and chiseled features, he looked Scandinavian, but his skin was too dark. Leaning over the counter, the man's piercing blue eyes were like wandering hands.

"So, what looks good?"

That question was about as loaded as a pizza with the works. The guy's lascivious grin was bad enough, but such an obvious double entendre was too much on an empty stomach. This guy was a player who'd break lots of hearts come summer. Anyone else would have been flattered by the attention, but Peter was only craving food.

"Just a couple slices. Whatever's ready."

"Coming right up. By the way, my name's Max."

"I'm Peter."

Ding. Ding. Ding. The oven timer signaled the end of the first round.

In one fluid motion, Max slid a wooden peel beneath the bubbling pizza and transferred it onto a round, aluminum tray. With surgical precision, he made three cuts with a wheel and pulled the pieces apart.

"For here?"

"To go."

Peter was digging through his wallet for some cash when Max reached across the counter and grabbed his wrist.

"Don't worry about it. Dinner's on me. I was going to throw most of this into the trash anyway."

"Thanks," Peter said, tossing a five-dollar bill into the tip jar. "See you around."

"Definitely."

Turning around decisively, Peter walked out the door and turned left toward the center of town. One by one, he pulled out each slice and peeled back the silver foil. The first piece satisfied his hunger, but he ate the other two anyway to pass the time. Eating and walking gave him something to do, but now that the meal was over, he was out of distractions. Crushing the empty paper bag, he collapsed onto a wooden bench in front of Town Hall and surrendered to the memories he'd been running from all day.

MOST OF his first morning on the Hill had been spent learning the complex protocols that would, in time, become second nature. New to their posts, most of the freshman staff spent the lunch hour frantically networking with one another. Rather than waste time forging such pointless alliances, John had decided to take a short walk through the park to clear his head. Boston had given him a taste of big city life, but in DC, he felt like a tourist who didn't speak the language.

John was about to head back to the office when he noticed a young woman sitting on a park bench. As if sensing his presence, she glanced up from a short stack of paperwork. Something about her austere look suggested she was probably fluent in the local dialect. When the girl glanced his way, as John knew she would, he tossed out a smile. Rather than acknowledge the greeting, she picked up her bag and turned away.

Radiating self-confidence, John lobbed his half-eaten lunch into the trashcan and moved over to the bench directly across from her. Men and women alike usually found it difficult to resist his good looks and charm. Playing hard to get would only prolong the inevitable. John would make this girl like him—if only to prove he could.

When it came to his appearance, John was the opposite of a Monet: the closer he got to someone, the better he looked. Although the young woman's eyes were locked on a memo, he could see that his presence was having the intended effect. Tucking a lock of brown hair behind her ear, she took a deep breath and exhaled. John was willing to bet she wasn't the kind of girl who was used to being wooed by a handsome boy. With any luck, all the attention would go straight to her head.

A small battalion of Japanese tourists marched down the sidewalk in formation. John hoped the clicks of their cameras and the sounds of their exotic voices would be enough to pique the young woman's curiosity. When she finally looked up again, he was ready.

"Would you happen to know how the cell service is around here? I'm counsel for Patrick Donovan, and I want to make sure the senator can reach me."

"I'm not sure," the woman said, looking up into the air and shrugging. "But with such an important position, you should definitely find out."

"Yeah, I just started today. What is it that you do?"

"Mostly I compile research and write briefing memos...."

Almost as an afterthought, she gestured to the files on the bench next to her. They'd been talking for less than a minute, but John had heard enough. This girl was a legislative aide—just one of the many drones that kept the hive buzzing.

"Nice. Well, anyway, I should probably be getting back." Rising, John buttoned his jacket and glanced at his watch.

"Good luck, counselor."

John appreciated the sentiment, but when it came to his career, he wasn't about to leave anything to chance.

Later that same day, she'd appeared at the door of his windowless office with her arms full of manila folders. John had just hung his diplomas and was unpacking the rest of his things when he noticed her studying him from the hallway. More annoyed than startled, he tried to push back from the desk, but his chair was already pressed against the wall. Swiveling to the right, he knocked his knee hard on the metal side. Fortunately, a forced laugh took the place of his usual expletive.

"So, we meet again," she said, stepping into the cramped space and handing him the stack of reading materials. "I went ahead and pulled some research for you on the senator's new energy bill."

"Now why in the world would you ever do that?"

John was too angry to be polite. He knew it was important to make allies on the Hill, but this borderline stalking was definitely a turnoff.

Offering to help him with his homework was a shrewd move, but he didn't have time to waste indulging a schoolgirl crush. John needed to shake this woman off, once and for all.

"Look, I'm not sure *what* you think you're doing, but I can manage on my own. I certainly don't need any help from you."

"Perhaps I should introduce myself, Mr. Wells. I'm Melody Donovan."

John cringed as he registered the magnitude of his mistake. He'd just snubbed the senator's daughter. Even with his good looks and so-called charm, he'd never get a second chance to make a first impression. Swallowing hard, he squeezed out of his chair and came around to the front of his desk. Melody shifted her weight, but held her ground.

"Look, Miss Donovan, I feel we may have gotten off on the wrong foot." John had always been pretty good at giving an apology without ever actually saying he was sorry.

"Which foot was that, Mr. Wells—the one in your mouth or the one that's halfway out the door?"

Ouch. John stepped back as her razor-sharp retort lanced his swollen ego. It was the second time today he'd underestimated her.

As if certain she'd made her point, Melody shut the door and took a seat.

"I know you're new and probably feeling out of place," she said in a noticeably more forgiving tone. "But I'll give you the same advice my father gave me when I started. Be who you are and not who you think people want you to be. You'll do great here—I can already tell. Just be careful not to lose yourself along the way."

BACK IN the present, Peter shivered inside his borrowed jacket. Melody's admonition nagged like a stitch in his side as he ran back up Commercial Street. The few lights around town were going dark. Safe in their houses, the locals were fast asleep.

After running full out for nearly six blocks, Peter stopped at Spiritus and sat down on the retaining wall to rest.

"So, how was the pizza?"

Max stepped out of the shadows hefting two loaded trashcans. The hooded sweatshirt he was wearing barely covered his broad frame. Despite Peter's initial antipathy, the idea of going home to an empty bed tempered the tone of his response.

"It was good. Thanks for not sending me away hungry."

It was getting late, and neither man seemed particularly interested in small talk. Lonely enough to spend yet another night in bed with a stranger, Peter let Max lead him back to his studio apartment. There was no logical order to what happened next. Strong hands tugged and pulled at Peter's belt—before they'd even exchanged a single kiss. Max was more than just a player; he was captain of the varsity. Scoring with the new guy was all that mattered.

"Wait a minute," Peter said, trying to pull away. He realized what he was about to do would make him feel even worse. Suddenly, going home alone didn't seem like such a bad idea.

"Wait for what? Come on, man. Just loosen up."

Powerful arms snaked around Peter's torso and sharp teeth nipped at his ear. Those muscles under his jacket weren't just for show. Max could easily force Peter to stay, but for someone like him, the chase was half the fun.

"No? You sure?"

Peter answered with a stone-cold stare.

"Not tonight, huh? That's cool. No worries."

Defiantly, Max gave him one last hard kiss and disappeared down the nearest alley.

Peter waited until he was out of sight before wiping his mouth with the back of his hand. A momentary lapse of judgment had almost led to another colossal mistake. At least he'd stopped before it was too late.

Back at the cottage, he stumbled, fully clothed, into bed. Turning off the light, he buried his face in a pillow and struggled with the reality of his situation. Melody's death had severed the ties connecting him to his former life. Everyone he'd loved was gone. Everything he'd worked for was lost. Like Bill Woodside, John Wells had become a ghost.

Chapter 10

THE GLASS in the window was opaque with a dense layer of condensation, and heavy droplets plinked off the tin roof like pennies falling into a jar. Drifting in and out of sleep, Peter listened to the sound of water sloshing through gutters and pulled the covers closer. The night was proving to be kinder than the day. Sleeping, he could still dream about the people he'd lost.

Too soon, dawn pulled back the dark curtain. Pounding rain on arid soil had released a smell so fresh and sweet it woke him. Even before his eyes were open, the memory of last night's run-in with Max blared like an alarm clock. Peter wanted to bury his head under a pillow and hide. Instead, he kicked off the covers and jumped out of bed. He was determined to make it through another day—even if that meant just going through the motions.

The patch of hardwood floor by the bed was cold, and the heat from the quilt was fading fast. Reaching into the wardrobe, Peter grabbed the first thing he saw—a weathered flannel shirt. The cuffs were frayed and the color faded, but it smelled like sunshine and salt. At every turn, Bill Woodside seemed to be watching out for him—ready to provide whatever comfort he could to another lost soul.

Unfortunately, that was when the lucky streak Peter had been enjoying since his arrival ended. Although the kitchen cupboards were fully stocked with dishes and cookware, any perishables had been disposed of long ago. Peter didn't relish the idea of walking into town, but there was no way he'd make it through the morning without coffee. Behind his eyes, a caffeine headache was already brewing. The longer he denied his body what it needed, the worse it would get. Cursing under his breath, he slipped on Bill's jacket and headed out the door.

A wicker basket sitting in the center of the porch stopped him short. Not quite certain what to make of the unsolicited delivery, Peter snatched it up by the handles and peeked under the wooden lid. Two home-baked muffins and a battered silver thermos were nestled beneath a red-and-white checkered napkin. Cradling the precious cargo under his arm, he unscrewed the top of the metal container and lifted it to his nose. Miraculously, the impending caffeine crisis had been averted.

Back inside, Peter poured himself a generous cup of coffee and sat down at a bistro table by the living room window. He had no idea who'd dropped off the care package, but since he only knew two people in Provincetown, the list of suspects was short. And there was a note:

I thought this might help you get through the morning. And don't mind the rain, dear. It helps the flowers grow. Florence

Peter refolded the sheet of paper and glanced out the window. Using his index finger, he followed the path of a raindrop racing down the glass. The smell of cinnamon and butter reminded him there was also food in the basket. While it was true that John's work schedule had rarely allowed for more than a quick cup of coffee, Peter had nothing but time. Eager to experience the simple pleasure of sitting down to breakfast, he spread the napkin on his lap and picked up one of the still-warm muffins. Holding it like an apple, he took a bite.

Ten minutes later, the basket was empty and his stomach was full. Fortified and caffeinated, Peter felt prepared to venture forth. Outside, a cold breeze off the water had collided with the warmer air on land to create a heavy fog. Slogging through wet grass and puddles, he cut across the yard and started off down the lane on an uncharted expedition.

Back at the office, Wilson would be busy fielding calls from the press and trying to contain the situation. The confluence of the senator's announcement and his daughter's tragic death was undoubtedly flooding the weekend news cycle. Overwhelmed and ill equipped to handle a crisis of this magnitude, the office staff would be looking for a strong leader to tell them what to do. But that was Stan's problem now. The biggest decision Peter had to make this morning was whether to turn right or left at Commercial Street.

Once past MacMillan Pier, the shops and restaurants gradually gave way to the shabby-chic studios of the East End. Even off-season, select pieces tastefully decorated the gallery windows. Peter stopped at an open door to watch an old man scrape thick, oily paste across a canvas. His silver blade lifted and curled the crusty layers of paint into a rolling wave that swelled beneath the artist's steady hand. Even unfinished, the scene conveyed more about the sea than a photograph ever could.

Using the public library and Pilgrim Monument as landmarks, Peter found he could wander off the beaten path and still find his way. Although there was a dearth of year-round residents, an aggressive strain of urban sprawl had blighted virtually every square foot of developable land. Garish McMansions and quaint cottages abutted one another. Seasonal occupants settled for window boxes instead of gardens. From just the right angle, Peter could usually manage to catch a glimpse of the harbor, but the general layout of the waterfront left him feeling a little claustrophobic. Craving open space, he turned up a side street.

Less than a mile from the center of town, hidden within an intricate maze of back roads, he discovered a tract of green space. It didn't appear to be a public park, but the cobblestone path leading away from the sidewalk was particularly inviting. As a kid, John had spent his weekends exploring the slag dumps that had, from necessity, cropped up around local steel mills. Like an astronaut traversing the surface of some distant planet, he'd hiked up and down the dunes of vitrified matter. Memories of those lost afternoons made Peter curious to find out what was hidden down the path behind a wall of trees.

With an equal amount of strength and care, Peter lifted the lazy arm of an oak and ducked underneath. Rising like a ghost ship, the remains of an old chapel sat squat in the middle of an open field. The structure of the building looked remarkably sound, but the whitewashed facade had faded to gray. Peter was just about to write the place off as an architectural relic, when he noticed a stained glass window hanging above the double doors. In spite of the overcast day, it radiated a vibrant spectrum of color that cut through the haze and gloom. Considering the general condition of the building, he wondered how something so beautiful and fragile could have remained intact. *Crash.*

Without warning, the doors flew open, and a man stepped outside. Provincetown certainly seemed to have more than its fair share of hot guys lurking about. Stealthily, Peter ducked behind the tree and watched. The man was dressed for work in tan boots, faded jeans, and a flannel shirt covered with sawdust. Soft curls of brown hair jutted out from beneath a dingy baseball cap. Although he appeared to be a few years younger than Peter, his beard was streaked with strands of red and gold that made him look older.

Even from a distance, Peter could see there'd been some kind of accident. A white cloth was wrapped loosely around the guy's left hand. Although the temporary bandage was crimson with blood, the man seemed oblivious to his injury. Crossing the yard in three long strides, he unlocked a shed and disappeared inside. Out of sight, Peter watched as the man reemerged carrying some tools and a wooden frame. Apparently, the chapel was in the early stages of restoration, but by the look of things, this was a one-man show.

After the man propped open the double doors with cinder blocks, Peter saw him step inside and position the frame on a makeshift table. As he stared intently into the empty form, his green-eyed gaze traced invisible lines that diverged and intersected to apportion the space. Once the complex pattern in his head was complete, he was ready to begin. The man's nimble fingers tested the shapes and contours of his collection of colored glass while a calloused thumb worried the sharp edge of a particular piece. Wedging it securely in his palm, he rubbed the shard clean on his jeans and held it up to the light. John knew from experience that first choices were the most difficult.

Something like a smile played at the corners of the man's mouth as he positioned the keystone in the center of the frame. *Red. Purple. Gold.* John felt his pulse quicken as the next three pieces fell quickly into place. Satisfied with his progress, the man unknotted the tourniquet. He blotted the wound a couple of times to make sure the bleeding had stopped, then tossed the soiled gauze into a pile of trash.

Unaccustomed to playing the voyeur, Peter followed the trail back to the road. The trek across town had kept him from obsessing over the loss of his job, but a painful splinter was slowly working its way to the surface. Watching this guy on the job, it was easy to imagine the rhythm of his life. At the end of the day, he'd sweep the floors and put away his tools, knowing he'd actually accomplished something. John had spent the last ten years of his life negotiating deals and crafting words. Now his career was over, and the only tangible thing he had to show for it was money.

Ironically, he was learning how to feel when there was no one around to love. Peter strained to hear some trace of Melody's voice. Closing his eyes, he tried to remember how it felt to hold David's hand. The memories were still there, but like old photographs, the images were already beginning to fade. Adjusting his jacket to block the wind, he trotted back down to Commercial Street. If there was one thing misery loved, it was company.

WALLS OF books absorbed the sound of his tentative hello. Reader's Cove was empty, but its oriental rugs and Tiffany lamps set the perfect mood for a dreary New England afternoon. More for effect than warmth, Peter rubbed his hands together and visually catalogued the shelves of reading material. *Funny. Light. Trendy.* Those were the adjectives used to describe the beach novellas the boys liked to nibble on between Tea Dance and dinner. During the summer months, literary giants like Armistead Maupin and Edmund White usually took a backseat to lesser-known authors with names like J.J. Smith or C.D. Powers. Gender-neutral initials effectively disguised the fact that suburban housewives wrote most of these "M4M" romances.

While waiting for Byron, Peter browsed through the stacks until one title in particular caught his eye. From the crisp dust jacket and crack of the spine, it was clear that *Inns & Outs: A Photographic History of Architecture in Provincetown* wasn't exactly a best seller. Even so, he was curious about the man and the chapel. Carrying the oversized volume to the back of the shop, he settled into a window seat that overlooked the harbor.

Flashing off the water, a refraction of light brought the seascape into perfect focus. Mother Nature was broadcasting in high definition. Colors seemed truer, and the smallest details were strikingly clear. The scene would have made a great postcard—if you could ever manage to get to your camera fast enough. Sure enough, a moment later the light changed, and the magic was gone.

When the show was over, Peter opened the book and began thumbing through the glossy pages. After a couple chapters, all the old sepia photos started to look alike. Luckily, his persistence paid off. Buried in the back, Peter discovered a brief epilogue that catalogued some of the proposed renovations around town. The oak in the black-and-white picture was less than half the size of the one he'd hidden behind an hour earlier, but it was certainly the same tree. Peter skimmed the text, but the only reference to the chapel was in a one-line caption: "*A Capela do Morro*, The Cavanaugh Foundation."

"Well, my heavens!" Byron said, emerging from the basement. "I'm surprised to see you out and about."

Like a teenager who'd been caught with a dirty magazine, Peter blushed and tried to hide the book under a cushion.

"Can I offer you something to drink?"

"Coffee?"

"No. I'm afraid all I have is tea."

Byron lifted a silver kettle from the hot plate on his desk and positioned a cup under the spout. As he poured, a blast of steam fogged up his glasses. Laughing at his own predicament, he put the pot back on the burner and wiped the lenses clean on his shirttail.

"A Capela do Morro," Peter said, repeating the phrase to set it to memory.

"The Chapel of the Hill," Byron translated. "Do you speak Portuguese?"

"Actually no. I walked by there this afternoon and saw someone working."

"Oh, yes, that would be Daniel Cavanaugh. He's been renovating the old place since his… well, since last fall."

Without saying more, Byron stared out the window and stirred his tea. Most people would have taken the hint that he wanted to change the subject, but Peter wasn't a man who was easily deterred.

"I'm really interested in finding out more about that project."

Peter had been in Provincetown less than a day, but his perspective on John's former vocation had changed. The US Senate was a lot like the chapel: an institution people once believed in was now in need of repair.

Drafting bills and lobbying votes—the entire legislative process—had irreparably fractured an already-faltering foundation.

John's life in DC was becoming a blur of paper and ink. Peter turned his attention to the view outside, but darkness had turned the window into a mirror.

"Are you okay?" Byron asked.

Honestly, John wasn't sure.

"I ran away from a bunch of problems that I don't know how to fix. Now, I'm here, and I've got no idea what I'm supposed to do next."

"Well, welcome to the *real* world, Mr. Wells! Most of us feel that way every single day. Gosh, I don't think I've had a plan since 1981, and I wouldn't have it any other way. It's called 'freedom' and it's delicious. Now, stop sitting around feeling sorry for yourself!"

Byron scurried back to his desk where he scribbled a note and affixed it to his daily planner. When he returned to his chair, he was noticeably more subdued.

"Give yourself some time. Stop trying so hard and just let things happen. You might be surprised at how much you enjoy yourself along the way."

"That all sounds great, Byron. Really, it does!" Peter blurted out. "But what the fuck does that actually mean? I mean, what exactly am I supposed to do—here, now, today?"

"Oh, you beautiful, silly man!" Byron said standing up and placing his arms akimbo. "Every seven-year-old kid knows the answer to that question. Go outside and play! Do whatever you feel like doing, or don't do anything at all. The important thing is to have some F-U-N! But don't cuss, dear. It isn't attractive on you."

Byron was right. Somehow, he seemed to know just what to say to cut through all the bullshit. In that regard, he was a lot like Melody.

"Sorry. I've got to go."

Without offering an explanation, Peter darted through the shop and out the door. The blowing rain felt like tiny bites on his face. He tried his best to avoid the deeper puddles, but it was a lost cause. His feet were soaked before he was halfway back to the cottage. Wet and cold, he was just about to unlock his door when a scratching sound beneath the floorboards caught his attention. Hopping off the porch, he peered into the crawl space, where a small mound of brown-and-white fur blinked back at him.

"Well, hey there little fellow."

Peter was careful to speak in a tone he usually reserved for small children and Republicans. At the sound of a human voice, the pup whimpered once and squeezed into a tight ball. Two chestnut-colored eyes watched Peter's every move. Above them, a gust of wind blew a song from the chimes on the porch. Cocking his head to the side, the dog listened.

"Do you like that sound?"

The animal responded to the question by stretching out his front paws and inching forward on his belly. After a few awkward crawls, the dog was right next to him. Without rising, the animal rolled over and pressed his head against Peter's leg.

The rain had started up again, and the temperature was dropping fast. Carefully, Peter reached down and stroked the coarse, mottled coat. He tried to convince the dog to follow him inside, but the animal just stared straight ahead. It was going to take more than words to earn his trust. With a sudden burst of inspiration, Peter bounded up the porch steps and opened the door.

Stepping into the living room was like dipping into a hot bath. Once the shivering had subsided, he began foraging for a treat to coax the dog in from the cold. The kitchen cabinets were still bare since Peter had been too busy thinking about the hot construction worker to remember to stop by the grocery store. In desperation, he grabbed the wicker basket and shook it over the counter, but there was nothing left inside. That was it—he was fresh out of ideas.

Just about to head back outside, Peter noticed a small wooden chest with the word "CHANCE" stenciled in block letters across the front. Acting on a hunch, he rushed over and dumped out the contents. The items from the box squeaked and bounced as they hit the wooden floor. Pay dirt! Bill Woodside had come through for him once again.

Peter grabbed the most colorful toy from the pile and bolted out the door. For a moment, he worried that the stray might have run away, but the pup hadn't budged an inch. The little guy seemed resigned to his fate.

Like a talisman, Peter held the object out in front of him and squeezed. The high-pitched bleat that followed was just the ticket. Pricking up his ears, the dog pranced forward and took the ball in his mouth. Side by side, they climbed the porch steps, but the animal stopped short at the welcome mat.

"It's okay, boy. You can go in."

A single flash of lightning unexpectedly lit up the sky. Glancing once over his shoulder, the little dog scurried through the open door.

Once inside, Peter stripped off his wet clothes as the dog circled twice in front of the hearth and curled into a ball. Collapsing onto the couch, Peter wrapped himself in a crocheted afghan and closed his eyes. As he drifted off to sleep, his new roommate let out a heavy sigh. It was good to be home.

Chapter 11

PETER WATCHED the morning unfold from the steps outside Marissa's Café. Provincetown sunlight danced on the harbor, and a cloudless sky was so blue it almost hurt. Across the street, a woman swept her sidewalk. In gray wool pants and a canvas barn coat, she hummed a tune to the scratch of straw on pavement. Peter listened and finished what was left of his coffee. Each time the café door opened, aromas from inside reminded him he was still hungry. Reaching inside a paper bag for another bagel, he felt an urgent nudge.

"Are you really a dog or just a weird-looking pig? No more! You've already had a plate of eggs and three pieces of turkey sausage."

It was hard to speak authoritatively with those sappy brown eyes staring back at him. Reluctantly, he broke off a chunk of bagel and held it out. Whipping his tail back and forth, the dog chomped it down in one bite. Peter could have sworn the animal was smiling as he licked a schmear of cream cheese from his furry lips.

Breakfast was a pleasant addition to John's usual routine, but that third cup of coffee was definitely a mistake. Almost crawling out of his skin, he walked briskly ahead while his canine companion ambled behind. There was no need for a leash or collar. They'd already decided to form a pack. In spite of his better judgment, Peter found himself talking to the dog. The animal cocked his head as if he understood, but Peter knew better. It would take time for them to learn each other's language.

With no particular destination in mind, they marched west along the water. Intermittent stretches of uneven sidewalk forced Peter onto a ribbon of asphalt that was barely wide enough to accommodate a car. Along the way, he noticed that some of the residences were marked with a cryptic blue-and-white ceramic tile that depicted a house on a boat. These so-called floaters were all that remained of a settlement that had once thrived on Long Point. After the collapse of the salt industry in the 1850s, the entire population picked up and resettled on the mainland. Peter imagined the time and effort it had taken to ferry each of the thirty-eight houses across the harbor. It would have been easier to just start over and rebuild, but families were determined not to abandon their homes to the sand.

After nearly a mile, Commercial and Bradford Streets merged at the moors. Deep channels fed tidal pools, and thick carpets of brown-and-gold sea grass showed hints of summer green. This part of Provincetown was exactly as he remembered it. The passing decades had not changed a stretch of land that was, by its very nature, timeless.

After looking both ways out of habit, Peter crossed the road and walked cautiously along the berm. Come summer, locked bicycles would cover the weathered fence that marked the entrance to the path like barnacles on a boat. The rough terrain and distance from the beach deterred casual tourists from venturing out to Herring Cove. Anyone who'd ever bothered to make the trip, however, would confirm it was worth the effort.

Standing at the crest of the first dune, Peter watched the dog take off at full speed toward a flock of unsuspecting gulls. The trail, untamed, wound circuitously across the partially flooded land. Schools of tiny fish darted through the tidal pools like flecks of sunlight, and blue crabs scurried sideways across the sand. Measuring each step, Peter trudged on.

The surface of the ocean was calm, but the water was a menacing shade of gray. Puffing out their feathers, seabirds huddled together against the cold. Peter's head felt thick and heavy, as if he'd slept too long or not enough. It suddenly occurred to him that it was Sunday—the day Melody would be buried. Her funeral would probably be a private affair with only immediate family present to mark her passing. Under normal circumstances, John would have been at the senator's side, ready to provide whatever support he needed.

"My best friend died."

The dog blinked twice in response.

Down shore, a wave broke hard, changing the silver sand to a deep shade of pewter. Its power spent, the surf sizzled and hissed as it receded. Peter kneeled down and picked up a handful of wet pebbles that glistened like jellybeans. Years ago, John had carried pocketsful home only to find that, dry, they were just plain rocks. Content to let them be, he tossed the stones to the ground and brushed his hands clean.

The Wood End Lighthouse looked white and majestic from a distance, but the closer he got, the smaller it seemed. Rather than retrace his path back through the cove, Peter decided to explore Long Point. Although he'd hoped to find some trace of the original settlement, the elements had restored the remote peninsula to its natural state.

"Grrrrr. Whoof."

It was clear from the dog's anxious disposition that he was less than eager to make the long trip back across the moors. Lucky for him, Peter knew a shortcut.

The breakwater had been built in 1911 by the Army Corps of Engineers to protect Provincetown from the tides and shifting sands. Massive stone slabs were stacked on top of each other to form an effective barrier that also served as a navigable bridge to the West End. It was over a mile long, but unquestionably the shortest route back to town.

Peter hopped from rock to rock until the land in front and behind seemed equally distant. Ten steps ahead, a seagull was working on lunch. It had been easy enough for the bird to snatch a mussel from the beach, but pecking had proven ineffective against the hard shell. Just when it seemed like a lost cause, the bird lofted, hovered, and released the mollusk. When the shell struck the flat stone, it shattered into pieces. Shrieking out a victory call, the gull swooped down and devoured the tasty treat inside.

Traversing the gaps between the uneven rocks was tougher than Peter had expected. Charting a course and choosing his next step was more important than enjoying the view. Once back on dry land, he dared a quick look over his shoulder to see how far he had come. Including the long trek across the moors, the two had probably covered about six miles. The acrobatics of walking in sand and balancing on rocks had taken a toll. Unused muscles ached, and his stomach was empty. Peter didn't need to look at his watch to know it was time for lunch.

THE WAITRESS at Bubala's scribbled down the order with a look that warned Peter that his eyes were bigger than his stomach. To prove her wrong, he added a side of clam chowder for himself and a hamburger, no bun, for the dog. Peter also ordered a beer to celebrate his first passage on foot across the harbor. The dog sleeping under the table would have to settle for a bowl of cold water.

Hiding out in Provincetown was an easy, albeit temporary, solution. John had left Boston without telling a soul, but it was time to make some calls or at least send a few messages. Cringing, he scrolled through the Rolodex inside his phone. The longer his contact list grew, the more overwhelming it all seemed. For the first time since his arrival, he was feeling like his old self again. Without thinking, Peter lifted his beer and drained the glass. There were a couple of family members who needed to know John was okay, but everyone else would just have to wonder.

By the time the food arrived, the e-mails had been sent. Arranging the plates on the table, the waitress watched as Peter disemboweled John's BlackBerry and tossed the pieces into a trashcan.

"Wow! You must be really mad at your phone."

"No. I just need to take a break from the rat race."

"Well, you've certainly come to the right place," the young woman said, retrieving his empty glass. "The next round's on me."

As the waitress went back inside, Peter leaned forward and stretched out his hand. Sighing heavily, he stroked the dog's coat and promised them both that things would get better. *Walk. Eat. Sleep.* It wasn't much of a plan, but at least it was easy to remember.

Peter had eaten his way through practically every dish on the table when he spotted Byron walking up the street. Arm in arm with another man, he was talking a mile a minute. It would take some time to get used to the fact that such public displays of affection were considered normal in Provincetown. The pair had almost passed by before Byron noticed his friend and called out an overblown hello. Waving, Peter forced a smile. Even though he didn't really feel like company, John was used to performing on command.

"My goodness!" Byron said, rushing forward. Somehow, he was able to talk and belly laugh at the same time. "Where have you been, young man?"

Startled, Peter jumped up from his chair as the little dog sprang to life.

"Where did you find him?"

"He was hiding under my porch. I was just taking care of him until…."

Peter's words trailed off as a painful realization took hold. The dog belonged to someone else. A knot in his stomach tightened as he imagined losing the pet he'd never wanted, but already loved.

"I told Florence this little mongrel would come home sooner or later."

"Come home?" Peter's beer buzz was making it harder for him to connect the dots. It took a few seconds before he remembered the box of toys in the chest by the door.

"Is this Chance?"

"It most certainly is! He disappeared about a month ago. Florence has been sick with worry."

Listening intently, Chance stared up at the trio of goofy humans and produced his best version of a smile.

"Well, this is definitely a cause for celebration!" Byron declared, rubbing his hands together in anticipation. "We're hosting a dinner tonight at our place! You bring Florence, and we'll take care of the rest."

Peter opened his mouth to object, but honestly, a quiet dinner with a couple new friends sounded better than eating alone.

"If you are coming to our house for a meal, then perhaps I should introduce myself?" Byron's companion quietly interjected. "I am Jasper Avellar."

"Sorry. I'm Peter Wells."

Jasper spoke with a heavy Portuguese accent. With salt-and-pepper hair and olive skin, Byron's partner was the physical embodiment of tall, dark, and handsome. Stretching out his throbbing legs, Peter listened as the couple talked—sometimes to him, sometimes to one another—about anything or nothing at all. There were no jarring calls or urgent meetings to interrupt the natural ebb and flow of the conversation.

When lunch was over, Peter said good-bye and watched each man go his separate way. Byron headed back to the bookstore while Jasper made his way to the pier to check his lines. While waiting for the check, Peter had an unexpected burst of inspiration. He knew he should probably head back to the cottage and rest before dinner, but his tired feet had other plans.

CHANCE TILTED his head and listened to the pounding bass of a hammer. Hugging the trunk of the oak, Peter watched from the shadows and tried to convince himself that there was no such thing as love at first sight. Still, he refused to be self-critical. Indulging a fleeting infatuation was better than wallowing in self-pity, or worse, feeling nothing at all.

Daniel Cavanaugh was hard at work repairing the broken steps. Despite the weather, he was shirtless, and a thin sheen of sweat covered his skin. Lifting his hammer, he sank a three-inch nail into the wood with one strike. He was just about to move on to the next riser when Chance let out a yelp and darted from behind the tree. Ready for playtime with a new friend, he ran circles around the yard, venturing a little closer with each pass.

Daniel pulled off his baseball cap and wiped the sweat from his face with a red bandana. He waited until the dog made a third pass, then tossed his hammer into the toolbox. Hearing the clang of metal, Chance dropped to the ground and rolled onto his back. Peter worried for a second that the dog might have stumbled into trouble, but before he could react, Daniel kneeled to scratch the animal's pink belly. With his paws flailing, the dog whimpered and squirmed in delight. Wishing they could somehow switch places, Peter called out a hello and walked into the yard.

Peter knew it was going to take more than just a squeaky plastic toy to capture this guy's attention. John would have been ready with the perfect opening line, but speaking first is always risky—especially when you don't have anything to say. After an uncomfortable pause, he decided to skip the small talk and stepped closer to inspect Daniel's work. A second window, presumably the one Peter saw being constructed, had already been completed and installed next to the first. Golden sunlight ignited the red-and-orange flames trapped inside the colored glass. In addition to the repairs to the steps, Daniel had begun the painstaking process of stripping the doors. Peter had imagined how he'd carefully applied a heavy coat of toxic gel to the surface and used a putty knife to scrape away the thick layers of paint. The exposed wood was pristine, but progress would have been slow. Even when this task was complete, it would take months to replace the rows of rotting boards.

THE CHAPEL hardly qualified as a tourist attraction, so the appearance of a visitor was an unwelcome surprise. The locals expected a certain amount of social interaction, but Daniel's neighbors had learned it was best to let him be. It had taken some practice, but he could usually manage a simple conversation at the Stop & Shop on a Saturday night. When questions came, as they always did, he knew how to keep his answers brief and to the point. Squatting defensively, he raked his hand through the dog's fur and waited. Daniel had spent every summer of his life in Provincetown, and he was used to curious strangers. It was just a matter of time before this one got bored and went away.

"SO WHAT do you think?"

"The place has good bones."

It wasn't much of a dialogue, but at least both men had established they were capable of speech.

Grabbing a remnant of a two-by-four, Daniel wrapped a sheet of sandpaper around the block and got back to work. After a dozen or so passes across the stripped wood, he stopped to brush away the sawdust. Yes. It would definitely take months, maybe even years, to finish the restoration, but he'd see it through to the end.

Peter's infatuation was quickly changing to respect. He'd just about worked up the courage to suggest grabbing a beer together, when Daniel vaulted up the steps and retrieved his hammer. Selecting a piece of precut lumber from the pile, he used one hand to hold the wood flush against the door while the other searched through his tool belt for a nail. Peter was only a few yards away, but he'd become invisible again. Nothing—not even a handsome stranger—would distract Daniel from his work. Most guys would have felt hurt or slighted by the brush-off, but Peter thought his intensity was kind of cool.

Disappointed, but not discouraged, he backed away slowly and followed the path to the road. Patience and time were two things Peter had in abundance. And besides, in a place as small as Provincetown, he was almost certain they'd meet again.

PETER WATCHED as Chance squeezed between two pickets in the fence and poked along the outer edge of the garden. Hovering just above the ground, his cold, wet nose took in all the delicious smells that told him he was home. Once he'd found the right spot, the dog clawed at the dirt with all his might to exhume a favorite bone. Peter's own muscles were like hothouse flowers—workouts at his local gym had been designed to make them bloom, but not grow. Now, after a long day of physical exertion, he was paying the price for his vanity. Hobbling toward the cottage, he spotted Florence on the porch and detoured to the house. The nap he'd been daydreaming about would have to wait.

Florence closed her book and tucked away a pair of bifocals as Peter pulled himself up the stairs. Before she could even inquire about his day, a brown-and-white apparition materialized at his heels.

"Are my eyes playing tricks?" the old woman asked the furry face staring back at her. Afraid he might vanish again, she waited until the little dog was curled up at her feet before she dared to reach down and touch him.

"My, but you're a dirty scoundrel. I should have known you'd be back."

Chance lifted his head a few inches and licked her frail hand.

"I found him last night during the storm. I took care of him today, but I'm sure you'll want to keep him here in the house."

"Oh no. I'm afraid that won't do at all, dear. Chance will have to stay with you in the cottage. That's his home. And he'll come and go as he pleases—always has and always will."

Peter had spent the last two hours trying to convince himself that owning a pet was too much responsibility. Florence would provide a better home—a place where Chance would be cared for and loved. It was easier to believe that than to admit how attached he'd already become to the dog.

Always the lawyer, he was prepared to argue a case against himself, but the look on Florence's face confirmed that the matter of custody had been settled.

"Byron phoned. He and Jasper will be expecting us around seven. It'll be a cold night, so be sure to wear something warm."

Peter shifted his weight to relieve the cramps in his legs. He'd been so busy worrying about Chance, he'd almost forgotten about the impromptu dinner party. It was still early, but the light was beginning to fade.

"The winter days are short and, more often than not, the sun saves its best light until it's about to set."

The colors of the sky reminded him of those rare occasions when John had managed to escape from the office at a decent hour. Sometimes, when the weather was good, he'd wander up the gravel path on the National Mall. Blinking in the distance, the light at the top of the Washington Monument pulsed like a red star.

"This was my son's favorite time of day—the gloaming," Florence said, patting the cushion on the chair next to her.

"Would you tell me more about Bill?"

It was only natural to be curious about the man whose clothes he wore and in whose bed he slept, but Peter was an outsider. Given his history, he had no right to start asking questions.

"Well, dear... I'm not sure what a mother can say about the child she's lost."

Using what little weight she had, Florence started her chair rocking.

"In the beginning, Bill had been too much with me. I could still see the distinctive lines of my son's handsome face reflected back in the mirror and the deep timbre of his voice sometimes echoed in my own Scottish brogue. To speak of him then, even to a stranger, would have been as natural as breathing. But now, most of those memories have been packed away. Lately, I've been more and more frugal about where and when I share them. Bill loved to read me poetry while we watched the sunset. Sometimes he'd pick something by Frost or Keats, but most often it was Walt Whitman. My son loved Boston and was devoted to his circle of friends, but he was never too busy to come home and spend some time with his old mum."

At just the right moment, the old woman smiled and held up the book that was resting on her lap. Shifting in his chair, Peter realized that at eighty-four, Florence's life had spanned the better part a century. Each passing decade had brought a mixture of good times and bad. She had taken it all in stride, but the death of her only child was a loss that had tested her mettle. Peter thought about his own mother's grief for the son she'd never known.

"Bill passed away last June. It was a long, hard illness, but he never complained—not my bonny boy. He was thankful for the life he'd been given. And I'll always be thankful for the privilege of being his mother."

The tone of Florence's voice made it clear that the story had ended. Looking at her face, Peter knew her sharing had come at a cost. There were no words of comfort he could offer to ease her pain. Losing people was an inescapable part of growing old.

"You stay here as long as you like, dear," she said, smoothing the invisible wrinkles from her skirt. The double meaning of her words was clear. "Let's meet at seven, and we can head over to Byron's together. I have a feeling that tonight is going to be glorious."

Peter made a wish on the twinkle in her eye.

As if sensing movement, Chance rolled onto his back and stretched. He opened his eyes a crack, then drifted back to sleep. Peter wondered what siren's song had lured the little dog away and what trials he had endured on his long journey home.

Chapter 12

WATER DRIPPED from Peter's hair as he stood in front of the wardrobe's open door. It felt good to be clean again and even better to have somewhere he needed to be. Without missing a beat, he pulled a brown cable-knit sweater from one of the piles and casually tossed it onto the bed. Less than twenty-four hours had elapsed, but most of the awkwardness he'd felt about borrowing Bill's things was gone.

The staccato clip of claws on the kitchen floor meant Chance was on the move. Although they were roommates, Peter hadn't quite figured out how to read the animal's ever-changing moods. One minute he was aloof, and the next, affectionate. In that regard, the dog was a lot like John. Apparently ready for company, the little pup scampered into the room and jumped onto the bed. Lying with both front paws hanging over the side, he watched as Peter got dressed.

Peter staggered across the floor, hopping and cursing as he struggled to pull rag-wool socks over wet feet. Falling backward onto the bed, he glanced over at the clock on the nightstand. Although he was perpetually late, he still had ten minutes to kill. In Provincetown, there were no motorcades or traffic jams to fret about. Virtually everything was within walking distance.

To pass the time, Peter rolled onto his back and began counting the wooden slats on the ceiling. Like picking a scab, he couldn't stop imagining David with someone else. Fixating on his ex-partner's infidelity was painful, but it was hard to resist the compulsion to reopen the wound.

More out of habit than necessity, Peter locked the cottage door and hurried up the path. Florence was waiting patiently at the front gate.

"Sorry I'm late," he said, glancing at his empty wrist. Peter reminded himself that he'd intentionally left John's watch behind.

"Why no, poppet, you're right on time. *Tis a braw, bricht, moonlicht nicht the nicht*," Florence said in Scottish as she stepped forward and took her escort's arm. "It's a beautiful, bright, moonlit night tonight!"

After walking together for a couple of blocks, Peter realized he'd seriously misjudged his new friend. Instead of burdening him with idle chatter, the old woman passed the time quietly humming to herself. Florence seemed to be one of those rare individuals who actually enjoyed some peace and quiet. With her, there were no expectations to live up to. All she wanted was his companionship.

It was easy to figure out where they were going since every house on the street was dark except one. Even from the sidewalk, he could hear the sounds of jazz and laughter. From what little he already knew of Byron, Peter could have guessed that a quiet dinner would be anything but.

"You look quite handsome in that sweater, dear," Florence whispered in his ear. "It brings out the color of your eyes."

The compliment proved to be an effective antidote for his unexpected case of the jitters. Jasper and Florence didn't seem like big talkers, but Byron would most likely fill any gaps in the conversation. Peter rang the doorbell and reassured himself that he could manage dinner with a few friends. After all, how bad could it be?

"Well, helloooooo! Our guests of honor are finally here! Welcome, friends!"

Peter had walked straight into an ambush. Too late, he realized that "dinner" had really been code for "party." The notion of being thrust back into the red-hot spotlight was somewhat disconcerting. John had never suffered from stage fright—he'd been playing the same character for years, and his lines were well rehearsed. Tonight, however, there was no script for Peter to follow or director to set his blocking.

Doling out hugs, Byron guided them into the living room where a dozen guests had fallen into an impromptu receiving line. Once introductions had been made, Peter tried his best to remember names and work his way into one of the ongoing conversations. He managed to nod in all the right places, but whenever it came time to answer an innocent question—like where he was from or why he was in Provincetown—words seemed to fail him.

After a couple of halfhearted attempts to socialize, Peter retreated to the far side of the room to nurse a glass of wine. He expected Florence to feel equally out of place, but she was giggling like a schoolgirl as a woman in a turban regaled her with an update on her love life. Byron, Peter's only other friend, was busy passing out hors d'oeuvres and refreshing drinks.

Although he'd just arrived, Peter already needed some fresh air. Unfortunately, Jasper and another guest were engaged in a heated debate in front of the door. At one point, the man reached forward and playfully covered their host's mouth to silence him midsentence. The intimacy of that moment reminded Peter of similar exchanges with Melody.

The wave of agoraphobia that followed swept Peter down a hallway and out the back door. A porch, partially enclosed by latticework and a dense patch of wisteria, took up most of the small yard. Judging by the volume and frequency of laughter inside, it sounded as if the party had kicked into second gear. Peter might be suffering from acute social paralysis, but he had to admit Byron's informal shindig was more fun than a black-tie event at the Kennedy Center.

The sigh Peter heard was not his own.

"So, we meet again."

Straining his eyes against the dark, Peter watched a figure emerge from the shadows.

"Although technically, we haven't been introduced."

Daniel Cavanaugh was a changed man. The grungy baseball cap was gone, and his tangle of brown hair had been washed and styled. In defiance of the temperature, the sleeves of his shirt were rolled up to the elbows, and he was wearing flip-flops. Without breaking eye contact, he placed his bottle of beer on the railing next to three empties and offered his hand. Peter made sure to shake it firmly and reminded himself to play it cool.

Proving the old adage that timing is everything, Byron appeared in the doorway.

"So there you are! Everyone's been wondering if you two ran off together. Well, not everyone—just me. But I'm someone, so that counts!"

Byron's eyes darted back and forth between the two men. From his body language, it was pretty clear that he'd moved on from the role of housemother to matchmaker. Still, considering Daniel's chilly reception at the chapel, Peter wasn't about to object to a little meddling.

"I think I… need another drink," Daniel grunted as he brushed past Byron and stepped back inside.

"Me too."

Decorated with an assortment of mismatched china, the dining room table glowed in candlelight. Most of the guests were already seated, making Peter feel as if he'd stumbled into a game of musical chairs. Before the music stopped, he hurried toward one of the last two vacant spots at the far end of the table. At almost the same time, Daniel emerged from the kitchen and plopped down next to him. Fortunately, the clinking of silver on crystal interrupted the awkward silence that followed.

"Good evening, everyone," Byron said, encouraged by the happy faces and the potency of his wine. "Before we partake of this glorious feast, I've asked our own, sweet Florence to lead us in a blessing."

Each guest took his or her neighbor's hands to form a chain. Inevitably, Daniel had to reach under the table and close the circle. Given that he spent most days pounding wood and cutting glass, his touch was surprisingly tender. Peter tried not to read too much into it and locked eyes on Florence, who was humming a sustained note. Once she was certain everyone had the key, she lifted her hands as a signal to start:

> Oh, the Lord is good to me
> And so I thank the Lord
> For giving me the things I need
> The sun and the rain and the apple seed
> The Lord is good to me.
>
> For every seed I sow
> There grows another tree
> And one day there'll be apples there

For everyone in the world to share

The Lord is good to me

Amen.

Peter hadn't sung the "Johnny Appleseed" song since elementary school, but he remembered most of the words. Even during grace, it was still a party. Inspired by the warmth of the occasion, Peter was just about to try to break the ice with Daniel when a gentle squeeze reminded him he'd yet to let go. Offering a casual apology, he released his neighbor's hand and quickly looked away.

"I know all of this can be, well, let's just say *overwhelming*, but you'll get used to it. I'm Lynn, and you're Peter, the new guy."

Turning toward the voice, Peter was surprised to see the woman on his left sorting her peas from her carrots and segregating them into neat piles. Encouraged by the open display of OCD, Peter picked up his fork and speared a piece of roast. The rich red meat had been grilled to perfection. Chewing it slowly, he tried to remember the last time he'd enjoyed a home-cooked meal.

"Okay, now it's your turn," Lynn said, gently prodding him with her elbow. "I said something clever, now *you* say something clever. That's called 'making conversation.' It's a new thing people are doing at parties. You should give it a try."

"Yes. I've heard of it, but I thought that was more of a European thing. It'll never catch on over here. Americans are too busy for that kind of nonsense."

"Not in Provincetown!" she exclaimed through a mouth full of food. "Good conversation is what gets us through the winter!"

Peter looked away for a moment to check in on the rest of the party. The food and wine were delicious, and everyone seemed to be having a great time. Only Daniel's attention seemed limited to the contents of his plate. Peter was eager to make another attempt at conversation with his enigmatic dinner partner, but Lynn kept pulling him back into her orbit.

"So, seriously, tell me something about yourself. There might be a quiz later, and I need some answers. What's your story? Byron only said you're new to town and staying in Florence's cottage."

This sort of interrogation was exactly what he'd been afraid of. Reflexively, Peter put up a wall and ducked behind it.

"Honestly, my life isn't worth talking about right now."

He expected another question or at least a sarcastic remark from Lynn, but his words just dangled in the air. Amidst all the laughter and chitchat, the silence around them was like a bubble.

"You know what?" she said without looking up from her food. "I think you might be right—this whole 'conversation thing' is overrated. Sometimes it's better to spend time with a new friend without all the blah blah blah. Am I right? Of course I'm right."

Grateful for the unexpected reprieve, Peter finished his wine and slumped down in his chair. He still didn't have any answers, but the alcohol made it easier not to care. From out of nowhere, Daniel produced another open bottle and refilled their glasses.

"Thanks, Daniel."

"Actually, I go by Danny. Byron's been calling me Daniel since I was a kid, and I've never had the heart to correct him."

Peter turned his body to the right, but avoided making eye contact. Instead, he studied his half-empty plate and idly wondered why the blond fuzz on Danny's forearms was so much lighter than the hair on his head. After a few seconds of reflection and another gulp of wine, Peter decided to risk a serious look. When he did, Danny was staring back.

"Hey there."

"Hey."

Mercifully, their attempt at conversation was interrupted. At the other end of the table, Byron delivered a punch line, and the room erupted in laughter. Although he hadn't heard the joke, Peter chuckled and turned away.

With plenty to eat and drink, the rest of the dinner went off without a hitch. One by one, the various courses were served as the elegant tapers burned down to nubs. After a few more glasses of wine, Peter discovered that offering a passable answer or innocuous remark was usually enough to keep the conversation going. *Movies. Books. Travel.* Although John had never made time for such activities, Peter was surprised at how much he enjoyed listening to other people's stories and perspectives.

After the last of the dessert plates and coffee cups had been collected, the woman sitting next to Byron stood up and announced it was time for her to go. Once the spell had been broken, the other guests quickly followed suit. As Jasper passed out coats, Peter quietly excused himself and ducked into a powder room beneath the stairs.

Trying his best to avoid an overdose of warm hugs and heartfelt good-byes, he washed his hands a second time and checked his reflection in the mirror. Even though the party had been a simple gathering, Peter was spent. Using one of the decorative towels, he dried his hands and opened the door.

The mood and music were noticeably more subdued. Floating around the room, Jasper tidied up while Florence sat next to the fireplace chatting with Lynn. Peter was crestfallen to discover that Danny had already left. Fortunately, he'd had plenty of practice masking disappointment.

While Lynn helped Florence with her jacket and scarf, Peter darted back into the kitchen to say a quick good-bye. He lingered for a moment in the doorway and watched his hosts huddled over the mountain of dishes soaking in the sink. With his hands encased in fluorescent rubber gloves, Byron quietly sang show tunes and washed as Jasper dried. The sight of their domestic bliss triggered a bout of nostalgia. Once, long ago, John had been half of such a pair.

Peter complimented Byron on the quality of the meal, but the amateur chef responded to his praise with a long list of culinary miscalculations. Leaning against the counter, Jasper grinned and shrugged. Ironically, it was the minor imperfections that had made the night so special. When it became clear that Byron was determined to undermine his own success, Peter decided to substitute actions for words. Breaking his rule regarding public displays of affection, he gave his hosts a quick peck on the cheek and said good night.

Florence was waiting for him on the porch, but she wasn't alone.

"Sorry to have just disappeared, but Douglas wasn't feeling well and needed some help getting home."

Peter lobbed a less than subtle smile in Danny's direction. The night air was cold and crisp, but he felt warm all over.

A quiet man, about the same age as Byron, Douglas was a part-time employee at Reader's Cove. His cheerful blue eyes were in stark contrast to his pallid color and sunken features. Signs of the illness that was ravaging his body were obvious to those who had seen them before. With new medications and better care, AIDS had been downgraded from a deadly disease to a chronic condition. Resistant to the miracle drugs, however, Douglas was living proof that the pandemic was far from over. When the funding for social programs dried up, his friends and neighbors had quietly stepped forward to offer their support.

Peter admired Danny's loyalty and compassion. If John had possessed similar qualities, Melody might still be alive. It was hard to admit, but David had probably been smart to cut his losses and get out before becoming another casualty.

A gentle hand guided him back to the present and walked him up the lane. More like chaperones than friends, Peter and Florence took the lead while Danny and Lynn lagged behind, speaking in hushed tones. With each passing block, it became clearer that the distance between the two men was something personal. Feeling the sting of rejection, Peter found he was eager to reach the fork in the road and part ways.

"Florence?" Lynn said, sidestepping the boys and taking her friend by the arm. "I've been meaning to ask you for your recipe for shortbread. Can I walk you home and copy it out?"

"Why of course, dear. I'll make us a nice cup of chamomile tea, and we can continue our chat."

Peter couldn't be sure, but it seemed like the game Byron had started on the back porch had gone into overtime.

Hands dug deeply into their respective pockets, the two men watched the women disappear around the bend. Danny's demeanor was a few degrees chillier than Bill's empty bed. Even so, Peter still hoped there might be a spark between them. Stay or go? It was a simple question, but he didn't know enough to make an informed choice. What Peter really wanted was for Danny to magically produce another bottle of wine and offer him a drink. Since that probably wasn't going to happen, he'd settle for a sign.

Wagging his tail until his body shook, Chance came scampering up the street. He looked at Peter, then Danny, and back to Peter again. When the little dog failed to get the desired reaction, he yapped twice to make his point.

"Wanna take him for a walk?"

Danny was alluring, but aloof. That, among other things, was part of the attraction. Walking side by side, the two men headed back down Commercial Street toward the East End.

"You tired?"

"Not really," Peter lied. "Are you?"

"I spend twelve hours a day doing construction. I could sleep standing up."

Anyone could see where this was headed. Danny was exhausted, and it was getting late. As much as Peter enjoyed being with him, it was probably time to call it a night.

"We could go back to my place, if you feel like hanging out."

Danny looked down at the sidewalk and ground a piece of gravel under his heel. In silent affirmation, Peter smiled.

Chapter 13

IT WAS hard to imagine getting lost in a place as small as Provincetown, but Danny seemed determined to try. Using detours and shortcuts—hopping fences and cutting through backyards—they zigzagged through the East End. When Bradford merged into Commercial Street, Danny made an unexpected left turn onto Snail Road. Peter's feet and legs were starting to ache, but Route 6, the outer boundary of town, was just ahead. It couldn't be much farther.

As if to prove him wrong, Danny pushed past some overgrown bushes and stepped onto an unmarked trail. Until now, Peter had been happy enough to follow along, but two guys wandering in the woods at night was like the beginning of a bad slasher flick. As if sensing his apprehension, Danny turned around and offered a mischievous smirk. It wasn't very reassuring but enough to rekindle Peter's interest. After all, he'd come too far to turn back now.

The light from the full moon was bright enough to illuminate the path, though Peter had a feeling Danny could easily find his way in the dark. Just up ahead, on the crest of a hill, Peter could make out the silhouette of a structure partially obscured by sand and an outgrowth of leafless shrubbery. Strings of brightly colored buoys hung on rusted lobster traps like lights on a Christmas tree. Covered in cedar shingles, the dune shack was reminiscent of a Hopper painting.

Peter did his best to keep up as Danny jogged ahead and disappeared inside. By the time he reached the door, the soft yellow glow of a lantern illuminated the hut.

"Park rule, battery power only, no flames allowed," Danny explained as he hung the lamp from a hook in the ceiling.

"This is where you live?"

Peter almost laughed out loud as he surveyed the space. The room was small—barely large enough for two people—with a makeshift bed that was nothing more than a thin mattress and sleeping bag on a rickety frame. Peeking out from beneath the cot, an old footlocker with a shiny new padlock was apparently all the space Danny needed for his possessions. The cracked wooden walls were covered with a dozen charcoal sketches of the beach and town. Compared to this dune shack, Peter's cottage was a mansion.

"I have a place in town, but I like to stay out here as much as I can. It's my Fortress of Solitude."

Peter smiled at the obvious comic-book reference. Hard and unmovable, Danny was a lot like the man of steel. Provincetown seemed remote and disconnected to a city slicker like John, but this was a place where you were literally unplugged from the world. Maybe spending time in this rustic shack would help Peter discover Danny's Kryptonite.

Outside, the wind suddenly kicked up, sending a spray of sand into the room.

"It must be a bitch to keep this place clean."

"You can't imagine," Danny said, tracing a smiley face on the dusty glass window above the bed. "One night, I fell asleep with the door open. By morning, the whole place was covered in an inch of sand."

The image of Superman snuggled up in his sleeping bag while the beach crept in was priceless. Collapsing into the only chair, Peter began to wonder what it would be like to wake up here in the morning.

"There are nineteen of these places scattered up and down the beach. Artists stay in them when they come out here to work."

"Like Thoreau at Walden Pond…."

Peter faintly remembered a predawn morning back in college when John had climbed out of a warm bed to drive the barren stretch of I-95 north to the state park in Lincoln. The day was bright and clear, but the weather was indescribably cold, even by Boston standards. Crunching through the permafrost, he blew off some postexam steam by throwing baseball-sized rocks onto the frozen surface of the pond. Each one landed with an eerie "THWONK" as sound waves reverberated through water and ice. Thoreau's little house had been carefully preserved, but it was no bigger than this dune shack. The idea of that kind of isolation was liberating but also disorienting. John Wells needed technology and modern amenities to anchor him to the present.

"How did you ever find this place?" he finally asked.

"I grew up in Boston, but my family was originally from Provincetown. My dad used to bring me here when I was a kid. We would camp out on the beach, and he'd teach me about the stars."

Danny's voice was strong and clear, but John's recent loss had given him a sixth sense about grief. Somehow he knew Danny's father was dead. Though his comments were brief, they'd been enough to shift the mood.

Peter was just about to suggest a moonlight stroll on the beach when Danny jumped up and switched off the lantern. Certain about what would happen next, Peter moistened his lips and waited. Things had been touch and go all night, but against the odds, the kiss he'd been imagining was about to happen. Maybe it really was true that some things were meant to be.

It took a couple of seconds before Peter realized he was alone. Looking out toward the waterline, he was surprised to see Danny running with Chance up and down the shore.

"Dammit!"

When it came to his love life, John was sick and tired of letting everyone else call the shots. It was time for Peter to take matters into his own hands. Without thinking it through, he sprinted across the hard, wet sand. Eyes wide to show his surprise, Danny seemed too stunned to react when Peter grabbed his shoulders and pulled him into a kiss.

Falling slowly, Peter felt the force of Danny's hands on his chest as his legs gave way.

"Shit!" he cursed, landing on the ground.

With clenched fists, Danny took a giant step backward. He was breathing hard, but not from exertion.

"What are you doing?"

"Well, right now I'm sitting here with a seashell up my butt, trying to figure out why you pushed me away," Peter said, sitting up and brushing the sand from his borrowed sweater. "I know I might be rushing things, but with all the wine and moonlight, can you really blame me for wanting to kiss you?"

"I'm not *gay!*" Danny spit out the last word like it was poison. Peter was suddenly sober and alert. *Florence. Lynn. Byron.* Once again, he'd been making assumptions about someone he barely knew. Danny Cavanaugh wasn't his soul mate. He was just a good-looking straight guy who was in the wrong place at the right time.

"I'm sorry. I misread the signals."

The apology had its intended effect. Even in the shadows, Peter could see Danny's features soften.

"A single guy living alone in Provincetown? It probably wasn't much of a leap. Anyway, there's no harm done."

Danny smiled and offered his hand. Rather than let himself be heaved off the ground, Peter jumped to his feet and shook it instead. This time, he made sure to let go quickly. If he left now, without saying anything else, he might be able to preserve a shred of dignity. Whistling for Chance, he mumbled a good night and headed up the trail. With nothing left to look forward to, it was going to be one hell of a long walk home.

Once safely away, Peter stopped and turned back for a look. The image of the dune shack against the moonlit ocean was the perfect romantic backdrop. Too bad wanting something wasn't enough to make it happen.

The sound of someone running snapped him to attention. Digging his feet into the sand, Peter braced for impact, but the shape of the shadowy figure on the trail was familiar. Chance's tail wagged frantically as Danny sailed over the last dune and slowed to a trot.

"Hey."

Winded from the brief sprint, he coughed and bent over to catch his breath. Always hungry for more attention, Chance scooted forward. This time Danny didn't disappoint.

"Look," he said, combing his fingers through the dog's coarse fur, "I was wondering if you might be willing to help me out."

Favors were an accepted form of tender on the Hill. In ten years, John had never given one away without the promise of something valuable in return.

"Sure. Whatever you need."

"Hold on a second," Danny said, chuckling. "Don't you even want to hear what you're committing to?"

"Well, if it involves you, it'll probably mean getting hot and sweaty."

"God, are you *still* coming on to me? You're relentless, Pete."

Both men began to laugh. The wordplay was adolescent, but it was the most comfortable Peter had felt all evening. Giving Chance a final pat on his belly, Danny rose to his full height and slowly backed away.

"Okay, Romeo. Just be at the chapel tomorrow by eight. And make sure you wear something you can get dirty in."

"Okay, so who's flirting now?" Peter called out over his shoulder as he trudged on toward the road. The echo of Danny's laughter was his only reply.

"Don't worry. I'll be there."

The butterflies in Peter's stomach were gone. Even with all the mishaps and blunders, the night had turned out to be pretty terrific after all.

Alone with his dog and a sky full of stars, he trudged on. Each step took effort, and his arms and legs felt like lead. He was almost halfway back to Route 6 when he came to a fork in the trail. One branch led to civilization, but the other snaked over to Race Point. What if he chose the wrong way? Was he already hopelessly lost?

Tired of waiting for Peter to make a decision, the little dog darted to the right. Chuckling at the irony of the situation, Peter decided to relinquish his position as pack leader and just leave it to Chance. Eventually, they'd find their way home.

Chapter 14

PETER FELT the gentle pressure of the little dog's body pushing against his legs. Shifting in bed, he kept his eyes closed and tried to hold on to a few more precious moments of night. But it was already too late—another day had begun. Although he'd only gotten a few hours rest, Peter felt remarkably alert. He'd fallen asleep and woken up thinking about the same thing: Danny. Despite his lowered expectations, the prospect of spending time with him was even better than a cup of coffee.

Exhausted from two long hikes, Chance rolled onto his back and extended all four legs in a prolonged stretch. Squinting at the clock on the bedside table, Peter felt a familiar rush of excitement. It was a new week, and he needed to get ready for work.

In the kitchen, a blue-black flame blazed beneath the front burner of the stove. Mechanically, Peter went through each step of his new routine—filling the copper kettle with water and packing a small silver ball with tea. Outside, the horizon glowed with traces of red and purple. He knew from experience it was later than it looked. Back in DC, John would already be riding the Metro and worrying about the crisis du jour. That bustling city, with all its drudgery and demands, seemed less civilized than Provincetown. The little fishing village was starting to feel like home.

Pulling the whistling teapot off the stove, he filled his mug to the rim. Even though the fireplace hearth was dark, Peter sat in front of it for comfort. The cottage was chilly, but the heat from the mug warmed his fingers and hands. After a couple sips, the hot liquid worked its way into his core. It would take time to break his addiction to adrenaline and coffee. Peter was finding it hard to get moving without the jolt that had always jump-started his days.

Back in the bedroom, a gentle thump announced that someone had finally decided to get out of bed. His mouth open in an exaggerated yawn, Chance appeared in the doorway.

"Good morning, boy," Peter said as he forced down another gulp of tea and returned to the bedroom. Keen on the idea of more rest, Chance jumped back into the warm spot he'd just vacated and curled into a ball.

"No way, José! Come on. It's time for work. Want some breakfast?" The mere mention of food was enough to pique the dog's interest. He could sleep later.

Skipping his usual shower, Peter pulled on a clean pair of underwear and looked for something to wear. Bill's wardrobe produced a suitable uniform—a heavy flannel shirt layered over a Red Sox T-shirt and a pair of canvas painters pants. Cinching his belt tight, Peter checked his reflection in the mirror and shrugged. With three days of scruff and his collage of mismatched clothes, he looked more Seattle than DC. Last night, however, he'd been thoroughly schooled about the deceptive nature of appearances. Danny's revelation was a huge disappointment, but in truth, Peter was probably better off. Without any romantic bullshit to contend with, he could just relax. That kind of freedom was almost as good as sex.

The rest of Provincetown was just waking up, but the Portuguese Bakery had been open for hours. Two bagel sandwiches—layered with egg, cheese, and salty sausage—were just enough to satisfy his hunger. Sitting on the wooden stoop outside the bakery, Peter shared his breakfast in unequal portions with Chance as shopkeepers barked at one another in their distinctive New England accents. Somewhere close by, a woman was calling a man's name.

"Peter? Earth to Peter?"

Lynn appeared out of nowhere, bundled up in a warm jacket with an overstuffed briefcase dangling from her shoulder.

"Sorry," he said, shaking himself awake. "I didn't hear you."

Peter sweetened his words with one of John's warmest smiles to hide the fact that he'd forgotten his new name. Lynn seemed not to notice and plopped down next to him. Not thinking, Peter handed her the large cup of tea he was drinking.

"You need this more than I do. I must have called your name five times, and you didn't even blink. Long night?"

"Yes. It was interesting, but not at all what I'd expected," Peter said, taking back his tea and leaning against the post behind him.

"It never is, honey. But be careful what you wish for, because you just might get it. I learned that lesson the hard way. I pushed and pushed to get funding for a big conference in Boston. Now, I'm spending every minute of my free time slaving away to get ready for it."

"In Boston?" The city—the real world—seemed like a far-off continent. "So tell me all about what you'll be doing there."

"I'm going to be the keynote speaker on 'Reflections on Creativity' at Harvard. A world-class panel will be discussing the connection between depression and inspiration—the chemical reactions in the brains of artistic people. That kind of stuff."

"Wow, very heavy. Are you a scientist?" It took a minute, but Peter was finally starting to connect the dots.

"Actually, I'm a clinical psychologist. I have a small practice across the street from Byron's shop. Stop by some time if you're ever in the mood to talk." Lynn's message was subtle, but clear.

"You know, I think I'd really like that, Lynn. Sorry, I mean.... Dr. Morris."

"Oh, please! I don't believe in standing on ceremony. Just call me Lynn."

To make her point, she stood up and gave Peter a friendly peck on the top of his head.

"Well, you won't be able to do that *if* I become your patient," Peter responded in a slightly flirtatious voice as she slowly backed away.

"Hah! The hell I won't! *When* you become my patient, I can do it all the time. This is Provincetown. Lighten up!"

Peter looked at Chance, the lone witness to the exchange, and laughed. His new life was starting to look like a funky kaleidoscope. Byron, Florence, Danny, and Lynn were all shiny crystals moving together to create something unpredictable, but unique. Though arbitrary, the complex patterns of their lives remained symmetrical because of the love each friend reflected back at the other. It was a corny metaphor, but it seemed to work.

Peter's body twitched with excitement. For the first time in years, he was about to use his muscles, rather than his brain, to accomplish something. Propelled by a newfound sense of purpose, he hurried along the winding roads to the chapel. Even from a block away, the generic sounds of construction reverberated through the crisp morning air.

Back on the job, Danny looked more like himself again. He was wearing a torn pair of overalls, and the brim of his baseball cap cast a shadow over most of his unshaven face. As Peter watched him work, the sweet mixture of caffeine and adrenaline quickly soured into anxiety. Unless Danny wanted someone to research a zoning ordinance or apply for a building permit, there was really nothing Peter was fit to do. Still, John had been massively underqualified when Donovan promoted him to chief of staff. He'd always been a quick study and was once again eager for a chance to impress his new boss. And besides, the men of his family had worked in coal mines and steel mills for generations. Manual labor was hardwired into his DNA. Hopeful that some latent muscle memory would eventually kick in, he stepped forward into the yard.

"Ever used a hammer?" Danny asked without making eye contact. This morning, he was all business.

"Sure. All the time," Peter responded with a macho affectation. Betting that Danny's sense of humor wasn't nocturnal, he decided to press his luck and lead with a joke. "I mean, come on. Most gay guys spend half their lives trying to get nailed."

"Ouch!" Danny said, pulling off his hat and raking his fingers through his tangled hair. "I really set myself up for that one."

"Yep. Just be glad you didn't ask if I knew how to use a screwdriver."

Danny smirked and shook his head. Peter was hoping for a little more repartee with his new buddy, but it was time to get to work. Pointing his thumb toward the back of the chapel, Danny handed Peter a heavy toolbox and explained his plan for the day. At work before dawn, he'd somehow managed to remove a large section of rotten wood from the facade. Now, with another set of hands at his disposal, he was gung ho to put it all back together.

Starting at the bottom, the two men began affixing new clapboards to the exposed frame. Danny measured and cut while Peter drove three-inch nails into the wood. After only an hour of work, both men were sweating freely. Peter was relieved to find that the job required more stamina than skill. Even so, he didn't know whether Danny's enthusiasm and the promise of progress would be enough to get him through the day.

The buzz of the saw and the pounding of hammers went silent at noon. It was time for their first real break. Danny reached into a cooler under his workbench and pulled out two bottles of water. Cocking his left arm, he hurled one across the yard. Like the wide receiver he had never been, Peter pulled down the pass.

"Nice catch!" Danny said, twisting off the cap and downing half his bottle. Wiping the sweat from his neck, he grabbed another and dropped to the ground beneath the shade of the oak tree. Too tired to walk over and join him, Peter sat down right where he'd been standing. The earth was hard and cold, but at least the grass was dry. *Pulse. Pulse. Pulse.* He opened and closed his right hand a couple of times to relieve the throbbing sensation. Looking down, he was surprised to see that angry red blisters had formed beneath the skin. How could he have worked so long without noticing the pain?

With no advance warning, Danny leaped to his feet and disappeared into the chapel. Apparently, break time was over. Peter slowly got back up and grabbed the hammer with his other hand. It would be nearly impossible to keep working with his injury, but he wasn't ready to give up yet. He was just about to tackle the next clapboard when Danny reappeared carrying a white metal box with a red cross emblazoned across the top. Stepping closer, he took Peter's hand and tested the blisters with his thumb.

"Are you trying to make me think you're some kind of tough guy?" Danny asked, tearing open a package of ointment with his teeth.

"That depends. Is it working?"

As Danny applied the salve to each small wound, Peter stared at the top of his head and wondered what it would feel like to run his injured hand through those soft curls.

"Maybe. But only a little."

Careful not to bind the dressing too tightly, Danny unrolled clean gauze around the hand and secured it with tape.

"There you go, big man. You'll live."

"Is that a threat or a promise?"

Danny pretended not to hear him and repacked the first-aid kit.

Peter smiled at his own joke and inspected the new section of wall he'd helped rebuild. It felt good to get his hands dirty, even if it was with his own sweat and blood. Linked by the same sense of accomplishment, Danny stepped forward and ran his hands across the smooth wood.

"This is really good work. We'll start on the other side tomorrow—after your hand heals up a bit."

"Wait. I'm done for the day? No way," Peter objected as pain spread up his arm like fire. Despite his injury, the idea of stopping now seemed out of the question.

Danny ignored his protests and began gathering up the tools. Peter tried to help, but there was only so much he could do with one good hand. In the end, he fell in line and accepted the assignment of clearing away remnants of wood and miscellaneous debris. Flexing the muscles in his back and arms, Danny hefted the wheelbarrow Peter had loaded and pushed it toward the dumpster out back. It took half a dozen trips, but in less than an hour, they were finished.

Danny double-checked the padlock on the tool shed and then wandered back to the center of the yard. The afternoon sun revealed the stark contrast between the old and new. With an unexpected swell of satisfaction, Peter realized he was now part of the history of the chapel. No matter what else happened, he could return here one day and see the planks he'd set with his own hands. It was a good way to end his first day.

Peter had just shaken loose the sawdust from his flannel shirt, when Danny stepped up next to him.

"It was really good to have you here today. I'd never planned to do all this work alone. This renovation was going to be a family project. My dad used to talk about it all the time."

The two men stood, side by side, reflecting on pasts that kept colliding with the present. *Yesterday. Today. Tomorrow.* Somehow, those words didn't seem to mean much anymore. Acting on instinct, Peter reached out and rested his injured hand on Danny's shoulder. Considering last night, it was a risky gesture, but hours of hard labor had established the foundation for a friendship.

"All right, then. So, I'll see you tomorrow," Danny said, heading back toward the shed. It was a statement, not a question.

Peter walked along the broken path, thinking about the way Danny's face crinkled when he squinted against the light. Stopping at the road, he clenched his hands into fists and let the pain fortify him. Last night, Danny had made it clear he liked girls, not boys. Indulging in a fantasy where they were more than friends wasn't just foolish, it was dangerous. When it came to his love life, the truth was literally staring Peter straight in the face.

Before he knew it, Peter was back on Commercial Street, standing at the door to Reader's Cove. Cupping his hands around his eyes, he peered through the window, but the bookstore was dark. Suddenly, Lynn's words at breakfast seemed prophetic. He desperately needed to talk to someone. Peter stopped and carefully considered what he was about to do. The thought of being clinically dissected was unsettling, but the alternative was decidedly worse.

Once the idea took hold, it was easy enough to find her office. Peter looked both ways and quickly crossed the street with Chance following at his heels.

The crash of the brass knocker against the door heralded his arrival. Standing on Lynn's front stoop, there was nothing to do but wait. Seconds passed and nothing happened. Leaning forward, Peter listened for some sign of movement from inside. More relieved than disappointed that no one was around, he had just turned to leave when the door swung open.

"I wondered what the hell that sound was," Lynn said, lifting the knocker and letting it fall. "No one *ever* uses this stupid whatchamacallit."

If Lynn was surprised to see him, she didn't show it. There was something about her casual demeanor that instantly made Peter nervous. As a child, John had been taught that doctors, like lawyers, should always project an air of superiority and detachment. Apparently, Lynn hadn't gotten that memo.

Nodding a greeting, Peter stepped inside the small living room that doubled as her office. Without waiting for an invitation, Chance squeezed between the humans' legs and scurried under the coffee table.

"Sorry about that. I'll get him."

"No, really. It's fine. Bill Woodside was a patient of mine, so I'm used to Chance hanging around."

To corroborate her story, Lynn opened a small tin canister on a shelf by the door and pulled out a biscuit. Grinning from ear to ear, the dog snatched the treat from her fingers and scarfed it down. Satisfied that at least one of her guests was now comfortable, Lynn sat down in her usual chair and invited her new patient to do the same.

Peter sank into the sofa across from her and surveyed the room. Space on Commercial Street was at a premium, and the office was surrounded on three sides by other buildings. Hanging in the only window, a large, ornate piece of stained glass functioned as a privacy screen. It let in sunlight, but effectively obscured the view from the sidewalk. Peter could tell by the distinctive pattern that Danny had crafted the piece. Another pang of jealousy, even more powerful than the one he'd felt last night, resurfaced as he considered the possibility that Danny and Lynn might be more than just friends.

When Peter finally turned his attention back to Lynn, she was waiting with an open notebook and pen. Clearly, she was ready for him to begin, but John was unaccustomed to talking about his feelings. As the trusted counselor, he was usually the one doling out advice.

Years of experience had probably taught Lynn how to recognize when someone was suffering from a malady of the heart. No two patients' scars could ever be the same, but Peter had a feeling that the first words were always the most difficult.

"My name isn't Peter. It's John."

Although true, the confession sounded dishonest. In less than a week, John's life had split in two. "I'm afraid you're going to think I'm crazy. Nothing I'm about to tell you is going to make any sense."

"Don't worry about that," Lynn said, putting down her notebook and pen. "For now, let's just talk about that guy I met at dinner last night."

At first, he spoke slowly, in starts and stops. John and Peter's memories were like before-and-after photographs that had been shuffled out of sequence. Through it all, Lynn was there. Sometimes she prodded him with a question, but mostly she just listened. By the end of the hour, Peter had said all he was ready to say—the rest of the story of David and Melody would have to wait. Lynn also seemed to know they were finished.

"Okay. Let's stop here. I know how difficult it's been to talk about your feelings, but this was definitely a good start. I only have one more question to ask. Are you going to be able to pull yourself back together?"

Peter wasn't sure how long he'd be able to keep his two separate lives from crashing into each other, but it helped that John's dysfunctional world was five hundred miles away.

"Honestly? I'm not sure, but I'm willing to give it a try."

In the time it takes for the Provincetown light to change, he was one whole person again. The chiming of a clock on the mantel signaled that their hour was up. Somehow, Peter had survived his first session.

"So, what happens next?"

"I have absolutely no idea," Lynn deadpanned.

Peter's face flushed red.

"Oh, no. I'm sorry," Lynn said, chuckling. "I was only joking. I have to keep reminding myself that I'm a psychologist, not a comedian."

"I'd like to come back and talk. I mean, if you're willing to take me on as a patient?" Peter tried not to sound desperate, but after today, he wasn't sure he could make it on his own. Looking tentatively at Lynn, he hoped he wouldn't have to.

"Of course. I'll go ahead and schedule you for a weekly session." She handed Peter an appointment card with the date and time of their next meeting. On the back, her phone number was written in blue ink. "I get the feeling there might be times when you need a friend more than a psychologist. Call me if you need either one."

"You picked up on that, huh?"

"Yes. I'm very psychic. I may even be the first psychic psychologist."

Lynn's weak attempt at humor was strangely reassuring. If she was cracking jokes, then things couldn't be as bad as they seemed. Chance got up from the floor, shook himself awake and smiled up at the two of them.

"Well, I sure was lucky to have found you," Peter said as he opened the office door and stepped into the real world.

"I'd say we were both lucky."

As Lynn closed the door, Peter hopped down onto the busy sidewalk. Walking up Commercial Street, he smiled and wondered whether this new friend might just turn out to be psychic after all.

Chapter 15

THE NEXT two months passed quickly. Peter's days fell into a satisfying rhythm of work and sleep. The weather on the Cape turned warmer, and the population multiplied exponentially. Locals found it difficult to endure the unending flow of traffic, but their trendy restaurants and boutique businesses relied on seasonal sales. Summer was the penance Provincetown paid for the tranquility it enjoyed during the other seasons.

In the early morning, while vacationers slept, Peter meandered through the empty streets on the way to work. Most nights he was in bed before nine. Danny had never formally asked him to sign on to the project, but Peter kept showing up anyway. In time, primitive shorthand replaced detailed plans and instructions. Weeks passed and work progressed, albeit slowly. Like so many other things in Provincetown, the expression of their friendship changed with the light. Usually bright, sometimes dark, but always intense.

Counseling with Lynn also continued. Although John felt secure enough to speak in her office, it was Peter who came and went from each session. Each week, he would struggle to resurrect the ghosts of his past, only to experience losing them again at the end of the hour. Peter seemed determined to hold onto John's grief as long as possible since it was the only thing that connected him to the people he'd lost. Progress was slow and rarely linear. Most days, it felt like he was running in sand.

That feeling was even more pronounced when Peter woke one morning and realized the day he'd been dreading had finally arrived.

Burrowing beneath the quilt, he reassured himself that he could make it through the next twenty-four hours—after all, it was only a day. Something about the turn of phrase triggered a realization. As far as his new friends in Provincetown were concerned, it was just another Friday in June. It could be that for Peter as well.

On any other day, he would already be hard at work, but this morning they were taking a road trip to Barnstable to find hardware for the chapel. After grabbing a hot shower, Peter pulled on a clean cotton shirt and khaki shorts. He was already down to the last notch on his belt. The inches from his waist had recently relocated to the muscles in his arms and chest. One of the perks of his new job was that he could eat anything he wanted and never gain weight. John had spent years starving himself to sustain a look that could only be described as mildly emaciated. Lately, his body had become an open hearth, burning far more calories than he consumed.

Perched on the steps of the Portuguese Bakery, Peter finished another deep-fried cinnamon stick and listened to the familiar sound of the old pickup as it idled down Commercial Street. Even at a distance, he could see that Danny was bleary-eyed and scowling. Frequently he'd shown up late to work with a thermos of coffee, complaining about another sleepless night. Peter closed the passenger door and fastened his seat belt without bothering to offer a greeting. Early on, he'd learned that Danny's moods were like the morning fog—a dense haze that usually burned away once the sun came up.

"Can we talk?" Peter asked, once they'd hit the highway. "You know, we see each other every day, but we don't really share much." His words came out in loud spurts as he competed with a rush of wind through the open windows.

"Whaddaya mean, Pete? I gave you half my turkey sandwich yesterday," Danny said with a playful grin.

Turning his attention back to the road, Peter fixed his eyes on the two parallel lines running down the center. In one lane was the person John had been, and in the other, the new man Peter was trying to be. Keeping secrets from Danny was like being stuck in the middle. The prospect of telling him the unvarnished truth was unsettling, but after two months, it was time to go one way or the other.

"I just think it might be nice if every now and then we took a break from work and talked. To be honest, there are some things I'd like to tell you."

"I already know everything I need to know about you," Danny said, looking straight ahead. Gripping the wheel, his knuckles were white.

The awkward silence that followed was heavy with what remained unsaid. It would have been easy to crack a stupid joke or change the subject, but Peter let the moment linger. Something about the situation felt a little too familiar. How many times had John lied to David to protect him from the truth?

"Maybe we could start with something simple," Peter offered by way of compromise. "I could tell you something about myself that isn't such a big deal. Like the fact that today is my birthday." He had blurted out the last part without thinking. Once it was said, however, he couldn't take it back.

"Is *that* what this is all about?" Danny said, trying to contain his laughter. "Is all this heavy drama just a play to get me to take you out for your birthday?"

"Well, Lincoln did sign the Emancipation Proclamation. So technically, slave labor is illegal. Maybe we could break the rules just this once and cut out of work early?"

Intentionally, Peter steered the conversation back to safer waters. Both men relaxed comfortably in their seats as the truck bounced along the country road.

"I'll make a deal with you," Danny said, making a hard left into the parking lot of the hardware store. "You help me pull down the steeple this afternoon, and we'll do something tonight to celebrate your birthday."

"Sounds like a plan."

It was just past eight, but the shop was already crowded with local contractors. Inside, an architectural graveyard of hinges, doorknobs, fixtures, and fittings was waiting. Relics from old houses and buildings protruded from weathered wooden bins like broken bones. Producing his list, Danny read out aloud as Peter scavenged. The look on both men's face betrayed their lack of optimism. Most of the debris was nothing more than junk.

While Danny wasted time sorting through piles of rusty hinges, Peter struck up an unlikely conversation with a crotchety old man who turned out to be the proprietor. After ten minutes of small talk and schmoozing, his new best friend offered to give them first dibs on a shipment that had just arrived from a demolished church in Chatham. From the back of the shop, Peter called out each time he found another hidden treasure. In less than an hour, they were finished.

Danny hung back and paid while Peter loaded crates into the truck. The acquisition of all this authentic hardware elevated the status of their work from common construction to true restoration. The project, like Peter's life, was starting to come together.

Danny strutted across the parking lot wearing his baseball cap and a smile. In an unprecedented display of affection, he grabbed Peter by the shoulders and gave him a bear hug. As far as they were both concerned, the morning had been a complete success.

Buoyant moods made the trip back enjoyable. As the truck raced up the highway, Peter entertained Danny with exaggerated imitations and made-up stories about the contractors at the shop. By the time they reached Provincetown, their stomachs ached from too much laughter. Getting away had been a pleasant diversion, but it felt good to be home. The pickup had just turned off Howland Street and onto Commercial when Peter spotted Lynn, balancing precariously on a bright-red bicycle. As Danny tooted the horn, she slammed on the brakes and came to a screeching halt.

"Hello, boys!" she called out in her best Mae West impersonation. In one fluid motion, Danny turned off the ignition and pulled his body up, and halfway out, the open window. Sitting comfortably on the driver's side door, he pounded a drumbeat on the roof of the cab.

"Today is Peter's *birthday!*" he sang loudly and out of tune. Lynn gasped and feigned a look of shock.

"What? No! This can't be possible. Today is *our* Peter's birthday?"

Peter slumped in his seat and stared straight ahead. He was pretending to ignore his friends' antics, but really, he loved the attention. Lynn parked her bike on the sidewalk and rushed to the passenger's side as Danny slid back into the truck. Peter felt his face flush red as they both pushed closer. Sandwiched between them, he was trapped.

"So, what are we going to do to celebrate?"

Peter wondered whether it was his friend or his psychologist asking the question. Lynn knew that he'd spent most of his life in a mad dash, leaping over challenges like a hurdler. Always ready for the next race, John had never slowed down long enough to celebrate anything. Now, after two months of intensive therapy, Peter was starting to realize that by running so fast he'd left himself behind.

"Shhhh! I can't tell you," Danny answered in a loud stage whisper. "It's a surprise."

Lynn raised an index finger to her lips to indicate that his secret was safe. Shifting in his seat, Peter was enjoying the pressure of Danny's shoulder against his arm.

"Okay. You can have the birthday boy tonight, but I get him this weekend. Dinner at the Crown & Anchor on Saturday. Be there at seven!"

"It's a date," Peter said with genuine enthusiasm.

Lynn gently squeezed his arm and smiled. For a split second, a look of concern drifted across her face. Peter searched her eyes for some kind of coded message, but whatever Dr. Morris needed to say would have to wait. Blowing both men a kiss, she hopped back onto her bike and pedaled up Commercial Street. Still chuckling under his breath, Danny started the pickup and shifted it into gear.

Back at the chapel, Peter stowed the hardware in the shed while Danny secured two tall ladders to the front wall. With hammers and crowbars in hand, the men began to climb toward the crumbling steeple. The road trip had been fun, but Peter was glad to be back on the job. In his case, the devil always found work for idle hands. Early on, he was painfully aware of the line Danny had drawn in the sand. Romance, even imagining the possibility of anything happening between them, had been strictly off-limits. But lately, when Peter least expected it, the clear boundaries around their friendship had begun to blur.

Perched above the treetops, it was easy to see the restoration in progress. The new cedar shingles burned orange and red. It would take two or three seasons before the rain and sun turned the roof a more respectable shade of gray. Unfinished, the clapboards that covered the exterior gave the place a rustic feel, but a few heavy coats of whitewash would restore its New England charm soon enough.

It took the strength of two grown men to pull away the rotted exterior of the steeple. *One. Two. Three.* Peter's hammer split through the thin layer of plywood hiding underneath. Grinning at him from the other side, Danny tugged hard at the exposed frame. Peter expected the shell to crumble to pieces, but it held fast. The fact that the structure was sound was a huge relief, considering what it would have taken to rebuild it from scratch. Another smile from Danny—even brighter than the first—was like lightning hitting the same spot twice.

It was late in the afternoon when a bank of fluffy white clouds drifted slowly across the blue sky. The Pilgrim Monument, a majestic pillar, stood proud and tall like its distant cousin in DC. The panoramic view captivated Peter, but Danny's attention was focused on finishing the job. Checking the framework one last time, he stole a quick glance at the ground. Then, with exaggerated care, he extended his left foot and searched the empty air for the next rung. Peter scuttled down the ladder and looked away to hide his obvious amusement. It didn't seem possible, but Danny Cavanaugh was afraid of heights.

"Well, we did it. Now, will you *please* tell me what we're doing tonight?"

Danny ignored the request and continued his backward descent. Waiting impatiently below, Peter tried to keep from looking up and enjoying the view.

"Don't worry about it, birthday boy. I'm on it. Just wrap things up here and meet me at the pier in an hour."

Danny sprinted across the yard and disappeared beneath the branches of the oak. With less than an hour to spare, Peter began pulling down the ladders and collecting the tools. It was the first time Danny had trusted him to secure the site for the night.

Luckily, Peter knew Danny's routine by heart. Working quickly, he cleaned up the yard and made sure everything was back in its proper place. As important as it was to prove himself, he was even more anxious to run home and get ready for their date. The sound of that word made him cringe. Despite all the hard-learned lessons, he was doing it again— indulging in fantasies. For a moment, Peter actually considered calling the whole thing off, but it was too late. Danny would be waiting.

Peter stopped at the cottage just long enough to shower and put out a bowl of food for Chance. The clock read six forty-five. If he left now, he would make it to the pier with a few minutes to spare. Knowing the best shortcuts through town was one of the advantages of being a local. After putting on a clean T-shirt and a pair of khakis, he pulled the door shut and raced across the path. Peter was almost at the front gate when he heard Florence calling from the porch. Stopping to talk to her would probably make him late, but he was willing to risk it.

Peter blushed when he saw the ornately wrapped gift waiting in the old woman's arms. Florence was beaming with anticipation as she stepped forward and presented it to him. All traces of his earlier impatience were gone. To hell with the time. Danny would wait.

"What's this all about?"

"A wee bird may have whispered in my ear that today's your birthday," she said with a wink.

"Well, if your source was Lynn, then it was more like a nightingale."

Like a kid at Christmas, Peter shook the package and tested its weight. Untying the blue satin ribbon, he lifted the lid and carefully separated the sheets of tissue paper. A bright yellow windbreaker with white piping was folded neatly inside. Light and water repellant, it was a must-have for anyone living on the Cape. Peter dropped the box and made a grand show of putting it on.

"Oh, it's perfect!" Florence announced, clapping her hands in front of her face.

"Thank you," he said, drawing the zipper halfway up and down again. "I'd love to stay and chat, but...."

"...you're running late to meet Danny." Florence finished his sentence. "I guessed as much by the way you're fidgeting about. Well, be on your way then. Lord knows the Cavanaugh boys have never been a very patient lot."

Peter wanted to stay and chat, but he really had to get going. If time was money, then he was overdrawn by almost ten minutes. Even so, he was willing to spare a few more seconds to let his true feelings show. Leaning forward, he planted a kiss on Florence's powdered cheek.

With the scent of lilacs lingering in the air, Peter sprinted down the lane with his jacket fanning out behind him like a cape. Rather than wishing the rest of the afternoon away, he was unexpectedly grateful to have been born on the longest day of the year.

Chapter 16

CLIMBING UP and down the ladder had forced Peter to stretch unused muscles. Now, he was paying the price. A spasm radiating in his left calf warned him not to run, but he ignored it and kept on going. *Bob. Weave. Duck.* The season didn't officially start until next week, but wandering hordes of tourists had already turned Commercial Street into a human obstacle course. Minutes were ticking away, and Danny was waiting. Pushing through the pain, Peter used a final burst of speed to dart down Ryder Street where the concrete beneath his feet changed to wood.

At this time of day, the pier was practically empty except for the few fishermen and whale watchers heading back into town. More industrial than commercial, it lacked the shops and restaurants that attracted a crowd. Peter stopped to catch his breath and look around for Danny. The sun was low in the sky, but he'd made it across town in record time. By his best estimate, he was no more than ten or fifteen minutes late. Peter was beginning to worry that Danny had gotten tired of waiting and left when he heard a familiar voice calling his name.

Waving from the deck of a schooner, Danny Cavanaugh looked like an authentic sailor. His baseball cap was gone, and a length of white nylon cord hung slack over one shoulder. As Peter maneuvered down the metal ramp connecting the jetty to the pier, Danny hopped over the side of the boat and rushed forward to greet him. Right on cue, an older man emerged from below deck and took his place securing the jib.

"Nice threads," Danny said, tugging one of the strings dangling from the hood of Peter's windbreaker. "Looks like someone knew you were going sailing tonight."

"Yes. I always like to dress well when I take to the sea," Peter said in a terrible English accent. "Although comfort is obviously more important to me than fashion, since I look like a giant lemon."

"Well, most guys in Provincetown *are* a little fruity. But actually, I think you look kind of great."

Peter's face flushed. Under different circumstances, he'd have savored a compliment from Danny—even one that was slightly backhanded. Given the current situation, however, it was just another painful reminder that his one-sided feelings were beginning to throw their friendship off balance.

When it came to the weather in Provincetown, June was like a petulant child. Days that started out sunny and warm often turned overcast and cold without warning. Tonight, it looked like Mother Nature was in a good mood—the skies were clear, and the wind was strong.

"Welcome!" a woman called out to them. "You can just climb on board whenever you're ready."

Following Danny, Peter used his arms and shoulders to pull the rest of his body up a ladder at the stern. Once on deck, he widened his stance for stability and tentatively walked toward the prow. It would take time and a little practice to get his sea legs. Straight ahead, two tall masts were dressed with sails, ready to take the wind. Glancing through a porthole, Peter could see a well-appointed galley and two small cabins below. Unlike the senator's floating mansion moored in Annapolis, this old sailboat was dignified. Made entirely of wood, there wasn't an inch of chrome or fiberglass in sight.

"Carol and Al, this is my buddy, Peter."

Like most of the locals, the long-married couple belonged to the sea. Despite the warmth of the evening, both wore light slickers to protect them from the heavy mist drifting off the water. The woman's hair was jet black and worn in a chic style that suggested she'd once cared about such things. Mostly bald, her husband was a foot taller, with a neat goatee peppered silver and gray. In the most natural of gestures, the man slipped his arm around his wife and pulled her close. It was good to see that the passing years had deepened, not diminished, their affection.

"It's very nice to meet you."

Peter extended his hand, but Carol opted for a hug instead. Holding on a second too long, she patted him twice on the back before letting go. John would have been naturally suspicious of such an intimate greeting, but Peter knew that most of the locals felt a strange kinship with one another. In Provincetown, hugs were more common than handshakes. If Peter had only known that he was about to be introduced to two of Danny's friends, he'd have practiced what to say. Rather than risk speaking to Carol off-the-cuff, he shifted his attention toward her husband. Noticeably cooler, the man's body language subtly conveyed the message that he'd appointed himself Danny's protector.

"Good to see you out here again, son," Al said, pulling a rag from his back pocket to polish a spotless brass fixture.

"Yes, sir. It's been a while since I took the boat out."

"Far too long to stay away from something you love so much," Carol said, putting her arm around Danny's waist. Peter knew they weren't talking about sailing. It was clear that this couple was a part of Danny's enigmatic past. Peter tried to fit this new piece of information into what little he knew about the Cavanaughs, but it was hard to assemble a puzzle without having ever seen the completed picture.

"Well, you're here now," Carol said in a noticeably lighter tone. "And we couldn't be happier to see you—to see *both* of you. So, welcome!"

Despite the smiles and warm words, Peter felt uncomfortable. Danny had given him more than he could have ever expected for his birthday—a rare glimpse into his very private world and an evening alone together. It was probably the closest they'd ever come to the fantasy Peter had conjured up, but the unrequited nature of his feelings had the potential to turn their cruise into a shipwreck. Since they were already on board, there was nothing Peter could do. Fortunately, the last months with David had taught John how to endure almost anything.

The position of the sun over Al's left shoulder signaled it was time to shove off. Carol squeezed Danny's hand and reminded him that a tub of her famous shrimp salad was waiting in the galley. Peter thanked her for the effort, but he was more interested in beer than food. Helping himself to a cold one, he stood a safe distance away from Danny and listened to the engines churn.

More deftly than Peter had expected, Danny maneuvered the vessel away from the pier and cruised up the channel. Once clear of the harbor, he killed the motor and quickly went to work. As Peter watched, Danny tugged at the knot that tied the halyard to the headboard. His eyes traced a clear path to the top of the mast. When he was sure that the rigging could run free, Danny pulled the canvas ties loose and hoisted the mainsail. Then, jumping back behind the helm, he spun the wheel hard and brought the boat around. Without warning, the heavy boom swung left and the sails unfurled. Peter braced himself for speed. Ready or not, their adventure had begun.

Skipping across the ocean on a current of wind was like flying. The crashing sound of the waves was almost loud enough to drown out the voices in Peter's head. Despite any earlier misgivings he'd had about spending time alone with his friend, he was actually having fun. Out on the water, his problems seemed to have less weight. Thirty minutes of sailing was almost as cathartic as an hour of therapy with Lynn.

Danny was visibly more relaxed as he captained the boat through Hatches Harbor and into a secluded cove. Ahead, off the port side, the Race Point Lighthouse was a white dot on shore. With one hand on the tiller, he tugged at a line to lower the mainsail. The drag of the water slowed their progress but not completely. Once the boat had glided to a stop, Danny pushed a red button and sank the anchor to the bottom. Hovering just above the horizon, the sun was a wild conflagration of color. Red, yellow, orange, and purple flames consumed the clouds.

Peter felt a shiver race up his spine. Looking over his shoulder, he was surprised to see Danny standing behind him, pushing an icy bottle into the small of his back. Smiling, he wiped the condensation off his jacket and snatched the beer away. Alcohol made it easier to relax and enjoy the moment, but it was his third on an empty stomach. It was a good thing the captain wasn't keeping count.

Laughing at his own prank, Danny grabbed a drink for himself and settled into a comfortable chair. It had taken some skillful navigation, but he'd managed to get them front-row seats for the sunset.

The colors of the sky deepened as the sun touched the water. Once it had set, they would turn around and head back to the pier. Peter just needed to hold it together a little longer. Nudging his feelings back into place, he sat down next to his friend and busied himself by peeling away the label on his bottle. Too bad that only took about ten seconds.

"Thanks for coming out here with me tonight," Danny said unexpectedly. "I haven't been sailing in over a year, and I'm glad this was something we could do together."

"There's nowhere I'd rather be."

Peter cringed as he felt the words slip out of his mouth. When it came to his emotions, honesty wasn't always the best policy. Even so, it felt like an appropriate response to Danny's affirmation of their friendship.

Peter finished what was left of his beer and sat down. Back on land, John's memories seemed like they belonged to someone else. But tonight, here on the water, the details of that other life were as clear and vivid as the colors of the sky.

"You know, you don't always have to keep everything bottled up. It's unhealthy."

The idea of Danny Cavanaugh lecturing about transparency was almost laughable, but Peter knew Danny was right. Even though he'd spent the last two months in therapy with Lynn, talking about John's past was like watching the same movie over and over. No matter how hard Peter tried, he could never change the ending.

"I spent last summer hiking through Alaska." Danny offered up a piece of information about his past to make the point. "I used to think running away was the only way to deal with things that were too painful to remember."

"Yeah. I know the feeling. But those are usually the things you never want to forget."

The conversation had reached a turning point. Without realizing it, the two men had drifted into open water. Now it was time to make a choice: turn back or sail on.

"My dad really loved this old boat. When the weather was good, we'd take my whole family out for the day. This cove was our favorite spot. I haven't been back here in a long time."

"What happened to your family?"

Peter had to ask the question even though he was afraid to hear the answer. Danny abandoned his untouched drink and walked over to the stern. Gripping the polished wooden railing with both hands, he stared down into the murky water.

"My parents and little brother were killed in an accident last year."

Peter rose from his chair and stepped forward. Standing side by side, the two men gazed at the afterglow on the horizon. It had been a spectacular sunset.

"My father was an amateur pilot. He flew us out here all the time in his Cessna to see his pet project, the chapel. My grandparents were married there, and my dad was really pumped to restore it. When dad retired a few years ago, he decided to buy it from the town. Every night he'd go over the plans with me and write notes about what needed to be done."

Danny stopped to collect his thoughts. When he continued, his voice was quieter.

"We'd planned to go home together, but at the last minute I bailed and decided to stay for a party. I said I'd take the morning ferry instead of flying with them at night. I'll never forget the last time I saw my mom—I was so anxious to meet up with my friends that I never even said good-bye. I just called out 'later' and waved to her as I headed out the door. They were almost back to Boston when a short in the electrical system blew out the instruments. Dad managed to fly by sight for a while, but he misjudged the altitude in the dark and…."

Peter closed his eyes and tried not to imagine the details. Stepping closer, he reached out and wrapped his arms around Danny. What few words of comfort he could offer would sound hollow.

"I lost my family, too," he confessed in a whisper. "Not the same way you did, but I had people who loved me and now they're gone." Peter felt as if he should say more. Even though he'd finally told Danny the truth, it had been less than a fair trade.

Beneath the cover of darkness, the two friends held onto each other as the boat rocked. Peter knew they would probably never be this close again. After a minute, Danny pulled back but not away.

"Wow, we're both a mess then, huh?"

Peter wiped his nose on the sleeve of his jacket and chuckled in agreement. Not surprisingly, it looked as though they were about to defuse the situation with humor and another round. Trying his best not to seem disappointed, he told himself that settling for a lasting friendship wasn't settling at all. Peter had almost started to believe that was true when Danny angled his head and leaned forward.

It's almost impossible to describe the intensity of emotion that fuels a first kiss. Like breath, something invisible passes between two people when their lips touch. Until now, John Wells had just been pretending to be someone else. But against the odds, that other part of him, this guy named Peter, had found someone to love. The possibility that Danny could feel the same way—a chance at happiness—changed everything.

Despite the obvious contradiction between his friend's words and actions, there was palpable heat behind the kiss. After what seemed like forever, Danny squeezed Peter's shoulders and pivoted to the right. Slipping back behind the helm, he pushed the red button again and switched on the power. While the anchor slowly ascended from the ocean floor, the twin outboard engines sputtered to life. There was no need to talk about what had just happened. Something about the matter-of-fact way Danny went about each task reassured Peter that he had no regrets.

On through the night, the boat sailed. It would have been easy to lose sight of the blinking buoys that marked the route. Even with the running lights, the sea was as dark as the shore. But Danny Cavanaugh knew the way. Sitting tall in the captain's chair, he studied the horizon and charted a course home.

"You know what?" he asked as they sailed into the harbor and the first lights of Provincetown came into view. "I think we should go ahead and paint the chapel tomorrow."

"Yeah?" Peter was afraid to say more and risk breaking the mood.

"We could invite all our friends and make it a group thing."

It had taken considerable effort for Peter to think and speak in the first person. In time, the lonely letter "I" came to replace the more familiar "us" and "we." Now, with a single word—"our"—he was part of someone's world again.

As the boat drifted up to the pier, Danny cut the motors and jumped to his feet. Unexpectedly, he guided Peter into the captain's seat and placed both his hands firmly on the wheel.

"Hold her steady, Pete. I just need to pull the mooring lines taut." Danny was still giving orders, but something about his tone of voice was different.

Standing alone at the helm, Peter adjusted his grip and looked up at the night sky. Could this really be happening? Was the universe offering him another chance to be loved? If the darkness knew the answer, it wasn't telling.

Chapter 17

LYING AWKWARDLY on his left side, David's features were frozen as he slept on the sand. Only the steady rise and fall of his chest confirmed he was still alive. Lonely fingers crawled across the beach blanket and melted into his empty hand. Above, a cold sun blazed in the cloudless sky as John tried to recall why they'd been apart so long.

Somewhere in the distance, just beyond the white water, a familiar voice was calling him by another name. Cupped hands shielded his eyes as he scanned the horizon, but it was hard to see the swimmer through the glare. Jumping to his feet, John walked carefully across the rocky shore and stepped into the swirling tide.

Out at sea, a mighty wave felt the ocean floor as it surged toward land. The drag from the friction of the sand invariably slowed the progress of the deeper water. Moving at different speeds, the surface of the wave crested and tipped forward. The sound, as it broke onshore, was like the crash of distant thunder.

Peter rolled over in his bed and rubbed the grit from his eyes. Pulling one of the extra pillows under his neck, he struggled to sort the fragments of his dream from reality. Slowly, the Sandman's dust began to settle. David was in DC sleeping with someone else while Peter was alone in Provincetown, tossing and turning. Well, maybe alone wasn't the right word to describe his current situation. After all, he still had Chance to come home to every night, and lately his prospects for love seemed to be improving.

Once fully awake, he couldn't stop thinking about Danny. A famous writer once said that you know you're in love when you can't fall asleep because reality is finally better than your dreams. That quote partially explained Peter's restlessness even though it was attributed to Dr. Seuss, a guy who'd successfully parlayed an overactive imagination into a career.

Tired of lying in bed, Peter relocated to the front porch in just a T-shirt and boxers. The sun had been up for a while, but the grass was still wet. Out in the yard, Chance darted from tree to tree, barking at squirrels. Unlike his master, the little dog was reveling in the morning. Peter lowered his body into an Adirondack chair and rested his mug of tea on one of the wide arms. Rising generously from the cup, steam filled the air with a rich, spicy scent.

His offer to show up early and help mix paint had been affably rebuffed. As usual, Danny had insisted on prepping the site. He was probably already there, anxious to get to work.

Peter swallowed a bowl of cereal in three mouthfuls and grabbed what was quickly becoming his favorite flannel shirt as he headed out the door. It was too late to avoid the traffic on Commercial Street, so he mapped out a detour using back roads. Despite his best efforts, it took twice as long as usual to reach the chapel. From the sound of things, Byron had rallied a small army to help paint. Peter tried not to calculate how many projects were left on Danny's list. Secretly, he was afraid their connection would waver once the renovation was complete.

Considering the short notice, it was an impressive turnout. Lynn and Douglas were passing out silver pails of whitewash while Jasper and his two brothers were already busy brushing on paint. Giddy from the excitement or the fumes, Byron stood on the chapel steps, belting out show tunes to a captive audience. Even Florence was doing her part by arranging food and drinks on the workbench-turned-picnic table.

Faces without names, neighbors Peter recognized but didn't know, greeted him with handshakes and smiles. Everyone seemed to be present and accounted for except Danny. Given his fear of heights, Peter was surprised to find him hanging precariously from a ladder, working shirtless in the sun. Even though it was still early, his forearms and chest were already speckled with white paint.

"Good morning, sleepyhead. It was nice of you to drag yourself out of bed and join us. I guess it's true what they say, most gay guys like to get a little *behind* in their work."

"Hardy har har—very funny, early bird," Peter replied, holding the base of the ladder steady as Danny climbed back down. "Too bad all those tasty worms didn't improve your sense of humor. You know it isn't like me to sleep in. Must've been all that sailing and the fresh sea air."

"Yeah, definitely. It could also have been the ten-hour day you worked yesterday and the six-pack you drank on the boat." Danny's playful grin took most of the sting out of his jab.

"Or maybe someone sent me home last night with something great to dream about."

Peter could almost feel the heat radiating from Danny's skin. Without meaning to do so, he'd given his friend an opening to either acknowledge the kiss or pretend it had never happened. Either way, it was the wrong time and place for a heavy discussion. Intentionally responding with a look that defied interpretation, Danny hefted the ladder and moved on to the next unfinished section.

Peter stared up at the rebuilt steeple and dug the heel of his boot into the soft earth. He should have been happy about the prospect of trading up from friendship to romance, but the ambiguity of their relationship pushed at the weakest part of him—the same spot where David had left a bruise. So far, he'd been doing a good job keeping his reservoir of anger from spilling over, but the steady trickle of insecurity and self-doubt was getting to be too much. Maybe it was time to let John step in and negotiate a deal that would allow him to keep all those feelings in check.

Back out front, Lynn was trying her best to strip away a layer of paint from one of the balusters. She had just finished slathering the thick jelly onto another post when Peter sidled up next to her and smiled. Picking up an old paintbrush, he stirred the congealing liquid inside a tin can while she worked. Even with good ventilation, the toxic vapors burned his nose and eyes.

"Whew!" Lynn said, pulling off her rubber gloves and tucking a stray tangle of hair behind her ear. Peter couldn't help but notice that her eyes were big and glassy. "I really need to get away from here and get some fresh air. Care to join me?"

Peter didn't really feel like taking a walk, but anything was better than standing around feeling sorry for himself. Answering with a shrug, he reluctantly followed her across the yard. More focused on the work than the workers, Danny would probably never even notice they were gone.

"So, tell me already. How was your birthday? Did you enjoy the sailing?"

"It was fine," Peter said, lifting the branch of the oak tree and walking a few steps ahead. There was nothing out of the ordinary about Lynn's questions, but something about her clinical tone suddenly made him feel vulnerable and exposed. Dr. Morris was a skilled psychologist. She could clearly sense when one of her patients was holding something back. Even though John had told her nearly everything about his past, Peter had never admitted his feelings for Danny. Pining for a straight guy, someone who could never love him back, was setting himself up for an epic fail. Lynn would undoubtedly counsel him to pursue a more conventional relationship, but he'd invested too much to walk away.

"Come on, Wells. You can do better than that. Tell me what you're feeling."

Peter was in no mood for an impromptu therapy session. Like a lab rat in a maze, he was tired of trying to explain himself and plowing into dead ends.

"It was absolutely fantastic! Is that what you wanted to hear? When I look at Danny Cavanaugh, I see fireworks. Every day I spend with him is like the goddamn Fourth of July."

Slapping down any vegetation that dared to stand in his way, Peter stomped off. Left or right? It really didn't matter which direction he walked; there was nowhere for him to go. Hot tears blurred his vision as Lynn walked up behind him and touched him on the shoulder.

"So it was fine," she said casually, without even a hint of sarcasm.

Peter couldn't help but laugh at her response. Once again, he'd misjudged someone. Lynn Morris was more than just his therapist—she was also his friend.

"Okay," he said more calmly. "Maybe it would help me if I talked out everything with you. Last night, on the water, something really amazing happened with Danny."

"Well, hallelujah!" Lynn exclaimed, lifting her hands to the sky. "Now, *that* I can work with."

John knew from experience how withholding the truth could be far more destructive than telling a lie. It was a relief to finally say out loud what Peter had been thinking for weeks.

"I just don't understand how I fit into his life. Sometimes, when Danny looks at me, I can feel him pulling me closer. But then, just when we start making a real connection, he pushes me away. Why can't he make up his mind about what he wants and stop jerking me around?"

"Maybe you should just man up and ask him instead of talking behind his back?"

It wasn't Lynn who posed the question. Speaking through gritted teeth, Danny stepped from beneath the shelter of the trees.

"Maybe he's working through his own stuff...."

"Maybe he isn't sure he can really trust you...."

"Maybe he's afraid to start caring again."

The air crackled with testosterone as the two men squared off.

In all the years spent fighting with David, John had learned how easy it was to objectify someone during an argument; anger destroyed empathy and transformed loved ones into targets.

Lynn cleared her throat to remind them she was still there. She reached out and took Danny's hand. Despite the dramatic vibrato, his face instantly softened. Mirroring the gesture with Peter, Lynn joined their hands and stepped away. "There," she said. "Now, talk." She walked back up the path to the chapel.

"I should have talked to you instead of Lynn. That was the wrong way to handle the situation."

"No, I'm the one who needs to apologize," Danny said, pulling off his cap. When he put it on again, he purposely turned it backwards so Peter could see his eyes.

Peter could tell from his body language that Danny was struggling to put his feelings into words. Now, unlike his knee-jerk reaction at the dune shack, he was ready to express himself with hands and lips. The very public display of affection that followed was direct enough to dispel some of Peter's lingering doubts.

"Let's do dinner tonight," Danny said, pushing his thumb into the calluses on Peter's palm. "No one else—just you and me. We can talk—really talk—and try to figure this thing out."

"Yes."

Overcome with happiness, Peter leaned in for another kiss, but Danny playfully pushed him away.

"Come on, Casanova. It's time to get back to work."

When it came to Danny, Peter always wanted more. Although it would be hard to make it through the afternoon, the promise of a real date tonight was enough to keep him going.

Like all the other volunteers, Peter had grossly underestimated how long it would take to finish painting. Even with so many eager hands, the chapel seemed to expand with every brushstroke. Thirsty, the unfinished wood drank in coat after coat of whitewash. After a few hours of repetitive motion, muscles stiffened, and the fluid enthusiasm of the crew hardened into grim determination.

Marked with streaks of war paint, the tribe of friends congregated in front of the chapel at the end of the day. In the failing sunlight, the oyster-white color of the exterior looked almost gray. There was still a bit of masonry left to repair, but overall the exterior now closely resembled the sepia photos in Michael Cavanaugh's notebooks. Despite all the challenges and setbacks, Danny and Peter had succeeded in restoring what had almost been lost.

It was just after dusk when the group finally disbanded. Bowing out of his belated birthday dinner with Lynn, Peter quickly rinsed out the brushes and locked up the shed for the night. Another long work day had left Danny completely spent. Asleep behind the wheel of the pickup, he reluctantly opened his eyes when Peter jumped into the passenger seat.

"So, where are we going for dinner—Spiritus or Bubala's?"

On any other night, it would have been more of a coin toss than a question. A creature of habit, Danny usually ate at places that specialized in cheese and grease.

"Well, smart-ass," he said, starting the truck and shifting it into gear, "I was actually thinking about taking you somewhere a little nicer. How would you feel about a proper sit-down dinner at the Lobster Pot?"

"Okay. First, that's *Mr.* Smart-ass to you. And second, I think that sounds perfect."

Just inside the entrance to the restaurant, a miniature ocean of creatures stared at Peter through a wall of water and glass. The place was unusually crowded—even for Saturday night—and a line of hungry tourists stretched out the door and onto Commercial Street. Without bothering to put their name in for a table, Danny grabbed a menu and ordered some side dishes to go. He waited until the waitress had written it all down, then pointed at two huge lobsters in the tank and paid the bill.

Cursing under his breath, Peter pulled Danny into the bar and reached for his wallet.

"Since you beat me to the punch by paying for dinner, you can at least let me buy you a drink."

"To hell with a drink," Danny said, waving to the bartender who sauntered over wearing a roguish smile. "You can buy us a bottle."

"Man, Cavanaugh. I know those damn seagulls can get pretty pissed off, but it looks like you boys really got clobbered today!"

"Nah, Randy," Danny said, rubbing off some of the dried white flecks. "It's just paint."

"So what are we drinking tonight?"

"In honor of the occasion, I've decided to forgo beer for bourbon."

On any other night, this kind of casual banter would have been entertaining. But after two consecutive days of emotional highs and lows, Danny looked like he was ready for a stiff drink. Ignoring the pushy tourists demanding service, Randy reached beneath the bar and pulled out a dust-covered bottle.

"If I'm remembering right, this was your dad's favorite."

Danny quickly filled two glasses and passed one to Peter.

"I couldn't have done any of this alone. If you hadn't come along, I'd still be up there pounding away. Thanks for not giving up on the chapel—or me."

Even over the clink of silverware and the chattering of voices, the sentiment behind the toast was clear. Danny took a small sip while Peter emptied his glass. The undiluted alcohol hit his empty stomach like a rock, sending ripples of heat through his body. Without pausing to enjoy the effect, he poured himself another.

More bored than thirsty, the two men drank in silence and watched as a trio of waitresses darted about, delivering orders and clearing plates. Across the room, a child let out a high-pitched squeal as a live, thirteen-pound lobster, was presented to him for inspection. The noble creature was probably a couple years older than the kid who would soon be tearing it apart claw by claw. Something about the ritual struck Peter as macabre. His appetite unexpectedly dulled, he reached again for the bottle.

"Hey, slow down, buddy. You aren't drinking ginger ale," Danny said, rimming the glass with the tip of his finger.

Fortifying himself with liquid courage, Peter desperately wanted to confess everything about his life back in DC. He'd just finished practicing what to say when Randy reappeared with a fresh bottle and three empty glasses. Without being invited, the bartender joined them in a round and listened intently as Danny updated him on the progress of their work. Peter had underestimated how much two months of self-imposed prohibition had weakened his legendary tolerance. By the time the food arrived, he was hopelessly drunk.

While Danny gathered the heavy paper bags and said his good-nights, Peter stumbled outside. He would have gladly paid a hundred bucks for a cool breeze off the water, but the air was unseasonably warm and still. Like a circus performer, Peter took a few steps forward on an invisible tightrope before stumbling into a freefall. Just as he was about to hit the pavement, Danny swooped in. Supporting Peter's weight, they shuffled down Commercial Street to the pickup.

With all the windows closed, the inside of the truck smelled of hot-buttered corn and biscuits. Peter turned to ask Danny where they were heading next, but all that came out of his mouth was a burp.

"Nice, Wells. *Very* classy."

Peter noticed Danny force back a smile and step on the gas. By the look of it, most of the tourists were walking off dinner. A surge of rowdy teenagers overflowed onto the narrow street from the even-narrower sidewalk. Danny sounded the horn in admonishment as one of the boys sheepishly smiled and waved an apology. Avoiding pedestrians was the first rule of driving in Provincetown. Peter closed his eyes and settled back into his seat. Tonight, with Danny at the wheel, he was ready to do something reckless.

Chapter 18

THE OLD pickup wound its way up Telegraph Hill where the houses were large and majestic. Peter had never been to this secluded part of town, but Danny seemed to know the way.

"I hope you don't mind, but Carol and Al asked me to drop by and check on the house. We won't stay long, but there's something I really want to show you."

First dinner and now an unscheduled stop. Things weren't going as planned, but Peter wasn't about to let a few detours derail the evening. The ocean breeze through the window was a few degrees cooler than the air in town. Leaning against the headrest, he decided to just sit back and enjoy the ride.

Buyers were used to paying outrageous prices for Provincetown real estate, but this quiet cul-de-sac, with its unobstructed views, was particularly desirable. Inebriated and impressed, Peter whistled when the truck careened around the corner and glided to a stop in front of the biggest house on the street. As the engine idled, he mentally calculated how much it would cost to buy and maintain such a property. Carol and Al had obviously done well for themselves.

Danny was halfway up the walk before Peter could even unfasten his seat belt. The grass and shrubbery were meticulously groomed, but like every other house on the street, the mansion was dark. Among the rich, there seemed to be an unspoken axiom: the more expensive the property, the less frequently it should be used. Still, there was something distinctive about this place that made it feel lived in.

Danny grabbed a spare key from behind one of the shutters and slid it into the lock. With a loud creak, the massive front door swung open, and he disappeared inside. Humming quietly to himself on the front porch, Peter glanced over his shoulder. The peace and quiet of the street was almost as disorienting as the commotion in town.

"It's okay. You can come in."

Following Danny's disembodied voice, Peter walked inside and closed the door. Almost full, the moon through the windows cast enough light to see by. Several of the larger pieces of furniture were covered with white sheets, and the air smelled like wet socks at the bottom of a hamper. With the start of the season just a few days away, it seemed odd that the house was not yet open for summer.

Danny maneuvered through the living room and punched a code into a keypad on the wall. A second later, the overhead lights blazed on, and the air-conditioning sighed through hidden vents.

"Wow," Peter said a little too loudly. The furniture and artwork rivaled anything he'd seen at the senator's Virginia estate.

"Yeah. I know. And you haven't even seen the best part."

Danny opened the back door and slipped outside. The mix of adrenaline and alcohol in Peter's bloodstream gave the scene a dreamlike quality. Back in the real world, their feast in the truck was getting cold. Those two lobsters at the bottom of the bag would still be alive if Danny had been craving pizza instead of seafood. Fate could be cruel, but Peter was determined to make sure their deaths had not been in vain. Now, more than ever, he wanted Danny to finish whatever he'd been dispatched to do.

A ten-million-dollar view was waiting just outside the door. Taking advantage of the elevation, the architect had incorporated a stone terrace where guests could enjoy the dazzling panorama. In the foreground, the weekend carnival continued on Commercial Street while the lights of Truro twinkled across the harbor.

"Hey, Houdini? Where'd you go?"

Standing alone, Peter searched the shadows. A metal staircase behind him twisted up the back of the house to an observation deck with an enclosed cupola. High above, like the ghost of a sea captain's widow, Danny was pacing back and forth, staring at the horizon. Still feeling a buzz from the bourbon, Peter grabbed the iron handrail and started to climb.

Danny was waiting for him at the top of the stairs. Despite his fear of heights, he plopped down at the very edge of the deck and dangled both legs in the air. As Peter joined him, he casually slid an arm around Danny's shoulder. The nebula of stars scattered across the sky reminded him of the night they'd first met.

Emitting what sounded like a sigh of relief, Danny leaned into Peter. Heads turned and lips touched. Everything about the kiss was perfect, but it left Peter wanting more. Shifting his weight, he pulled Danny closer and caressed the gooseflesh on his arm. Although their story had started off as a comedy of errors, it looked as though it was going to have a happy ending.

Drunk on moonlight and bourbon, Peter's hands went searching for more skin to touch. But like a replay of his reaction at the dune shack, Danny's body unexpectedly went taut. Once again, Peter had misread the signals and tripped a silent alarm. He tried to dial things back, but it was too late. Without warning, Danny jumped to his feet and pushed open the door to the cupola.

Peter was tired of waiting. Taking a page from John's playbook, he charged over and slid his arms around Danny's waist. "Just relax and go with it. I'm sure Carol and Al won't mind if we hang out in their house for a while and enjoy this incredible view."

"What are you talking about?" Danny asked, breaking free. Even in the dark, Peter could see his face was contorted with rage.

"Oh, come on. Drop the act. I know you want this as much as I do. Why else would you have brought me here tonight?"

Peter was afraid to hear the answer, but he was done playing games. It was time to stop pretending to be someone else. Finally ready to argue his case, John stepped forward as Danny switched on the lights.

"This isn't Al and Carol's house."

Charcoal sketches—more primitive versions of the drawings at the dune shack—were tacked to the walls. Affixed to the top of an eight-track cassette player, the words "Danny's Tunes" had been scrawled in magic marker across a yellowed piece of masking tape. A blunt realization took hold as Peter picked up a picture frame sitting on a bookcase constructed of milk crates and planks of wood. Frozen inside the photo, a mother and father stood on the deck of a sailboat, smiling at their sons. Waves of curly brown hair partially obscured the older boy's face, but the baseball cap on his younger brother's head looked familiar.

After almost a year, Danny Cavanaugh had come home. Captaining his grandfather's sailboat last night had reminded him that the biggest part of his family's history was waiting on this hill. At first, he'd been excited to show Peter the house, but his impulsive decision to bring him here was starting to backfire. Ever since he'd returned to Provincetown, Danny had been selectively editing his memories. Now there was someone he couldn't run from, pushing him to admit the truth about the story he'd been telling.

"Sharing the chapel with you wasn't enough. You had to have it all—every last part of me."

Danny's footsteps on the metal staircase, loud and heavy, reverberated like the beat of a snare drum. Hurling out a series of curses at his own stupidity, Peter stumbled after him. By the time he reached the lower terrace, Danny was spoiling for a fight.

"Please listen to me—I'm sorry." Peter's voice was urgent. "I got so caught up in my own feelings that I never stopped to consider what you might be going through."

"That's because you were never really my friend. Pretending to care about me was just part of your master plan to make me open up so you could get inside my pants."

"Are you serious? Is that what you honestly think?" Peter asked, grabbing the top of his head to keep his throbbing brain from exploding. "We worked together, day and night, for two whole months before we even kissed. Christ, I got further with the sex-crazed pizza guy my first night in town."

Peter laughed at the absurdity of the accusation, but it still hurt. Ironically, the bond between the two men had never been stronger. What Lynn had once told him during therapy was true. The fastest way for a couple to connect was to fuck or to fight. Clenching his fists, Danny stepped forward. It was clear from his body language that they were about to get even closer.

"This relationship was about a lot of things, Dan, but it was never about sex. I know you're scared, but why can't you just admit that you have feelings for me?"

Foolishly, Peter had broken the first rule of engagement by disregarding the adversarial nature of the conflict. Lowering his guard and putting another's needs first had been a novice mistake.

"How many times do I have to say it? I'm not gay," Danny said in a quiet voice as he stared out at the water. "And even if I was, what makes you think I'd ever want a relationship with a guy like you?"

Danny shut the door all the way and locked it. Peter's worst fear—that he was unworthy of love—had just been confirmed.

The truth was like a stone in his shoe as he limped through the house and out the front door. The renovation of the chapel was essentially complete. One minute, Danny Cavanaugh was a part of his life, and the next he was gone. There was nothing left for Peter in Provincetown now. It would take less than ten minutes to pack the wrinkled suit hanging in the back of Bill's closet. Tomorrow morning, he would jump onto the ferry and become John Wells again.

Until then, Peter needed to find something to dull the pain. On autopilot, he glided back into town where pretty boys packed the streets. Cycling back and forth between bars, their fragmented conversations and laughter reminded him of happier times. As expected, Peter's rugged good looks and rock-hard body turned heads. The hours these men spent at the gym were nothing compared to his long days of manual labor. While he didn't particularly like being objectified, it felt good to be the center of attention.

Surprisingly, it was a woman—not a man—who caught his eye. Standing beneath the portico of the Crown & Anchor, her voice seemed louder than all the other background noise and chatter.

"Actually, it's called a *tondo*...."

Peter's head was still aching as he cut between two cars crawling up Commercial Street and shoved past a cluster of strolling pedestrians. It was impossible, but she was here—standing just a few yards away—with the same straight brown hair falling to her shoulders.

"That's *seven* minutes...."

Not stopping to think, John sprinted ahead. The senator's call had come early in the morning. In all the chaos and confusion, Donovan had made a terrible mistake. Could it all just have been a bad dream? Nothing mattered anymore except reaching her. Somehow, she'd found a way back to him—now, when he needed her most.

"Melody!"

Turning around, she smiled and reached out to take his trembling hand.

"Are you okay, Peter?"

Blinking hard, he reminded himself that Melody had been John's best friend—not his. When he opened his eyes again, Lynn Morris was holding onto him, wearing a worried look. Peter's smile was dazzling, but his eyes were ready to overflow. Reaching out, he pulled her into his arms. His mind had played a cruel trick, or maybe, like the banner on the pier in Boston, the universe was sending him a sign.

David. Donovan. Danny. Every guy he'd ever loved had ended up breaking his heart. Like Melody, Lynn was the only person in the world offering him unconditional love and support. Peter would never try to change Danny, but John had always been an expert at adapting to succeed. It was finally time to become the man that Melody and the senator had always wanted him to be.

Taking Lynn's face in his hands, Peter leaned in. Her smooth skin and soft lips reminded him of every girl he'd kissed in high school. Although he'd been living under an alias for months, he suddenly felt like a stranger to himself.

"Peter... don't... this isn't right."

Lynn was saying what his body already knew. What he was doing would undoubtedly make him feel worse, but like a drowning swimmer, Peter couldn't let go.

"John. Stop. I'm here with you. You're going to be okay."

It was Dr. Morris speaking. Summoning a secret reserve of strength, she quickly brought the situation back under her control.

Peter's arms went limp. It would take more than a few words of comfort and a hug to fill the void. Luckily, there were at least three hundred guys waiting to welcome him with open arms. Without offering an apology or explanation, he stepped off the sidewalk and headed for the one place in Provincetown where he truly belonged.

Chapter 19

THE LINE for Purgatory stretched up Carver Street and around the block onto Bradford. Ignoring the gibes of the waiting crowd, Peter nodded to the bouncer, who recognized a fellow local and waved him in. Upstairs at Gifford House, friends were enjoying nightcaps on a quaint covered porch, listening to Ella Fitzgerald or Dead Kennedys on the jukebox. But beneath their feet, in the bowels of the building, men leered at half-naked go-go boys through a smoky haze. The music blared at a volume that made conversation impossible, but it didn't matter. Guys didn't come to Purgatory to talk.

The club probably had more patrons than legally allowed, if anyone had cared enough to check. Peter skirted around the edge of the dance floor and headed straight for the bar. Although his head was still spinning, he was hell-bent on washing his short-term memory clean with alcohol.

Like most of the service staff in Provincetown, Randy was behind the bar working a second job. Without waiting to be asked, he poured Peter a double bourbon and reluctantly took the twenty-dollar bill from his hand. He scarcely had time to pop open a beer for the next customer before Peter was pointing at his empty glass. Always happy to oblige, Randy served up another round and slid two fives and ten ones across the counter. It was an old bartender's trick to fool the management: take a friend's money and pay it all back in change. Normally, Peter would have refused the drink to avoid getting tangled in the strings that usually came with anything free. Tonight, however, he pocketed the cash and threw back the liquor.

The first glass partially numbed the pain, but John needed to find a more permanent way to separate himself from Peter. The faces around him confirmed he'd come to the right place. The guys cruising him were interested in his body, not his name.

A legion of sweaty men welcomed him as he pulled off his cotton T-shirt and tucked it into the back of his jeans. Some primal instinct warned John to stick to the periphery of the dance floor, but that wasn't where he wanted to be. Pushing past the weaker swimmers, he kept inching forward until the bar was out of sight. Strobe lights hanging from the ceiling, radiated flashes and bursts that overexposed the images in his head. Warm bodies pressing up against him created a feeling that was the opposite of claustrophobia. With the threat of loneliness looming, it was a relief to be surrounded by men.

Lost in the sensation of floating, Peter moved his body in time with the music. *Dance. Smile. Touch.* The purity of the experience—the promise of even more contact—intensified with each new partner. Peter threw back his head and reached toward the ceiling as an open invitation to be taken. Almost instantly, two strong arms snaked around his chest and a chin pressed into the soft muscle of his shoulder.

Although it had been almost two months, the guy from the pizza shop was eager to pick up where they'd left off. With designer drugs coursing through his veins, Max kissed Peter hard on the mouth and slid a free hand down the front of his jeans. It was hard to judge the passing of time when every song sounded the same, but things felt like they were moving too fast. John tried to convince himself that this was what he wanted. Going through the motions, he grabbed a tuft of Max's blond hair and closed his eyes. The other dancers watched with envy and begrudgingly gave up a few precious feet of space for the two men to go at it. Even for Purgatory, it was quite a show.

Max was like a kid in a toy store. After a few minutes of playtime, he was ready to move on. There was no need for clunky excuses or empty promises—one minute they were together, and the next he was gone. A couple guys stepped in to take his place, but Peter made it clear that he'd had enough. His halfhearted attempt at hedonism had seemed more like combat than sex. Pushing through the crowd, he wiped Max's sweat from his skin and pulled his T-shirt back on.

Randy reached over the heads of half a dozen patrons to pass Peter a beer. He pressed the intensely cold bottle against his forehead before gulping it down. Instead of the usual numbing effect, the latest round of alcohol amplified the lights and music. Grabbing at random bodies, Peter stumbled forward and tried, unsuccessfully, to gauge how much he'd already had to drink. He was almost to the exit when the room began to spin and his legs gave way. Swooping in from the shadows, a pair of arms caught him as he fell.

The faint smell of lavender on the sheets confirmed that he was home. One by one, each sweat-soaked article of clothing came off. Observing intently, Chance snatched up one of the discarded socks and scampered off to the living room. Peter was vaguely aware of the clunk of shoes hitting the hardwood floor as the lamp on the bedside table went dark. Vaguely wondering how he'd managed to get home, he rolled over and drifted off to sleep.

SINCE HE was always up before dawn, there was never any reason to close the blinds. Squinting, Peter turned away from the window and threw off the quilt. His memory of last night was foggy, and his mouth tasted like cotton soaked in vinegar. Propping himself up on his elbows, he was about to attempt a quick trip to the bathroom for aspirin when he realized there was somebody next to him in the bed.

Tangles of brown hair pressed against the white linens. Asleep, Danny looked half his age. Afraid of waking him, Peter stayed perfectly still, but Chance had other plans. At the first sign of movement, the little dog charged into the room and catapulted onto the bed. Moving in slow motion, Danny rolled onto his side and pulled an extra pillow under his arm. After an exceptionally deep and cavernous yawn, he opened his eyes.

A rabble of butterflies fluttered inside Peter's nervous stomach. He didn't want to think about what would have happened if Danny hadn't rescued him from Purgatory. Passing out in a leather bar could have been the equivalent of a death sentence.

"All right. I'm ready," Peter whispered. "Let me have it."

Danny started to say something but looked away. When he turned back, there were tears in his eyes.

"Danny. I'm so sorry. Please don't cry." Peter was afraid that, yet again, his reckless actions had hurt someone he loved.

"I can't help it. Your breath stinks so bad it's making my eyes water."

"Oh, is that right?" Despite the crippling hangover, Peter snatched a pillow and covered Danny's face to muffle his adolescent laughter.

Neither man was in any condition to put up much of a fight, but both were determined to try. Lunging forward, Danny used his superior weight to pin Peter to the bed. Only inches apart, it suddenly seemed impossible to resist the force of gravity. The kiss that followed didn't explain Danny's meltdown at his parents' house, but any unanswered questions would have to wait. If the last few months had taught Peter anything, it was to savor each moment of happiness—no matter how fleeting. Cradling Danny's head with one arm, he pulled the heavy quilt around them and drifted back to sleep.

It was almost noon when loud knocking startled them awake. Danny jumped out of bed and disappeared into the bathroom with his clothes. Somehow, Peter managed to pull on his jeans and grab a wrinkled shirt as he hurried to the door. Waiting on the porch with a wicker picnic basket, Florence Woodside was a burst of sunshine.

"Thank goodness you answered, dear," she said, slipping past him into the kitchen, "I was beginning to worry that you'd fallen ill."

Peter fumbled with his buttons while Florence unloaded food onto the counter. By the time he'd finished making himself presentable, she'd lit the stove and begun cooking. Thick slabs of bacon in the cast-iron skillet were starting to crackle when Danny appeared in the doorway, fully dressed. Even with his shoes on and his hair combed, it was obvious that he'd just rolled out of bed.

"Well, now. It's about time you boys came to your senses and realized you belong together," Florence said with a cluck of her tongue and a wink. "And by the look of it, you've probably spent a good part of the morning working up an appetite."

Without saying more, she finished fixing the meal while Peter stifled a laugh. Looking as though he might actually die of embarrassment, Danny put his baseball cap over his still-wet hair and skulked over to the table. He was about to sit down when Peter pulled out his chair. Danny responded to the chivalrous gesture with a smile as he brushed the back of his hand against Peter's leg. Peter caught Florence's smile as she delivered the food, piping hot, to the table.

At first, it was enough to spend time together eating, but after ten minutes of silence, Florence must have decided they needed a side order of conversation. Spearing her eggs with a fork, she tossed out a few open-ended questions about the chapel. Peter knew Danny couldn't resist talking about his favorite subject. Before long, he was regaling them with a story about one of the local carpenters who'd shown up to work dressed head-to-toe in women's clothing. Although she'd seen the man herself the day before, Florence feigned disbelief while Peter laughed between bites of food. In less than an hour, the skillet was empty and their stomachs were full.

Florence playfully slapped Danny's hand as he soaked the last bite of biscuit in bacon grease and stuffed it into his mouth. Rising from the table, she touched both men on the head as if they were boys getting ready to leave for school. Peter walked her out and kissed her powdered cheek. Once she was safely away, he closed the door and assessed the situation. Danny seemed relaxed and happy, but he usually looked that way after a big meal.

Stepping gingerly across the hardwood floor, Peter grabbed onto the sides of Danny's chair to steady his nerves. The uncomfortable silence that had settled over the room was actually more painful than a hangover. After what seemed like forever, Danny leaned back and pressed his head into Peter's stomach. The gesture was enigmatic but enough. Ready to trust his instincts again, Peter led Danny back into the bedroom and closed the door.

The day was almost over by the time they emerged from the cottage. With Chance ambling behind, the two men walked up Bradford Street and along the edge of the moor. At the breakwater, Peter sat down on an empty bench and watched as his dog crept through the tall grass, looking for a smaller animal to chase. A storm at sea was causing the waves to break hard on the rocks. Although there were plenty of issues to discuss, it was hard to know where to begin.

"There's something I've been afraid to tell you," Danny said in a whisper. It was clear from his tone how much he wished they could just skip ahead to the future and let all his memories fade like cedar shingles. "I haven't been honest with anyone—even myself—about the real reason I stayed behind the night of the accident."

Peter slouched forward and burrowed his feet in the sand. For two months, he'd been living under an alias to avoid sharing anything about his other life. Now, in light of Danny's imminent confession, those omissions seemed doubly dark.

"I said that I'd decided not to fly back with my family—to stay in Provincetown—so I could go to a party. But that was the same lie I told my parents to hide the fact that there was someone here I wanted to be with...."

Danny wandered away from the bench and walked onto the breakwater. Part of him longed to keep right on going, all the way to the other side, but the rising tide and failing light made it too dangerous. Stepping carefully from slab to slab, Peter followed close behind.

"So, this person you wanted to spend time with. Was it a guy?"

"Yes," Danny said, raking a hand through his hair. When he spoke again, his voice sounded loud and unnatural over the crash of the surf.

"His name was Kyle, and he was visiting from London. At first, he was just a friend, but by the end of summer, we were spending almost every night together. My parents must have known—or at least suspected—but I was afraid to admit what was going on. If I had told them the truth, they might have totally freaked out or just invited him to dinner. I'll never know how they would have reacted, but either way, they probably would have stuck around until morning."

Peter took Danny's hand and held on tight. It was almost high tide, and the pelting spray from the ocean felt like rain. Even though the gray stone slabs beneath their feet were dark and wet, the shore was only a few yards away. Holding on to each other in silence, the two men waited until the sun had set before making their way back to land.

As they retraced their steps to the cottage, Peter struggled to find the words to explain how his own white lie on the Metro platform had set into motion a series of events that ended in tragedy. Danny of all people would understand. But how could John ever defend his decision to run away and live under an alias?

Although Peter had constructed an emotional breakwater to protect himself from the truth, his past was like the rising tide. Sooner or later, it would crest and pull him under.

Chapter 20

SEPTEMBER MARKED the return of cooler temperatures and peaceful days. Gradually, the throngs of tourists thinned and the techno-beat sound track of summer faded into fall. The town had benefited from the usual financial windfall, but most of the locals were eager for the season to end.

Despite Peter's lingering apprehensions, there was still plenty of work left to do at the chapel. Once the exterior projects were complete, Danny redoubled their efforts to restore the sanctuary. The planked ceiling and walls were intact, but there were decades of grime to scrape off the floor. With unfaltering patience, he showed Peter how to pull even the most stubborn baseboard away from the lathe-and-plaster walls. Then, using crowbars and restraint, the men carefully urged each wooden pew from its assigned row and swept the nave clean. Workdays were shorter and break times longer, but after almost a month of sanding and three coats of varnish, the heart of pine floors glistened like honey.

Danny left most of the carpentry work to Peter and devoted July and August to the formidable task of creating seven new stained glass windows. Every night, he'd stay up late studying books on period designs and sketching out original patterns on butcher paper. Agonizing over the color and shape of each piece of glass, he had somehow managed to finish the central window above the altar before Labor Day.

There was always another job to tackle, but with the shadow of his past behind him, time was the one thing Danny could afford to waste. Late in the afternoon, when the weather was fine, they would cut out of work early to ride bikes along the shore or hike across the breakwater. Danny showed Peter all his secret spots and taught him about the sea and the stars. After a summer spent camping at the dune shack, Peter knew the night sky well enough to call out the constellations by name.

Before long, October's chill forced them back to the warmth of the cottage. Snuggling beneath a heavy quilt on the comfortable bed, Danny shared stories with Peter about growing up on the Cape and the family he'd lost. Provincetown accepted their union as the perfect ending to a tumultuous courtship. Soon, it became apparent to Peter and Danny that they were the last ones to realize they were meant to be together.

Late one Sunday afternoon, Peter climbed the stairs to the Porchside Lounge at Gifford House. No matter how busy, their band of friends had made it a rule to meet for drinks and dinner at least once a week. While a handful of loyal patrons listened to Etta James croon about love on the jukebox, Peter wandered outside with a beer to wait. Since Carver Street, like the bar, was almost empty, he'd easily spot the gang making their way up the hill. Gripping the bottle by its neck, Peter downed the contents in three long chugs. The warm rush that followed quickly quelled his impatience. Danny and the others would be along soon enough. He was just about to head inside when he noticed a stranger sizing him up from the other end of the porch.

"Hello," the man said, advancing. An "A-lister" in Provincetown after Labor Day was like a straight couple at the Boatslip. It happened infrequently and was usually by accident. Still, Peter was feeling friendly, and Danny was running late. Surely, there would be no harm in striking up a conversation to pass the time.

"Hi. My name's Peter," he said, offering his hand.

The stranger seemed to hesitate for a second before taking it. Leaning in, he mumbled something, but his words were lost in the buoyant laughter and music wafting through the open door.

"Sorry, but I didn't catch that," Peter said, raising the nearly empty bottle to his lips. Something about the man was unsettlingly familiar. Maybe talking to strangers wasn't such a good idea after all.

"I asked if there was someplace less public we could go?"

Peter shook his head and turned back toward the bar. "I'm afraid not. I have a boyfriend I'm crazy about. But thanks for asking." The words danced in Peter's ears as he willed Danny to hurry up.

"Mr. Wells," the stranger said in a low voice. "John. I'm not quite sure what's going on here, but I need to speak with you in private."

In the time it took to exhale, the wall between Peter's two worlds came crashing down. Taking a deep breath, John snapped to attention and switched into crisis-control mode. It was obvious this guy wanted something. Once John knew what that was, he could barter for his silence. It would be a simple transaction—just another deal to negotiate. Without missing a beat, he steered the stranger down the staircase. They'd just started walking toward Bradford when Danny rounded the corner.

Before John had time to react, Peter's friends converged. Lynn skipped forward to peck him on the cheek as Byron took him by the arm. Once again, everything was moving too fast.

"Wait! Stop!"

Byron froze dead in his tracks, and Danny's smile hardened into a grimace. From Peter's tone, it was obvious that something was off. Glancing over his shoulder, he stiffened as the stranger casually stepped off the sidewalk and into his world.

"Good evening," the man said with an air of practiced diplomacy. "I'm Robert Archer. Peter and I were colleagues on Capitol Hill."

"Actually," John said, quickly retaking control, "we didn't really work together. Rob spent the summer interning in my office a couple years ago."

"Sorry, but it's *Robert*. I'm a little sensitive about my name. I'm sure you understand."

"Of course," John said, tossing out his best smile.

The reason for Archer's unexpected appearance in Provincetown was masked beneath his polished public persona. But the trouble with hidden agendas was that they never stay hidden for long. John needed to sequester this witness before his inquisitive group of friends launched into a cross-examination. Eager to keep that from happening, he kissed Danny lightly on the lips and whispered a few words in his ear. Lynn suggested giving Peter a few minutes alone to catch up with his friend.

John's shoulders dropped in relief as he watched them walk away. The sound of their banter and laughter bolstered his confidence. If everything went as expected, he'd be back with Danny and the others before they'd even finished the first round.

OUTSIDE MARISSA'S Place, Chris was stacking metal chairs so he could sweep the porch. The café was dark except for a single light burning in the front window. With Archer following at his heels, John nodded to Chris, who responded by gesturing toward the open door.

As expected, the place was empty. That would make it easier for John to speak frankly without worrying about being overheard. Walking straight to the counter, he grabbed a ceramic mug and a tea bag. The boiling water he poured into the cup quickly turned as dark and muddied as the thoughts swirling in his head. Ready to skip any pleasantries and get right down to business, Archer took a seat and pulled out the chair next to him. John chuckled out loud at the proposed seating arrangement and sat down at the next table.

"Okay, Robert. We're alone now. Why are you in Provincetown?"

"The senator asked me to find you," he said. "Given the circumstances, he thought it best to send someone you knew to speak with you on his behalf."

John may have been out of the game for a while, but he still knew better than to show his reaction. Inwardly, a rush of memories carried him back to Boston. It was hard to believe that almost six months had passed since that horrible morning. Peter reminded himself to stay focused on the present and took a sip of tea.

"Mr. Wells," Archer said, leaning forward, "I'm afraid I'm going have to ask you to come back with me to DC. Tonight."

John exploded into laughter. Interlacing his fingers behind his head, he smiled and made direct eye contact with this lowly messenger.

"You can't possibly be serious. What makes you think I'd ever accede to such an outrageous demand?"

Archer sat in silence—unable or unwilling to say more. John was ready with a dozen rebuttals, but he paused to consider the potential consequences of spurning the senator. One way or another, Patrick

Donovan always got his way. John was no longer his loyal foot soldier, but openly refusing him meant provoking the wrath of a man who could, quite possibly, become the next president of the United States.

"Robert, what you're asking is impossible. Even if I agreed to go, I've made no arrangements. And Provincetown isn't the easiest place to travel to or from—especially this time of year."

"We've anticipated that," Archer said, rising from his seat as though the issue had already been settled. "There's a private jet fueled and waiting at the airstrip. We'll leave as soon as you're ready."

John was determined not to let this young upstart push him around. Despite the risks of defying the senator, it was time to send Robert home with his tail between his legs.

"As I'm sure you'd expect, the FBI has been conducting a full investigation into the circumstances surrounding Melody Donovan's death. You can return with me voluntarily, or I can make sure you become a person of interest in that investigation. The choice is yours."

John had grossly underestimated his opponent. Whoever had coached Archer knew precisely which buttons to push. The senator had left him with only one option.

"I'll meet you at the airstrip in an hour."

Archer nodded his assent and headed out the door. Visibly pleased with his success, he was ready to move on to his next task.

Brooding at the same table where he'd first met Byron, John struggled with the reality that in less than two hours he'd be back in DC. The control and order that world offered had a certain appeal, notwithstanding the inevitable loss of personal freedom. The rules of the game never changed and were always followed. He'd been naive to believe the last few months were anything more than a brief time-out.

The short walk up Carver Street gave him barely enough time to construct the story he was about to tell. It probably wouldn't take very long to tie up the loose ends in DC, but experience had taught John that the safest place to hide a lie was behind the truth. Since Peter had already told Danny and the others about his former position on the Hill, he could just say there was an urgent legislative matter that required his attention. A vague explanation would be enough to satisfy Lynn and Byron, but nothing short of an Academy Award-winning performance would fool

Danny Cavanaugh. Now, more than ever, Peter needed to keep up appearances, but John's legendary smile had gone missing. Preoccupied with his thoughts, he almost didn't notice his boyfriend waiting for him on the corner.

"So what was that all about? And don't even try giving me the bullshit speech you've been rehearsing. I could see you mouthing the words from a block away."

"I have to go back to Washington to take care of something important," Peter said, trying his best to avoid making eye contact. "I won't be gone long—just a couple of days."

"But what if you go and decide not to come back?"

"That's not going to happen. I'd never just pick up and disappear."

Peter put both hands on Danny's shoulders as John silently warned him not to make promises he couldn't keep.

"Let's just skip happy hour and head home to bed," Danny said, forcing a smile. "Maybe I can talk you out of making this trip in the morning."

Taking a deep breath, John steadied himself and widened his stance. If Danny was already apprehensive about his proposed travel plans, then he was about to feel even worse. A cold gust of wind off the harbor reminded Peter that summer was over.

"You don't know how much I'd love to do that, but there's a jet waiting for me at the airport."

"What!" Danny screamed. "Are you out of your mind? There's no way I'm letting you fly out of here at night."

"Really?" Peter snapped. "Because I don't remember asking for your permission."

His reaction was out of character, but he'd been backed into a corner. Empathizing—caring about Danny's feelings—would make it impossible for John to do what had to be done.

"I know this is difficult for you, but I'm going. There's no point in discussing it any further." Like kerosene on charcoal, his words were turning the fiery exchange into a conflagration.

"Go then," Danny said, throwing up his arms in surrender. "Get on that stupid little plane and fly away. Run back to wherever it is you came from and just forget all about me."

Always the lawyer, John was ready to argue, but something held him back. Confessing everything now, after so much time had passed, would be like trying to reset a broken bone that had already healed. Even if Danny could manage to forgive Peter, they'd be right back where they were in July. Maybe it would be easier on both of them if John simply ended things once and for all rather than inflict that kind of pain.

JOHN WELLS made his way back to the cottage alone. It seemed odd to put on his own clothes, but it was time to return the things he'd borrowed from Bill. One by one, shirts were hung and sweaters refolded as Chance sat on the bed and watched. Once he was finished, John stuffed his rumpled suit into his carry-on bag and slipped out the door.

A rainbow-colored taxi was waiting for him on Commercial Street. The driver, a middle-aged woman with short salt-and-pepper hair, wore a cynical look that said she was more interested in a fare than in chitchat.

"To the airport." It was a statement, not a question, since her passenger was carrying a suitcase and the next ferry didn't leave until morning.

Florence. Byron. Lynn. As the cab skirted around the outer edge of town, John tried not to think about the people he was leaving behind. In less than ten minutes, the cab made a right turn into the airport. Even from the road, John could see the taillights of the silver jet flashing. Passing a wad of cash through the window, he grabbed his bag and slammed the door shut without a thank you or good-bye.

"Damn tourists," the driver said out loud as she shifted the cab into gear and headed back to town.

Handing his bag to the waiting captain, John climbed the metal staircase and ducked inside the plane. Even in the dim light, he could see the obvious look of satisfaction on Robert Archer's face as he pulled out his cell phone.

"Good evening, Senator. I have Mr. Wells with me. We'll be at your office first thing in the morning."

Right on cue, the engines powered up and the jet lurched forward. John pushed his head back into the seat cushion as the plane gathered speed and hurtled down the runway. At the last possible moment, it lifted off the ground and soared over the dunes. The inky-black ocean below mirrored the darkness of the sky.

DANNY LEANED against the gate to the runway. It was too late to take back his angry words or to stop the guy he'd fallen in love with from leaving. Walking toward the pickup, he pulled off his brother's baseball cap and stuffed it into his back pocket. Like all the other relics from his past, it was just another painful reminder of what had been lost.

Chapter 21

ALTHOUGH HE'D barely slept, getting up early was a habit John couldn't seem to break. The room was unfamiliar, but that was to be expected in a hotel—a place where strangers came and went without any expectation of permanency. Standing at the window, he watched the sunrise and methodically dressed in the same clothes he'd worn the night before. Less than five miles away, in a quiet house on a tree-lined street, an extensive wardrobe of suits and ties hung neatly on wooden hangers. It would have been easy to make a quick stop on his way from the airport to the hotel, but to do so meant risking a run-in with David, and John had had enough drama for one day. In the end, he decided to make do with what was in his bag. Besides, the Mayflower Hotel was accustomed to accommodating important guests and could easily manage to have his clothes cleaned and pressed for his meeting in the morning.

The doorman whispered a polite good morning as John wandered out the hotel's front entrance. The morning sun was like a weak cup of coffee, but none of the pedestrians on the sidewalk seemed to notice. Hustling to work while chattering on cell phones, they were far too busy to care about something as inconsequential as the quality of the light.

John turned right on Connecticut Avenue and walked around the outer loop of Dupont Circle. He'd been gone for six months, a significant amount of time in a world that lived by terms and administrations rather than by seasons. Even considering his extended leave of absence, the faces that passed by looked all too familiar. Hair and clothing styles might change, but by the look of it, this fresh batch of political drones wasn't so very different from their predecessors.

Hoping for a quick hit of nostalgia with his caffeine, John stepped through the door to his favorite coffee shop. The young woman behind the counter had taken his order a hundred times before, but he'd never gone to the trouble of remembering her name. Wearing a perpetual smile, she delivered her stock greeting as John shifted uncomfortably in line and perused the menu. Like almost everything else in the city, there were too many choices and not enough time. After nearly thirty seconds of awkward silence, he placed his order and stepped into an adjacent corner to wait.

John leaned against the wall and watched a steady stream of customers come and go. Electronic reading devices and tablets had made printed books and newspapers virtually obsolete. Human contact was becoming passé, and "PDA" now stood for personal digital assistant—not public display of affection. Why bother taking the time to actually speak to someone when you could peck out a quick text message on a miniature keyboard?

At the far end of the cafe, baristas referred to patrons by their orders—not their names. Exotic variations of caffeinated beverages appeared to be one of the last vestiges of individuality and self-expression. John spotted his tea on the counter, steeping self-consciously. Slipping a cardboard sleeve around the recycled paper cup, he maneuvered through the crowd like a congressional page delivering a message on the floor. The nostalgia he'd been waiting for came rushing back as he recalled the weight and feel of a good ceramic mug.

"John? John Wells!"

A familiar voice called out his name as a hand spun him around so fast that the boiling water inside his cup sloshed over the top.

"Ouch!" he cried out, shaking his scalded appendage.

Eric Sloan grabbed a plastic lid from the service area and affixed it to the top of the paper cup. A fresh wave of customers surged through the door, pushing the two men closer. Suddenly claustrophobic, John headed for the nearest exit.

"Hey, wait up!" Eric said, tossing his untouched beverage into the trash. The sidewalk was even more crowded than the coffee shop, and the air was heavy and stale. Cursing under his breath, John slowed his pace and told himself it was time to stop running. Though unexpected, this encounter would simply be the first in a series of loose ends that needed to be secured.

Eric put an arm around his friend's shoulder and guided him down a quiet side street. The click of his wingtips on the pavement set the tempo. Even as their pace slowed, John's heart quickened.

"My God. I can't believe my eyes. Well, *you* were certainly the talk of the town this summer. Your vanishing act back in April was terribly dramatic. No one had a clue about where you'd gone or what you were doing."

Eric was asking a question, not making a statement. He expected his friend to share all the salacious details, but even John's dazzling smile barely hid his indignation. He'd been back less than twenty-four hours and was already playing in a high-stakes game. Politics was like poker: you were either in or out.

In an unexpected move, Eric ended the interrogation and began recapping the major events of his own social calendar. John pretended to care, but the comings and goings of relative strangers seemed inconsequential. Blinking hard, he strained to hear the sound of the surf in the whirl of traffic, but the city air smelled like exhaust, not salt.

"A lot has changed since you left."

Instincts tingling, John tried to discern the hidden meaning behind the words. Like a true politico, Eric was unreadable—a model of perfection in an imperfect world. If John wanted him to expound on his cryptic remark, he'd have to offer something in return.

"So, when can we get together and catch up?"

"The sooner the better," Eric said, slowly backing away. "Are you free tonight? We're all getting together for *Aida* at the Kennedy Center. Why don't you join us?"

"Thanks. I'd love to."

Despite his dour mood, John had no other choice but to accept the invitation. Being seen with a Sloan in public was his ticket back into the fold.

"Perfect!" Eric called out as he darted across the street. "See you this evening."

John waited the requisite beat before heading back to the hotel. Inside the elevator, he leaned against the velvet-padded walls and counted the passing floors. Up-tempo and cheery, the well-chosen Muzak playing in the background was more of an annoyance than a distraction. He'd been away for less than an hour, but the attentive chambermaid had already cleaned the room and hung his freshly steamed suit in the closet.

Shave. Shower. Dress. Like a soldier cleaning his gun, John reassembled the various components of his morning routine. At any given moment, he was acutely aware of tasks that would be left undone and promises that would not be kept in Provincetown. The locals would wait a week or two for Peter to return, but eventually they'd give up and simply write him off as another failed transplant.

John fastened the top button of his shirt and pulled the knot of his tie tight around his neck. The choking sensation was unpleasant, but he was determined to endure whatever pain came his way today.

Even though the Hill was only a few stops away by Metro, there was a shiny black sedan waiting out front. Sliding into the backseat, John stared out the tinted side window and prepped for his impending meeting. He may have missed Melody's funeral, but he felt as if they were driving to her wake. Patrick Donovan had appointed John as his daughter's protector, but he had failed them both. Now the time of reckoning had come.

In a rare moment of reflection, John let himself imagine what Melody had been feeling on that last night. Too late, he realized how easy it would have been to pull her back into the world of the living. Why couldn't he have just stayed with her instead of bolting?

Nervously adjusting the lapels of his jacket, John felt the distinctive outline of an envelope. Almost as an afterthought, he pulled a sealed letter from his breast pocket and made a mental note to deal with the contents later. It was only when the car turned onto Massachusetts Avenue that he gave it a second look and noticed the familiar handwriting across the front. John was just about to tear it open when the car came to abrupt stop. Quickly composing himself, he tucked the envelope away and stepped out onto the sidewalk where Archer was waiting.

Rather than waste time with small talk, the two men brushed past security and walked through the doors of the Hart Office Building. At the third floor, John charted a course back to his old stomping grounds but was visibly surprised when Archer turned left and continued on.

"I don't understand," John said, changing direction and hurrying to catch up. "I thought the meeting with Senator Donovan would be in his office."

"Actually, the meeting is with Senator Matthews. He's quite anxious to speak with you."

John was a smart guy, but nothing about what was happening made sense. Naturally, he'd assumed that Donovan had summoned him for personal reasons. But why would Sam Matthews—a man he hardly knew—go to so much trouble to arrange a meeting? Even though they'd never been formally introduced, their brief encounter in the lobby of the Metropolitan Club must have left a lasting impression.

Archer escorted John through the polished walnut doors of the junior senator's private office. Straight ahead, the dome of the US Capitol loomed like a full moon in the window. It was the perfect backdrop for a man with lofty political aspirations. Sitting at his desk, Matthews smiled graciously to indicate that he was almost done with his phone call. John stood squarely in the center of the room and listened. He knew right away that their meeting had already begun.

"Yes, Madam Speaker," the senator said a little too loudly. "We're all looking forward to November and are counting on your continued support. Even with the rest of the party standing behind us, it's going to be a long, hard road to the White House."

His mission accomplished, Archer quietly excused himself as Matthews said his good-byes. Rising from his chair, the handsome, young Texan floated across the room and gestured toward a conversation area strategically positioned in front of the fireplace. John unbuttoned his suit jacket and took a seat. According to the rules of etiquette, he was expected to dole out some kind of tribute for the honor of a private audience. But it had been a long night, and he was in no mood for platitudes.

Sam Matthews had mastered the art of making whomever he was with feel like the only person in the room. In the present case, that just happened to be true. Strength and character radiated from the senator. He'd obviously been blessed with an abundance of qualities that would eventually catapult him to the top of the Hill. Lesser men would have felt compelled to speak, but John had developed a tolerance for such greatness.

"John Wells," the senator said, sounding like someone who was trying too hard to make a good first impression. Matthews invoked his full name with bravado—as though saying it out loud would give him some kind of power.

"It's good to see you again, sir."

"Oh, we both know that's not entirely true," Matthews said, leaning forward in his chair and planting both elbows firmly on his knees. "Considering all the unpleasantness in Boston, I'm surprised you even agreed to take this meeting."

"Well, Mr. Archer was rather *persuasive* in convincing me to return. In fact, he made certain that I couldn't refuse."

"I've already spoken with him about his lapse in judgment," the senator said, shaking his head from side to side. "Robert is a valuable member of our team, but he needs to learn how quickly threats can turn valuable allies into dangerous enemies."

It was a shock to hear Matthews make such a frank admission and even more surprising that it sounded genuine. John warned himself not to make any hasty judgments about the senator's scruples as he watched Matthews retrieve a thick manila folder from his desk and toss it onto the coffee table like a live grenade. John was naturally curious about the contents, but he knew when to be patient and listen. Everything he needed to know would be explained in due course.

"A lot has changed since you left…."

"Since I was asked to leave."

"Yes. I stand corrected," Matthews said, quickly conceding the point. "That was a serious miscalculation that has, quite frankly, put the entire campaign in jeopardy."

"What do you mean?" John asked, barely able to contain his fervor. Knowing there was a problem only he could solve was more than just a salve for his bruised ego. Now that there was a chance for absolution, the senator had his undivided attention.

"We'd like to reinstate you as Patrick Donovan's chief of staff so that you can get the senator back up to fighting weight. That won't be easy, but if you're successful, I give you my word that once I'm president, you'll have a place waiting for you in the West Wing."

"Once *you're* president?" John blurted out the question without thinking.

"I'm not sure what rock you've been living under, but as I said, a lot has changed. I'm now the Democratic nominee. Senator Donovan has graciously agreed to serve as my running mate."

For the first time, John realized that Peter had spent the last six months without a telephone, television, or computer to connect him to the rest of the world. Working on the chapel and falling in love with Danny had consumed all his time and attention. After the shellacking John had gotten from Donovan and Wilson, national politics had been the last thing on his mind. Even considering that his candidacy was most likely the result of backroom deals and parliamentary maneuvering, the reversal of fortune Matthews had just described meant he was in a position to make good on his promises. Jealousy might be a green-eyed monster, but ambition, its dark brother, was a blind creature with an insatiable appetite. This was like the ending of some forgotten Greek play where the fallen hero is miraculously restored. With one word, John could accept Matthews's offer and have it all.

"Why don't you drop by Patrick's office for a chat? If you think his political image is salvageable, then we'd like you to jump right in and get started."

"There'd need to be some immediate staff changes for me to even consider the offer," John said, testing the limits of his new bargaining position. "I'd have to have broad discretion about who stays and who goes."

"Of course, you'll have to fire Stan Wilson. But I'm guessing you can probably live with everyone else?"

John's smile sufficiently answered the question.

"Good," Matthews said, hurrying back to his desk to prepare for the next round of calls. "This went better than I'd expected. I know it's a lot to ask, but do you think it's possible to put the last six months behind us and work together?"

"Anything is possible."

Standing a little taller than when he'd entered the room, John shook the senator's outstretched hand and wondered to himself whether what he'd just said was true.

Chapter 22

THE LIGHTS of the Kennedy Center danced across the still surface of the Potomac. Standing on the observation deck, John studied the silhouette of Roosevelt Island in the distance and watched the headlights from the cars on the George Washington Parkway. Six months ago, this view had impressed him, but now it just reminded him how many stars were missing from the city sky.

Eric Sloan made it a rule to arrive fashionably late to everything, so John's promptness gave him some much-needed time to think. The rest of his day had been less dramatic—albeit more informative—than his morning meeting with Matthews. With an untouched coffee in hand, he'd wandered the familiar halls, listening intently as staff debriefed him. Even though Donovan had returned from Boston in a haze of grief, he was determined to recommit himself to the campaign. But each personal appearance and rally confirmed that it was Melody, and not his political legacy, that had been meant to endure.

There were never any direct attacks or loose talk that could be traced back to a source. Finally exposed, Patrick Donovan's image simply tarnished like a piece of neglected silver. Much too soon, Stan Wilson stepped in and hired the sons of an unremarkable congressman to fill the vacancies left by Melody and John. Although the men were full of confidence and swagger, the overabundance of hot air being blown at the senator was never enough to lift his fallen spirits.

Summer came and brought with it the usual infusion of fresh, young interns. Warmer weather and slower days explained away many of Donovan's minor shortcomings, but his frequent absences from committee meetings and uncharacteristic silences during hearings became more glaring under the blazing June sun. It didn't take long before everyone realized that John had been the real wizard behind the curtain, pulling all the levers. By Independence Day, theories began circulating about his unexplained disappearance. Some thought he'd resurface as a key advisor to a governor or offer himself up to one of Donovan's enemies as a formidable resource to be used during the primaries. Whatever he ended up doing was beside the point. In the end, John Wells was posthumously credited with having choreographed the career of one of the most esteemed statesmen in the country.

By early August, Stan's grand machinations were in ruins. Few were able to discern the senator's positions on the headline issues, and even fewer seemed to care. Eager to cash in on whatever measure of clout the Donovan name still carried, the Democratic leadership flipped the ticket just days before the convention and bet on Matthews to win. The pairing of youth and experience looked good on paper, but in real life, the striking contrast between the two politicians was disconcerting to voters.

Somewhere nearby, the exaggerated inflection of a man's voice evoked fresh memories of Byron and Provincetown. Reflexively, John tossed back the rest of his drink and handed the empty glass to one of the many staff whose job it was to dispose of such things. Even though he'd yet to meet with Donovan, he had already made his decision. Being needed wasn't quite the same as being loved, but it was close enough.

The overhead lights flashed once, and a melodic chime encouraged the audience to start making their way into the theatre. At just the right moment, with all eyes watching, five men dressed in stylish black tuxedos appeared at the far end of the Grand Foyer. Leading the way, Eric Sloan smiled at friends and shook hands with a select few as he worked the red carpet. John admired his friend's practiced way with people, but he was ready to impress with his own natural attributes. Charging onto the field, he maneuvered around several clusters of minor socialites and sidled up to Eric just as he was finishing a conversation with the British ambassador.

"For god's sake, Wells. I know you have your hands full dusting off Patrick, but you can't expect to hobnob with the crème de la crème wearing your livery."

"Sorry," John said, glancing at all the other men around him in similar suits and ties. "I had a late meeting and didn't have time to change."

Before Eric could respond, the overhead lights flashed three times in succession and another chime rang out. Without further ado, the two men ascended the central staircase. Once inside the Sloan family box, John brushed past the other guests and brazenly claimed the catbird seat in the front row. Handing him a crystal flute of perfectly chilled champagne, Eric sat down beside him and whispered into his ear. What was being said was beside the point. At the first intermission, the news would quickly circulate that John Wells, the prodigal son, had returned.

The auditorium faded to black, and the orchestra began to play. Shakespeare had it right when he wrote, "All the world's a stage and all the men and women merely players: they all have their exits and their entrances." *Adultery. Betrayal. Death.* The last six months of John's life had all the elements of grand opera. Ironically, he was now facing the same choice as Aida: live a life of power and privilege in Washington or give it all up for love.

A jolt of emotion suddenly roused Peter from the political stupor of the last twenty-four hours. Somewhere in Provincetown, Danny was waiting. Then again, perhaps he'd already hooked up with some other drifter or hopped a plane to London to find Kyle. In the end, it might be best to think of their time together as a brief intermission. Peter didn't really believe that, but like any good performer, he was fully committed to his role.

Less than halfway through the first act, Eric got up from his seat and discretely signaled for John to follow. Despite the quality of the performance, there were other pressing matters that required his attention. A private elevator just outside the box transported them to the parking garage where a sleek limousine was waiting.

Conditioned air wafted from invisible jets, but the drive up Rock Creek Parkway was too smooth, and John missed the feeling of the wind on his face. There was no point in trying to open a window, since the luxury automobile had been designed to keep the real world out. Sealed safely inside, John watched Eric peel off his jacket and unknot the bow tie around his neck. He knew it was a rare privilege. There weren't many people in DC who'd ever witnessed a Sloan shrugging off the mantle of responsibility that came with that name.

"It really is good to see you again," Eric said, passing John a single Scotch and raising his own glass in a toast. "To your return. As usual, your timing is impeccable."

"Thanks for the invitation. Considering my extended absence, I'd half expected you to have forgotten all about me."

"Quite the contrary," Eric said, leaning in to refill John's empty glass. "You'd be surprised to know how much time I spent thinking about you and that kiss at Halo."

Averting his gaze, John turned his head and squinted at the tinted windows. Unexpectedly, his comfortable leather seat had become a casting couch. Eric's posture and tone made it clear what he wanted as quid pro quo for the evening, but he'd never be crass enough to actually say it out loud. John figured he could easily filibuster for a few minutes until they reached the Mayflower.

"Well, I'm sure I was fodder for some interesting gossip," he said, redirecting the conversation and giving Eric a backdoor through which he could gracefully retreat.

"Don't play coy, John. It doesn't suit you."

Despite his education and good breeding, Eric was on the verge of making an ass of himself. Turning in his seat, he reached out and casually brushed some lint from John's shoulder. The fact that the Sloans were notoriously aloof made the gesture seem especially intimate. John's first instinct was to knock Eric's hand away, but there was no reason to overreact. Like most political crises, the situation required finesse and diplomacy, not brute force.

"I'd be lying if I said I wasn't tempted," John said, intentionally modulating his voice. "But what about Stefan? Is it really worth risking your relationship for a casual fling?"

Eric let out a hearty laugh and reached for the bottle of Scotch. John felt a rush of euphoria as the tension in his muscles unknotted. This unpleasant exchange had merely been a momentary lapse in judgment. Smiling, he accepted another drink—this time a double—and prepared an appropriate segue.

"I keep forgetting you've been away," Eric said, inching closer. "Stefan and I parted ways in May. He's still living in the guesthouse, but except for the occasional conjugal visit, the relationship is over."

"I had no idea," John said, reconsidering Eric's proposition in light of his revelation. "Honestly, I'm not sure how anyone manages to survive a breakup. When the life you've built with someone shatters, it's hard to imagine ever finding a way to put the pieces back together."

"Oh, please. Let's leave all that melodrama for the opera. Stefan was charming, and he was certainly devoted, but I need to be with someone with greater aspirations. It took me awhile to realize it, but I think you just might be that man."

The seduction that was playing out was fueled by a desire more primal than lust. Power, after all, was the ultimate aphrodisiac. Without stopping to think about what he was doing, John grabbed the back of Eric's neck and pulled him closer until their lips touched.

Everything about the kiss felt wrong, but there was no reason to stand on principle anymore. If he was going to sell his soul to Matthews, why not throw in his body for good measure? Although a Sloan/Wells coupling would undoubtedly catapult him to the very top of the social ladder, there was a serious glitch. John no longer had a heart to offer. Peter had already given it away.

A canopy of dense branches blocked out the moonlight as the limo came to a stop at the end of a tree-lined street. Although his eyes were closed, John knew intuitively they were nowhere near Connecticut Avenue or the Mayflower. Breaking off the kiss, Eric slid over to his side of the backseat and pulled on his jacket as the driver came around to open the passenger door. Even as he stepped out of the car, John realized he'd never mentioned where he was staying. It was no wonder, then, that Eric had delivered him to the last place on earth he wanted to be.

Except for the empty flowerbeds, the stone house looked exactly as it had in April. Shuffling through a pile of freshly raked leaves, John clutched the lamppost at the end of the walkway and held on tight. Caught up in all the excitement, he had almost deluded himself into believing he could step back into his old life, but too much had happened for that to be possible. This wasn't home anymore.

The scraping of claws on concrete and the jingle of a metal collar reminded him of Chance. Turning toward the sound, John was surprised to see David stumbling down the sidewalk, tugging at a long, nylon leash. At the other end of the tether, an enormous bloodhound lumbered forward, voraciously sniffing at the ground.

"Good evening," Eric said, skirting around the limo and taking his place next to John. It was an unseasonably warm night, but David's icy stare seemed to chill the air a few degrees. Ignoring Eric entirely, he focused all his attention on John.

"What are you doing here? You disappear for six months, without even a phone call or e-mail, and then just show up unannounced?"

The old hound shook her head back and forth until her long ears slapped loudly against her head.

"It's still his house," Eric interjected. "He has every right to be here."

One look from John silenced him. Despite all their differences, there was at least one thing on which he and David could agree: this was a private matter.

"Eric, please. I think it would be best if you left."

John knew it wasn't the response his friend expected to hear, but Eric let the words glance off his battle-tested armor. By the look on his face, it was clear he was having second thoughts about starting a romantic relationship with someone who was his equal. Rather than stay where he wasn't wanted and let a perfectly good evening go to waste, Eric jumped back into the limo and called out an order for the driver to take him to Halo.

Alone at last, David and John stared at each other in silence. A rush of memories and emotions struck with immeasurable force, but the anger and rage that had fueled so many of their prior exchanges was gone. Despite everything—or maybe because of it—some trace of their emotional connection had endured.

"Who's this good girl?" John asked, lifting and scratching the old dog's drooping jowls. Quivering with excitement, the animal nudged closer and covered John's hands with sloppy kisses.

"Her name's Maggie," David said, in a noticeably warmer voice. "She's usually a little skittish around strangers, but she really seems to like you. So what are you now—some kind of dog whisperer?"

"Secretly, I've always been an animal lover. I was just never very good at finding time for anything that required too much attention. I think you'd be surprised to see how much my priorities have changed."

"That's great, John. I'm happy for you," David said, urging his dog toward the darkened house. "But before you say anything else, you should know that for me, everything is still the same."

It was painfully clear that the passing of time had not softened David's heart. Stinging from the blow, John ignored his better judgment and followed him up the walk. There was no way he was going to repeat his past mistakes and run off again. Right or wrong, he was going to stick around and see this through to the end.

"It looks like you finally got what you were after. I mean, you've wanted a dog for a long time."

"I decided to stop overthinking and just do it," David said, unleashing Maggie with one hand and pulling out a shiny new house key with the other.

"I'm sorry I didn't see how important it was to you."

"Yeah, well, we both know that you were always too caught up in your career to notice much else. But hey, I'm not looking for an apology from you—at least not anymore."

David opened the door, but only a foot. Without waiting for her master, Maggie squeezed through the narrow gap and trotted off toward the kitchen.

"Disappearing into thin air was a really shitty thing to do."

"Please, David. You know why I had to leave the way I did," John said in a voice that was more caring than critical. "And besides, I checked our joint account each month and made sure there was enough money for you to take care of the house and the bills."

There would never be enough time for John to say what was on his mind, especially since David didn't seem particularly interested in listening. Relationships were, by their very nature, complicated and messy. The neat-and-tidy ending he'd hoped for only happened in British novels and romantic comedies.

"You can't come in," David said without much conviction. "Call me tomorrow morning, and we'll arrange a time for you to stop by and get some of your things."

"Okay."

In ten years, John had never walked away from a tough negotiation, but this conversation was going nowhere. Past words, spoken and unspoken, could never be changed. Shoving his hands into his pockets, he turned and began the long walk to the nearest Metro stop. Somehow, he knew there could be no closure with David—not now or ever. John's past mistakes had left tiny cracks in David's heart. Looking back, it should have come as no surprise when it finally shattered.

The night doorman at the Mayflower stood vigil over an empty sidewalk. John drifted through the lobby and made his way up to his room. Grateful for the darkness, he climbed into bed and pulled the covers over his head. It was only his second night back in the city, but he'd already managed to misplace his smile.

Sleep, when it finally came, was like a secret door to the one place in the world where he'd truly felt loved. Curled up on his side of the bed, Peter Wells hugged his pillow and dreamed of the guy with curly brown hair who had offered him his heart.

Chapter 23

JOHN GLANCED nervously over his shoulder to make sure the cab was still waiting. As he slipped and slid across the wet grass in expensive leather shoes, John glanced at the faceless names etched into the milky stones. He'd visited this cemetery in Virginia two years earlier, after Mary Donovan, the senator's mother, passed away in her sleep at the ripe old age of ninety-four. Holding Melody's hand, John had spent most of the well-planned funeral imagining a day in the distant future when they would lay her father to rest. How painfully ironic it was that she, the strongest and most resourceful person he'd ever known, had been the first to go.

Up ahead, the surname "Donovan" was emblazoned across the front of a small mausoleum. Hidden in one of the oldest parts of the cemetery, the family plot was landscaped with colorful mums and adorned by marble statues. Although John wasn't sure exactly where to look, it only took a few seconds to find her grave. Melody's copper headstone shimmered in the sun like a shiny new penny.

He traced the raised letters of her name and let a fresh wave of grief carry him back to April. Reaching into the breast pocket of his jacket, John pulled out the plain white envelope he'd discovered on the drive to the Hill. More than six months had passed, but he clearly remembered finding the letter on the floor of his hotel room in Boston. Tired and distracted from a long night with Paul, John had assumed it was just another piece of business that could wait. Now, he realized the profundity of his mistake.

The sound of tearing paper seemed like an omen. The words he was about to read would most likely shred what little composure he had left. Still, knowing the truth would be better than struggling through the rest of his life with so many unanswered questions. Tentatively, he unfolded the single sheet of stationery and began to read:

Dear John,

By the time you read this, I'll probably be dead. I know you'll feel like you've failed me in some essential way, but like the other losses you've suffered over the last few days, this unexpected ending was beyond your control.

I've spent the last ten years trying to live up to my father's impossible expectations. If my parents had had other children (a son), then maybe things could have been different.

When every day is about duty and service, you eventually reach a point where life doesn't seem worth living anymore. Still, even at my darkest moments, I always knew you'd be waiting for me at the office with a smile and a hot coffee. Your friendship and love gave me enough strength to bear the unbearable.

Last night at dinner, though, my father tried to convince me that the only way he can win in November is by sending you away. My whole life has been about politics, and I've seen too many national campaigns to pretend not to know what happens next.

Dad seems ready for it all, but I can't imagine going through four more years of hell without you at my side. So I've decided to take matters into my own hands—before the glare of the political spotlight gets too bright.

The hurtful things we said to one another this afternoon were just words. After so many years together, I know what's in your heart.

Rather than over-obsess about what you could have done to prevent this, channel all that energy into changing your life. Don't settle for success when you've got a shot at true happiness. Despite everything that's happened, it's not too late for you to become the man you were meant to be.

John Peter Wells. What can I say that hasn't already been said except that you were my one true love.

Now, go and live—for yourself and for me.

Until we meet again,

Melody

John refolded the letter and slipped it back into the envelope. *Matthews. Archer. Sloan.* The names of the players had changed, but it was the same old game. Brushing away tears, John stared up at a cloudless sky and tried to think of a way out of the mess that had, once again, become his life. Like Melody, he'd reached the point of no return.

THE REST of the morning was spent in forward motion. There were boxes of memories to pack away and a life to sweep clean.

While the rest of the senate was in session, Donovan sat alone at his desk, rummaging through a towering stack of mail. Six months ago, the venerated statesman would have been far too busy forging policy to bother with such a mundane task. Currently, however, his afternoons were free, except for required appearances at luncheons and fund-raisers, where he faithfully stood a few steps behind Matthews.

Even though the polished wooden doors were wide open, John knocked and waited. Startled, but not surprised, by the appearance of his former chief of staff, Patrick Donovan stood and offered what passed these days for a smile.

"Good afternoon, sir. You're looking well."

"I look like hell," the senator said, settling back down into his chair. "But I appreciate you making the effort to convince me otherwise."

"Well, old habits die hard."

Time and distance had stripped away the hypnotic effect of the senator's title, but there was no point denying the residual affection John felt for his former mentor. It was hard to watch the once-powerful hands quiver as the old man fumbled with a manila envelope lying conspicuously on the credenza. After considerable effort, he finally managed to pull out a familiar black-and-white photo.

Side by side once again, Patrick and John stared intently at the image. Preserved forever, the smiles on the faces in the picture reminded them of happier times.

"You two kids were practically inseparable. I never stopped to think about how much my daughter relied on you for support."

"We were always there for each other," John said, touching the glossy paper. "We were like family."

That simple declaration unexpectedly brought a vision of the senator's impending future into focus. Power and influence were inadequate substitutes for love and companionship. John had made a lot of mistakes in his life, but there was still a chance to escape a similar fate.

"The coroner ruled her death an accident," Donovan said, placing his hands in his lap as he steadied himself to speak. "A large quantity of prescription antidepressants just stopped her heart. It was late at night, and you know how champagne always goes straight to Melody's head. With all the stress and excitement, she must have gotten overwhelmed and swallowed too many of her pills."

Grabbing hold to the edge of his desk, the senator finally asked the questions that had been haunting him for months.

"Was Melody's death my fault? Did my ambition drive my child to take her life?"

The unequivocal answer was in the breast pocket of John's jacket. Unknowingly, Melody had sharpened his blunt sword with her letter. In one fell swoop, he could use her words to bring down the man who had brought ruin on them all. With the senator's career in decline, memories of his daughter were all he had left. For the first time since his return, John didn't need time to think about what to say.

"Melody respected your patriotism and unfaltering commitment to public service. You might not have always been the perfect father, but she knew how much you loved her."

The senator's eyes were full of relief, not gratitude. In the end, he'd looked to his trusted counselor to do what he did best—spin the truth. But it was something deeper and more enduring than loyalty that had stayed John's hand. In the end, he'd discovered his love for Melody was stronger than his bitterness.

Their business concluded, John hurried from Donovan's office to an even more important meeting at an out-of-the-way bistro in Chevy Chase Village. Sitting patiently at their usual table, the daytime version of David was noticeably more affable than his nocturnal alter ego. Despite any unresolved feelings about the dissolution of their relationship, both men understood there were things to discuss and decisions to make. The most important issue to resolve was what to do with the house. Even though memories of the life they'd once shared haunted the place, it was still David's home. By all rights, the property belonged to John, but he was more concerned with fairness than equity. Rather than waste time arguing about money and the division of assets, he surprised them both by simply signing over the deed.

John spent the next five hours packing his things and loading them into a rented SUV. Driving down the street for the last time, he looked back and saw David standing alone on the sidewalk. Without question, he knew which one of them had gotten the better part of the bargain.

Epilogue

IT TOOK almost a week to wrap up his business in DC and crawl up the coast of New England. *First. Second. Third.* After the first hundred miles, driving a stick became almost second nature. The trip back to Provincetown by land was decidedly different than it had been by sea. Now, there were directions to follow and highways to navigate. And, of course, this time he was running toward something instead of away.

Gravel crunched under the hot rubber tires as he pulled his newly purchased jeep into the empty parking lot and turned off the ignition. Reports of theft were almost unheard of off-season, but he decided to lock the doors anyway. After all, everything he owned was packed inside the car. Taking a shortcut between two buildings, he stepped onto Commercial Street just as a run of drag queens whizzed by on roller skates. Holdovers from summer, the girls were a welcome sight.

The next hour passed in a blur as he methodically reassembled the scattered pieces of his life. As expected, Byron was all sunshine and smiles while Lynn was angry to the point of tears. Only Florence, with her unique brand of Scottish drollery, seemed unaffected by his unexplained absence.

"Were you away, my bonny lad? I was so busy with my social calendar that I hadn't noticed you were gone."

Her only tell was the slap she gave his hand when he planted a kiss on her cheek. Though playful, it was a clear warning about the kind of retribution that would follow if he ever went AWOL again. The family reunion was nearly perfect—an authentic Norman Rockwell moment—except that the person he wanted to see most was missing.

Searching for a guy who didn't want to be found wasn't easy, even in a small town. The doors of the chapel were chained shut, and the distinctive wooden sailboat moored at the pier was a ghost ship. Reluctantly, he hiked all the way out to the dune shack, but like the settlement on Long Point, the place had been abandoned to the elements. Acting on a hunch, he hurried toward the West End as the shadows lengthened and the afternoon light deepened from yellow to orange. Up ahead, at the very top of Telegraph Hill, all the grand houses were dark but one.

The features of the man who answered the door were the same, but his curly, brown locks were gone.

"You cut your hair."

"You went away."

"I came back."

"It'll grow."

Hand in hand, the two men made their way to the breakwater. Peter loved that Provincetown had been built at the very tip of a peninsula. It was one of the few places he knew of where you could see the day begin in the east and end in the west. Watching the sun kiss the water, he sat Danny down on one of the benches and told him everything. The improbable story brought both of them to tears, but by the time it was finished, all his doubts and fears about their relationship were gone.

"So what do I call you now?" Danny asked, running his hand through the bristles on his head. "Peter or John?"

"It really doesn't matter anymore. When I'm with you, I know exactly who I am."

WILL FRESHWATER was born and raised in a small steel town outside Pittsburgh. He graduated cum laude from Boston College and was awarded a Juris Doctorate from the University of Pittsburgh School of Law. Will has lived and worked in Boston, Philadelphia, Washington, DC, and Tampa. Although he has spent the better part of the last twenty years working as a successful corporate attorney, Will can happily confirm that his true vocation is writing. He currently resides in Morristown, New Jersey, with his husband, Stephen, and their golden retriever, Rory. Favorite Son is Will's debut novel, and he is hard at work on his second novel.

You can contact Will at https://www.facebook.com/willlivestowrite.

Also from DREAMSPINNER PRESS

http://www.dreamspinnerpress.com

Loving Jay

Renae Kaye

Romance from DREAMSPINNER PRESS

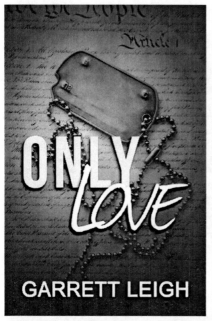

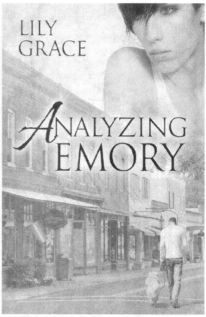

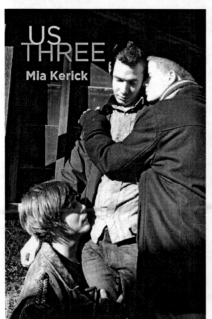

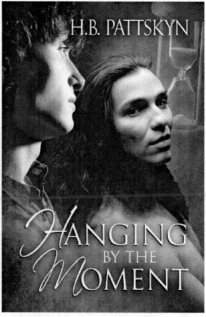

http://www.dreamspinnerpress.com

Romance from DREAMSPINNER PRESS

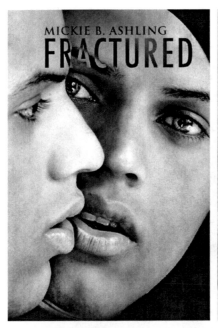

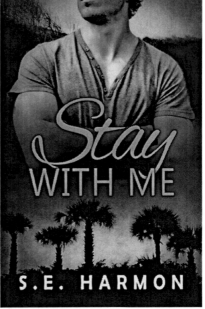

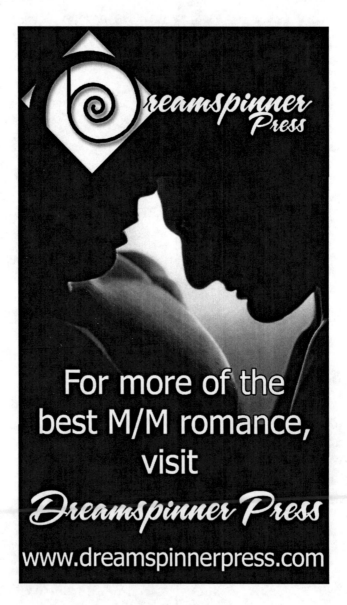

CPSIA information can be obtained at www.ICGtesting.com
Printed in the USA
BVOW04s1612040315

389970BV00009B/46/P